When I was a kid, my pa[...] of specialists to find out what was wrong with me. I wasn't afraid of anything, not spiders, snakes, heights, wild animals—nothing. That's when they figured out that if there was a fear gene, I was missing it. So I guess you could say I'm fearless. Like if I see some big guy beating up a little guy I just dive in and finish off the big one—and I can, because my dad trained me to. He figured if I was going to keep getting myself into trouble I might as well have the skills to protect myself. And my dad knows trouble—he's in the CIA. At least I think he is. I haven't seen or heard from him since, well, since something happened that changed our lives forever.

Anyway, you'd think that because I'm fearless my life would be pretty great, right? Wrong. In fact, if I had three wishes, one of them would be to know fear. Because without fear, I'll never know if I'm truly brave. That wouldn't be my first wish, though—my first wish would be to have my dad back. For obvious reasons. My last wish . . . well that's kind of embarrassing. I'd like to end my unlucky seventeen-year stint as Gaia-the-Unkissed. Do I have anyone in mind? Yeah. But I'm beginning to think it'll never happen. . . .

Don't miss any books in this thrilling series:

# *FEARLESS*™

Available from SIMON PULSE

# FEARLESS™

# Double Edition #5
## Kiss (#5) & Lust (#29)

## FRANCINE PASCAL

SIMON PULSE
New York   London   Toronto   Sydney   Singapore

First Simon Pulse edition September 2003
*Kiss* text copyright © 2000 by Francine Pascal
*Lust* text copyright © 2003 by Francine Pascal

Cover copyright © 2003 by 17th Street Productions, an Alloy, Inc. company.

SIMON PULSE
An imprint of Simon & Schuster
Children's Publishing Division
1230 Avenue of the Americas
New York, NY 10020

Produced by 17th Street Productions,
an Alloy company
151 West 26th Street
New York, NY 10001

Fearless™ is a trademark of Francine Pascal.

Printed in the United States of America
10 9 8 7 6 5 4 3 2 1

ISBN 0-689-85953-8

*Kiss* and *Lust* are also published individually.

# Double Edition #5
## Kiss (#5) & Lust (#29)

*KISS*

*To Nicole Pascal Johansson*

I'll probably never have kids. I'm not just saying that. There are a few really good reasons to think so:

1. I can't even manage to get a guy to kiss me, let alone . . . all that;

2. I seem to have very, very bad family karma (if you believe in karma, which I don't, but it's kind of a fun word to say);

3. Somebody tries to kill me at least once a week.

If you knew me at all, you'd know I'm not being a wiseass when I say that. Let me give you a quick example: I went on the first real date of my life recently, and the guy tried to murder me—literally—before the night was over. So, really, what are the chances I'm going to stick around on this earth long enough to find a guy to love me so much that I'd actually want to have kids with him in the far distant future?

But if by some miracle I ever

did have kids, I would never, never, never have just one.

I remember this old neighbor of mine telling me how great it was to be an only child, how you got so much more support, love, attention, blah, blah, blah, blah. How you didn't have to share your clothes or fight over the bathroom.

I would die to have a sister or brother to share my clothes with. (Although to be honest, what self-respecting sibling would want any of my junk?) I fight over the bathroom with *myself* when I'm feeling really lonely.

The summer I was thirteen, the year after my mom . . . and everything, it was over a hundred degrees practically the entire month of August, so I used to go to this public swimming pool. All the lifeguards, and lifeguards-in-training, and lifeguards-in-training-in-training, and swim team members chattered and gossiped and giggled while I sat on the other side of the pool. I never made a single friend. One day I overheard my foster creature at the time say, "Doesn't it seem like all the other kids at this pool arrived in the same car?"

That, right there, is the story of my life. I feel like the whole rest of the world, with all their brothers and sisters and parents and grandparents and uncles and aunts, arrived in one big car.

I walked.

The neighbor I mentioned earlier, the one who was so psyched about only children? I think he neglected to consider how the whole scenario would look if you didn't have parents.

Gaia sucked in a few shallow gasps of air, raised a pair of wide, haunted eyes to his, and whispered, "I see dead people. . . ."

**the color of fear**

# "MRS. TRAVESURA?"

At first Ella Niven didn't realize the voice was speaking to her. Then she remembered. *Travesura* was the Spanish word for "mischief." It was the name she'd given when she'd first made the appointment.

# Flesh Crawler

She looked up from her magazine. The stunning Asian receptionist was smiling down at her. "The doctor will see you now."

Ella nodded. Setting down the magazine, she grabbed her purse and the shopping bag resting beside her chair and followed the woman.

There were several other women in the posh waiting room. All were reading magazines. All were the indeterminate age of the extremely wealthy—somewhere between thirty-five and death. Clearly most of them had consulted the plastic surgeon many times before this.

Ella noticed that most of the women also had shopping bags with them. She recognized the familiar logos of Chanel, Saks Fifth Avenue, Bergdorf Goodman, and a couple of other Fifth Avenue boutiques, all glimmering like badges of honor.

Ella's own shopping bag was from Tiffany. As she crossed the room, she was acutely aware of each of the other women taking note of the robin's egg blue bag in her hand.

The receptionist led her out of the waiting room and into a long, gray corridor. At first Ella thought the walls were made of slabs of marble—but was shocked to realize they were actually enlarged, black-and-white close-ups of human flesh. A gigantic palm here. A colossal kneecap there. She'd never considered how the wrinkles and creases of one's skin could look like striations in rock.

Up ahead, the corridor ended in a pair of brushed-aluminum doors. The receptionist indicated that Ella could continue on alone. When Ella was within a yard of the metal doors, they glided open soundlessly.

The office was large and spare. Floor-to-ceiling windows wrapped around two sides of the square chamber, giving a panoramic, sixty-story view stretching from Central Park to the East River.

As Ella entered, the doctor was standing behind a large, black desk that gleamed like highly polished onyx. Oddly, it was bare except for a light blue folder that seemed to float—weightlessly—above the slick surface. It must have been an optical trick.

The doctor was tall, and pale, and bald. He wasn't dressed in a physician's white coat, as Ella had expected. He wore a black suit over a black turtleneck.

Drawing closer, Ella discovered that her initial impression was wrong again. The man *wasn't* bald. His hair was white, but cropped exceptionally close to his skull. His skin was the same ghostly color. That's what had created the illusion of baldness.

Still, the doctor's eyes were his most remarkable feature. They were deep set and a light shade of yellowish green. They gleamed like cat's eyes beneath his brow. In all her life she had never seen eyes that color.

Not on a human, anyway.

"'Mrs. Travesura,' I presume?"

His tone of voice made it clear he knew it wasn't her real name.

She nodded cordially. "How do you do."

The doctor didn't answer but gestured to the chair opposite him—an artsy contrivance of chrome bars and black leather straps.

The doctor sat down. "I understand, from our initial conversation, that there is a certain . . . procedure . . . that you wish me to perform."

"That is correct."

"Now. If I am not mistaken, you are . . . shall we say, *employed* by a certain L—"

"Exactly," Ella interrupted. She needed to shut off this particular line of inquiry as quickly as possible. "I am. He, however, is not to be contacted under any circumstances. I must shield him from this undertaking. It is of utmost importance."

The doctor nodded, but he looked skeptical.

Ella knew he had past connections to Loki. That's

how she had found him. But if he were to contact Loki directly, Ella knew her plan would be derailed instantly. Loki would accuse her of deep, twisted jealousy. But the fact was, when Ella succeeded with this plan, and Tom Moore arrived at the bedside of his poor, disfigured, comatose daughter, Loki would be forced to give Ella the credit she was due.

For now, she needed to change the course of the conversation. She cast her gaze at the mysterious blue folder and gestured toward it.

It worked. "Ah . . . the portfolio," he explained, placing his hand lightly on the folder. "It represents my . . . *side business,* if you will. 'Before' and 'after' photographs of some of my more *interesting* accomplishments." He slid it across the desk toward her. "Care to take a look?"

Ella stared down at the ice blue folder in front of her, but she didn't touch it. She didn't need to see what was inside.

"Oh, c'mon . . . go ahead." He pushed the folder a few inches closer to her. "Aren't you in the least bit curious?" His tone was friendly. Flippant, almost. But— glancing back up at him—she saw that the man's eyes had locked on her with the cold, intense scrutiny of a snake. It was as if he were mentally willing her to look at the pictures. Daring her, even.

When she didn't respond, he reached forward and started lifting the cover. "Just take one little—"

"*I'm familiar with your work,*" she interrupted.

The doctor instantly snapped his hand away. The folder whispered shut.

He shrugged. "Suit yourself."

Ella had the feeling she'd just failed some kind of test. She tried to regain ground.

Sitting up taller, she leaned forward slightly, bowing her shoulders so that her cleavage was displayed at its most alluring angle. "Believe me, Doctor," she began in a persuasive voice, "I wouldn't be here if I weren't already *highly* confident about your . . . skills."

If the doctor noticed her breasts, he made no show of it. His eyes remained locked on her own.

"And yet," she went on—leaning forward a little more—"regardless of your expertise, I think you may find this particular . . . patient . . . to be an *extremely* unwilling subject."

"Many such patients *are* reluctant," the doctor agreed. "At first." His eyes seemed to sparkle at some dark, private memories.

"This one is different," Ella stated firmly. She was growing annoyed. Why wasn't he looking at her chest? She leaned forward even more. "You might as well know, Doctor: You're not the first . . . professional . . . I've contacted in this matter. Others have tried to treat this patient. They failed."

"My success rate is impeccable," the doctor assured her. "And as I informed you at the outset, Mrs.

*Travesura*, one gets what one pays for." He stressed this last phrase meaningfully.

Ella took the hint. Reaching down, she picked up the Tiffany shopping bag that was lying at her feet. She placed it on the desktop, sliding it toward the doctor across the slick surface. As she did so, her hand accidentally brushed up against the folder.

Despite herself, she flinched.

The doctor noticed this, and his lips curled in mild amusement. He took the Tiffany bag, glancing inside.

Ella watched him and waited. She didn't expect him to react at the sight of the money; he was no doubt used to seeing such large sums of cash. She was waiting for him to notice what *else* was in the light blue bag.

The doctor's smile faded. Reaching into the bag, he removed a small, rectangular device. It might have been a cellular phone, except that it had a tiny LCD monitor where the earpiece should be. He held it up, a question forming in his bile-green eyes.

"It's a tracking device," she explained before he could ask. "Satellite technology. Effective within a fifty-mile radius. It allows you to pinpoint the precise location of a radio transmitter." Opening her purse, she withdrew a tiny metallic chip about the size of an aspirin. "*This* transmitter, which will be planted on the subject tonight."

She paused to gauge the doctor's reaction. It was crucial that he go along with the plan.

"Interesting," was all he said. He placed the tracking device down on his desk and sat back in his chair, steepling his fingers together on his chest.

Keeping her voice steady, Ella continued: "You will use the device to track the subject. There is a telephone number on the back. Once you have completed the job, you are to go to the nearest pay phone and call this number. Is that understood?"

The doctor stared at her over his fingertips. "Perfectly."

Was he mocking her? She couldn't tell. But she didn't care now. This transaction was drawing to a close.

"Good," she said. "Well—uh, *Doctor*—I believe that about covers it."

She stood up. So did he. She would not let him try to shake her hand. The thought of being touched by `those long, bloodless fingers made her flesh crawl.`

There was only one more matter to square away before she could leave.

She placed her hands on his desk. "I have to make sure we're perfectly clear on one point," she informed him, trying to make her voice as threatening as possible. "You may be as . . . *thorough* . . . as you desire. In fact, I encourage you. But it is of the *utmost importance* that the subject makes it through the procedure. *Alive*."

The doctor stepped around his desk, smiling widely and warmly. "Your concern, Mrs. Travesura, is quite touching," he said, his voice dripping with sarcasm. "But it's unnecessary."

He suddenly dropped his smile—and with it, his act. "The subject will live. I can assure you of that." His voice was much colder now. Deader. As devoid of life as his skin. "There's no challenge in it for me otherwise."

He nodded at the folder, still sitting on his desk. "*They* all lived," he informed her, his voice ringing with chilling pride.

# GAIA MOORE MOVED QUICKLY ALONG

## shortcomings

West Fourth Street in the direction of Washington Square Park, not bothering to slow her pace for her friend, Ed Fargo, who wheeled along a yard or two behind her.

As she walked, Gaia switched the strap of her beat-up canvas messenger bag from her left shoulder to the right. It was a smooth, fluid movement—one she made often over the course of her day. If she was doomed to have the overdeveloped deltoids of a Russian gymnast, at least she'd make sure they were *equally* overdeveloped. Being a supermuscular freak was bad enough. Being a lopsided one was too much to bear.

Gaia was painfully self-conscious about her body. Even now she was aware of her muscular arms and shoulders, although they were safely camouflaged beneath the bulky yellow-green Polartec parka she'd started wearing since the weather turned cold.

Long ago she'd given up trying to fight it. No amount of doughnut scarfing could erase the six-pack definition of her abdominals. Her genetics were simply stacked against her. Her muscles were as much a part of her as her blue eyes and her light hair and her extreme devotion to chocolate.

"Jesus, Gaia, could you slow down? The speed limit is thirty miles an hour, last I checked."

Gaia cast a glance back at Ed. "Why don't you speed up? You've got *wheels*, for God's sake."

It was a game they played. If she'd actually slowed down for his benefit, Ed probably would have clocked her. He appreciated pity exactly as much as she did.

The chess tables were coming into view. Gaia hoped there would be a new face today so she could earn some money for lunch.

Over the past three months she'd developed a reputation among the chess players. When she'd first arrived on the scene, it had been fairly easy to score a twenty-dollar game. That was in late August. Now the only regular who would play her for cash was old man Zolov, an international master. Since Gaia had helped save Zolov's life back in September, the "undefeated chess champ" of Washington Square suddenly began losing to her at regular intervals. A little *too* regular. It seemed as if they'd traded the same twenty dollars back and forth ten times in the past week.

And then there was Sam Moon. Sam could also get a game off her, but he was a different story entirely. They had played only once. They played to a deadlock until she'd freaked out and forfeited her king. Sam wouldn't take her money, but he had walked off with her heart that day.

Impatiently Gaia gathered her long hair from where it blew in her eyes and mouth and threw it behind her back. She'd forgotten to bring a hair band.

Maybe if she were lucky, Zolov would let her win today.

If she were really lucky, Sam Moon wouldn't show up at all.

Ed had caught up and started badgering her the way he'd been doing all day. "Gaia. Do the line from the movie. *Pleeeease?*"

And maybe—if she were really, *really* lucky—a certain someone would get his wheelchair caught in a sewer grate any moment now.

She glanced in annoyance at her self-appointed best friend. What had she done to deserve him?

"I'm not going to do it, Ed. So you can stop asking."

"Please, Gaia? I'm going to Pennsylvania tonight, so I won't get to see you for a whole four days. Besides, I promise I won't laugh this time. I promise."

"That's what you said the last time. *And* the time before that." God, why had she ever attempted that stupid imitation? She was just fooling around in the cafeteria at school, and Ed acted like it was the most hilarious thing he'd ever seen in his life. He wouldn't shut up about it.

"That was the old me. I've changed since then. I swear."

"The only thing you've changed is your underwear—and that's debatable."

*"Guy-uhhhhhhhhhh . . ."*

"Oh, sure, whine my name. That'll convince me."

"I'll pay you."

"You don't have enough money."

"Oh, you might be surprised."

"I doubt it. Seeing as you can't even afford socks that match." She gestured at his feet.

Ed shot her a confused look. "What are you talking about?"

"Your socks. Are you celebrating Christmas a month early? Or did you get dressed in the dark this morning?"

Gaia had walked a good ten paces before she realized Ed was no longer at her side. She spun around.

16

He'd stopped in the middle of the sidewalk and was bent over in his seat, staring down at his feet with a strange, aggravated expression on his face. "Aw, man. You're kidding me, right?"

Gaia put her hands on her hips. "Kidding you? You put them on, elf boy, not me."

Ed squinted up at her. "Great. Thanks. Make fun of the color-blind guy. Go ahead."

Gaia cocked her head. "You're not color-blind," she pronounced.

Ed frowned, crossing his arms. "I think I would be the one to know."

Gaia stared at him. Her hands slipped from her waist, flopping at her sides. "Seriously? You're color-blind?"

"Hey—don't worry. You can't catch it." Ed slapped his wheels, gliding toward her once more.

"It's just that you never told me."

"Hmmm, that's funny. It's usually one of the first things I say to people: 'Hi, I'm Ed. I'm color-blind.' I think it's good to get one's physical shortcomings out of the way, y'know, *up front*." He rolled to a stop in front of her feet, then peered furtively around the park. "Now, uh, Gaia, don't let this next bit of info freak you out, *but . . .*" He leaned in toward her, shielding his mouth with one hand conspiratorially. ". . . I'm *also* in a wheelchair."

Gaia was too busy looking at Ed's feet to think of a

good comeback. One green sock, one red. Could he really not tell them apart? Not at all? She raised her gaze to his eyes, studying them, not sure what she was looking for. They were a dark brown with gold lights. Eyes the color of a double espresso, she found herself thinking. Inwardly she groaned. *Guess you don't need those refrigerator magnets to write crappy poetry.* The point was, Ed's eyes didn't *look* color-blind. They looked . . . well . . . like regular, everyday eyes.

Regular, everyday, *annoyed* eyes.

"Please, by all means, Gaia. Keep staring at me like that. It does wonders for my self-esteem."

"Sorry—" Gaia barely had time to scoot out of the way as Ed blew past her. "It's just that you're the first . . . I mean, I never knew a person who was color-blind. What's it like for you?"

God, I must sound ridiculous, Gaia thought, stepping after him. Why don't I just say, Hey, Ed, you can't see colors, and I can't feel fear. Let's start a club!

Once she was beside him again, Ed looked up at her, amused. "Are you feeling okay, Gai?"

"Yeah. Why?"

"Because you asked me a question."

"And?"

"*And* . . . didn't you sort of stipulate way back when that we wouldn't ask each other questions because if *you* ask *me* something, that would mean *I* get to ask *you* something in return?"

18

This time it was Gaia who stopped in her tracks. "Right. You're right, Ed. Forget that I asked."

"No, no, no, no, no," Ed said, swiveling around to face her with a mischievous grin. "Not so fast. You can't back out now. A deal's a deal." He rubbed his hands together gleefully. "So—I believe the category is color blindness. What's the question gonna be?"

*"Does it make you jealous?"* She was startled to hear her own voice saying those words. She hadn't meant to say them out loud.

Ed blinked a couple of times. "Jealous?" he repeated, sounding confused. "What do you mean?"

Gaia chose her next words carefully. "Do you ever feel . . . upset . . . that other people can . . . experience something that you . . . can't?"

"Upset? Not really." He shrugged. "After all, it's not like being color-blind means everything looks black and white to me. I mean, I still see things in color. For example, I can tell that jacket of yours is the color of mucus. It's just that certain colors look alike to me. Mostly I have difficulty telling reds from greens." He pointed down at his feet. "Obviously."

Gaia self-consciously eyed her jacket. "Do you ever wish you *could* tell the difference?"

Ed nodded. "Well, sure. There was a pretty ugly incident involving hot sauce a few years back." He grimaced at the memory. "But most of those taste buds grew back. Eventually." He scratched the

19

back of his neck. "Traffic lights pose a theoretical problem, but I figured out at a young age that red is on top, and green is on the bottom. Aside from that, I don't really think about it too much . . . except when I commit the very occasional fashion faux pas and some heartless person goes and points it out to me." He shot her a fake-hostile glance but quickly leavened it with another shrug. "But—honestly?—I can't say I'm jealous of people who aren't color-blind."

"Why's that?" Gaia prompted.

Ed bit his lip, thinking. "Hmmm . . . I can't explain it all that well, but it's sorta like this: I can't imagine a world with more colors than I see it in already. I just can't. And . . . well . . . I don't think you can truly be jealous of something if you can't imagine having it in the first place. Besides"—he ran a finger across the arm of his wheelchair, adding casually, almost to himself—"there are better things to be jealous of."

Gaia gave him a rare smile. What *had* she done to deserve him?

After a moment he looked away self-consciously. "Uh . . . did any of that make sense?"

She nodded. "Yeah. It did."

"Good." Ed sat up a little taller in his seat. "So, I believe now it's *my* turn to ask *you* something."

Gaia took a deep breath, then let it out slowly. "Shoot away." Part of her almost wished he would ask her one of her secrets. Considering all he'd witnessed over the past three months, she supposed it was a wonder he hadn't guessed them all already.

Ed stroked his chin thoughtfully, gazing skyward. "Let's see now. . . . I get to ask the mysterious Gaia Moore a question." He was clearly savoring the moment. "Anything I want. . . . Anything at—"

"You got five seconds, Ed."

"Okay, okay!" Ed scowled at her. Then he snapped his fingers. "Here's one: Where'd you learn how to—no, no, scratch that." He waved his hand in the air as if erasing an imaginary chalk mark. "I got a better one: Why don't you ever talk about your—" He stopped himself short again, reconsidering. "No, not that one, either. How about—"

Gaia let out a low grumble.

Ed looked up at her, as if he were just struck by an idea. "Say. Can I ask you to *do* something instead?"

Gaia cocked a wary eyebrow. This actually represented an easy way out, but she didn't want him to know it. "I suppose. . . ."

Ed grinned evilly. "Do the line from the movie."

"Except that."

Ed pointed at her with both hands. "Oh, no! You can't back out of it now. A deal's a deal."

Gaia glanced at her watch. "Wow, what do you know? It's already the end of lunch period."

21

"Gaia!"

She sighed, resigned. "Fine. But you better not laugh this time."

Ed pantomimed zippering his lip.

Gaia held up a warning finger. "I'm not kidding, Ed."

Now he crossed his heart, holding up three fingers in the Scout salute.

"All right." She moved a couple of steps to a nearby bench, plopping down on the hard, cold slats. Clearing her throat, she cast a wary eye around the immediate area. Aside from a cluster of `sooty-looking pigeons` pecking at the ground nearby, this particular section of the park was empty. Thank God.

Ed repositioned his wheelchair in front of her for a better view.

Gaia sucked in a few shallow gasps of air, gripped the neckline of her coat with two white-knuckled fists, raised a pair of wide, haunted eyes to his, and whispered, over a trembling lower lip: *"I see dead people. . . ."*

`Ed the Expressionless Eagle Scout` managed to maintain his deadpan for an entire second and a half. Then he let out a guffaw so loud, it echoed clear across the park, sending the pigeons exploding skyward in a frenzied, flapping cloud. It was a wonder he didn't flip himself over backward.

Gaia slapped her hands down on the bench, standing up in annoyance. "What's so funny? I thought I was pretty good that time."

"Good?" Ed was doubled over now, his face bright pink. "*Good?*" He could barely choke out the word through his laughter.

"Okay, that's it." Gaia kicked the side of his wheel with her boot and huffed off. "I'm outta here."

A few seconds later she could hear him behind her, struggling to catch her. "Gaia—wait—please—" All the laughing had left him panting for air. Good. She purposely picked up her pace. "Please—Gaia—wait up—I'm sorry—I'm sorry, but—it's just that—if you could *see* what you—"

She turned around. "Spit it out, Ed."

Ed placed a hand on his chest, taking a moment to catch his breath. "You have got to do the most terrible impression of being scared I have ever seen in my life."

He cracked up again.

Gaia hoped the sudden flush in her cheeks appeared to be a reaction to the cold.

*Ed, my color-blind friend, you have no idea. . . .*

I used to think you could pretty much divide people into two categories: those who believe in love at first sight and those who don't.

I was a proud member of the second category. I used to think you fell in love with your brain. . . . Um, that came out wrong. Let me rephrase. I used to think your brain was in use when you fell in love. You sort of decided it over time, like I did with Heather. I saw her, I thought, man, that girl is beautiful. I talked to her, I thought, yeah, and she's smart and funny, too. I spent some time with her and thought, hey, we actually like a lot of the same stuff. I kissed her and thought, yo, this is fun. After that, as far as my brain and I were concerned, we were in love.

Then I met Gaia Moore. Every time I've ever had anything to do with Gaia, my brain has said, shit, this girl is nothing but pain, misery, and trouble. And in this case my brain was totally right. But in spite of my brain's lack of cooperation, I've fallen in love with her. It happened the first time I ever saw her. It was like a clap of thunder, a bolt of lightning, a monsoon, all those cheesy metaphors I never believed before (although there actually was a monsoon going on at the time). There is no good reason for me to love Gaia. There are only good reasons against it. Every day I struggle to release myself from it. Every day I try to convince myself that it will go away.

So anyway, I guess you could say my brain is sticking with the second category, claiming that no, there is no such thing as love at first sight. My heart has betrayed it in favor of the first category, arguing, yes, absolutely, it's the only kind of love there is. And now my brain and my heart aren't even on

speaking terms anymore. When I
said "divide people," that wasn't
exactly what I had in mind.

I told my friend Danny about
this theory, and he told me he
also had a theory for how to divide people: those who divide
people into two and those who
don't.

Her arms were around him, her heartbreaking **hell** scar pressed **hath** against his chest, her **no** lips **fury . . .** against his ear . . .

**". . . AND MEDEA, SO CONSUMED**
was she by her bitter jealousy, so desperate was she to take vengeance on
her unfaithful husband, Jason, that
she murdered her rival with a gift of
a poisoned cloak and then went on to
kill her own children. . . ."

## A Good Idea

Heather Gannis glanced up at the
animated face of her literature teacher, Mr. MacGregor,
who was talking much louder than necessary and
brandishing a paperback edition of Euripides. Jesus,
why were parents so up in arms about violence on television? The seriously grisly stuff was happening in
these Greek plays.

She heard a snort of laughter from the back of the
room. She turned quickly, recognizing the laugh before seeing its owner. Ed Fargo, her former true love,
was laughing at something Gaia Moore had written on
the corner of his notebook. The sound of it was corro-
sive in her ears.

Gaia could make Ed laugh. It was a rare ability and
another affront to add to the long list.

Heather wasn't superstitious. Unlike the ancient
Greeks, she didn't believe in fate. She wasn't religious and
had little tolerance for the wu-wu astrology and
Ouija board crap many of her friends were into.

But for Gaia, she made an exception. Gaia, with her
fairy-tale yellow hair and her long, graceful limbs, was

too terrible to accept at face value. How could one girl captivate Heather's boyfriend, enslave her ex-boyfriend, humiliate her, nearly get her killed, and completely destroy her self-confidence in less than three months? Gaia was a clear message from Somebody Up There that Heather deserved punishment.

Since Gaia had arrived in September, her evil had radiated. First there were the slashings, culminating in Heather's own near death. Then there was the stuff that happened to Sam. Then Cassie Greenman. Heather, like the rest of the school, was haunted by her murder.

All these tragedies weren't a coincidence. They just weren't.

". . . So for Monday, I'd like you all to read *Oedipus Rex*." Mr. MacGregor wrapped up his lecture just as the bell rang, signaling the end of a very long day at Central Village High. "Have a great Thanksgiving holiday, folks."

The classroom burst into cusp-of-vacation activity. Heather sighed as she jotted the assignment in her notebook. She had a feeling that play was going to be another doozy.

"Hey, chick."

Heather glanced up as two of her friends, Carrie Longman and Melanie Young, materialized at her desk. "Hey," she said, digging around to find a smile. "Whatsup?"

"You feel like Ozzie's?" Melanie asked.

Heather carefully piled her books and zipped them into her backpack. Her eyes landed momentarily on her empty wallet. A large mochaccino at Ozzie's cost over three bucks. Her friends thought nothing of buying two of them a day. Heather couldn't keep up, and she refused to let anybody else buy one for her. The old Gannis pride kicked in triple strength when it came to shallow displays of fortune. Or lack thereof.

Besides, she had something important to do this afternoon. Something she'd put off for too long.

Heather stood and smoothed her long, slim, blood-colored skirt. She strode out of the classroom, and her friends followed close behind. "Can't make it. Sorry," she said breezily.

"Oh." Carrie hovered at Heather's locker, taking a moment to regroup. "How about Dean & Deluca? They have those excellent caramel brownies. We can go to Tower Records after and get started on Christmas shopping."

"You all go. Maybe I'll catch up later," Heather said noncommittally. "I've got something I need to take care of this afternoon."

Melanie and Carrie stared at her in silence, obviously hoping she would elaborate. She didn't feel like it. She slammed her locker shut. She pulled on her black nylon jacket and slung her backpack over her shoulder. "See ya. Leave your cell on, Carrie."

Once Heather was rid of them, she slipped into the

bathroom. She got weirdly obsessive about her appearance every time she was about to see Sam, although she knew her boyfriend was even more oblivious to her subtle efforts than most guys.

She studied her face and her hair. She applied a coat of lip gloss and ran a brush through her long, smooth hair. No perceivable difference. Staring at the high neck of her white T-shirt under her soft, black V-necked sweater, she suddenly had an idea. Ever since "the incident"—the slashing that had put her in the hospital late in September—she'd worn a scarf or a shirt or sweater with a high neck every time she left her apartment. Now she discarded her jacket, dropped her backpack on the floor, and pulled both the sweater and the T-shirt over her head at the same time. She pulled the two garments apart, folded the T-shirt neatly into her backpack, and put the sweater back on.

She spent another minute gazing at her reflection. Yes, that was a good idea.

# SAM TIPPED BACK HIS HEAD AND

**Choose** rested it on the top of the park bench. He closed his eyes and soaked up the low, late autumn sun. For the end of November, the air was sweet and warm. Probably almost sixty degrees.

Wednesdays were his favorite days. His classes ended early, so he allowed himself to hang out at the chess tables. That was one of the great things about college—those one or two class days that left you lots of time to waste. He'd already hustled twenty bucks off an unwitting stranger, then given it right back to Zolov in a rout. It was a weird form of charity, but whatever. Hustle from the stupid and lose to the smart. 'Twas the season.

"Hey, handsome."

He lifted his head and blinked open his eyes. Heather was bearing down at twenty feet, beautiful as ever in her red skirt and whispery black jacket. He heard the dry acorns cracking under the heels of her boots.

"Hi," he said, rubbing his eyes. "How's your day?"

"Okay," she said. "The usual high school plundering of spirits. How 'bout you?"

He laughed. Heather was so cool, so together. Never awkward or at a loss for words. "Oh, you know. Wasting some more of my youth at the chess tables." He paused. "Looking forward to tomorrow."

Instantly he felt annoyed at himself for having gilded the truth like that. He was looking forward to the gauntlet of the Gannis family Thanksgiving in the very plain sense of the phrase—observing that it would take place in the near future. He wasn't looking forward as in eagerly anticipating it.

"Oh, yeah?" She angled her head coyly, causing a curtain of shiny chestnut hair to fall forward over her shoulder. It reminded him of sex, which started that tingly feeling spreading through his body, which in turn made him feel guilty about what had happened the last time they had sex. And the first time they had sex.

"Looking forward to my dad's dry, stringy turkey? My mom's sickly turnip-brown sugar thing?" she challenged. "Looking forward to Phoebe eating nothing and complaining about Binghamton? Lauren talking on her cell phone straight through dinner? Hmmm." She appraised him with one lifted eyebrow. "Are you telling me the truth?"

Sam laughed again, wishing his heart would listen to reason once in a while. "Well. *You'll* be there."

Heather awarded him a little smile. She pointed to the spot on the bench next to him. "Is this seat taken? Do you mind if I sit?" Her tone was light, but he registered that her eyes were serious.

He scooted over fast, feeling ungentlemanly. "Of course. Definitely. Sit."

She sat and dropped her backpack on the other side of her. She wasn't so close that any part of her was touching him, but neither was she so far that he couldn't feel her warmth. "Listen. There's something I need to talk to you about." She turned to face him, nailing him with her odd-colored eyes. They weren't blue, but they weren't not blue, either.

"Sure, of course." He was getting nervous now. He was saying "of course" too much. "Talk away."

"It's kind of serious. Just to give you fair warning. It's something we've been needing to talk about for a while now."

"Of c—" He clamped his mouth shut. He felt like strangling himself. "Okay. I'm warned."

Heather took a deep breath. "I know that you have some kind of . . . *relationship* with Gaia Moore."

Sam could tell it was painful to her to say the name, and he felt awful.

"I know that you know her somehow, and I need you to tell me what's going on between you."

Sam swallowed. Jesus, Heather had a knack for getting right to the point. He hoped his face didn't betray his dire discomfort. He needed to choose his words carefully. He cleared his throat. "There's nothing going on."

*Liar. You think about her every hour of every day.*

"I barely know her. I've hardly ever spoken with her. There's never been anything . . . romantic between us."

*But you wish there were. You dream about her at night.*

Sam glanced up, reminding himself that he was

having a conversation with Heather and not with himself.

"So what *is* there between you?" Heather pressed. "Why was she there the night we . . ." She trailed off and then started again. "How did she know you'd been kidnapped? Why did you need to leave in such a hurry the last time we were together in your room?"

All the saliva in Sam's mouth had dried up, and from what he could tell, it was never coming back. He tried swallowing again. "Honestly, Heather, I don't know. The last couple of months have been so strange. I really don't know anything about her." That last bit, finally, was a sincere answer.

"Have you ever . . . *been* with her?" Heather stopped and tried again. Here was a girl who accepted no cowardice, particularly not in herself. "Have you kissed her? Hooked up with her? Had sex with her?"

"No," Sam answered firmly. *But God, how I've wanted to.*

Heather looked relieved but no less serious. "Okay, here's the really important thing I need to say to you." She pulled one sleeve of her sweater up over the palm of her hand. "I don't like Gaia Moore. I hate her. I think she's dangerous, and I wish she'd stay away from you." Heather caught her breath for a second before she rushed on. She was nervous, but admirably determined. "I need you to tell me now that whatever there is between you is over. That you won't have anything

35

to do with her anymore." She fixed him with her eyes again. "Because if you can't, it's got to be over between you and me. You have to choose."

Whoa. Sam looked down at his jeans, pressing his hands into his thighs, raising his shoulders up around his ears. This was hard-core. This was much more than he'd ever expected. He had to think.

Heather was not only offering him a choice; she was offering him a way out. He could be free of the guilt and the craziness. He could be free to figure out what the hell was going on between him and Gaia.

"So is it over?" Heather asked, her voice quiet and wobbly.

Sam turned to her. The answer he'd been contemplating withered in his throat. Her eyes were round and glazed with tears. Her jacket had fallen open, and the low V neck of her sweater revealed a long, jagged rent in the delicate white skin along her collarbone. The cut through which she'd lost so much blood and nearly her life. It was still angry red in color. Still unhealed.

His mind flashed back to that night. Finding Heather in the park, lying in a puddle of her own blood. The strange, dissonant whirlpool of hospital sounds and smells and colors, then the unsettling piece of information that a girl from Heather's class, a girl named Gaia Moore, had seen the gang member with the knife in the park and she'd passed up an easy opportunity to warn Heather.

Sam's gaze was riveted on the wound. He couldn't seem to look away. All the while Heather kept her head up, seemingly unaware of what he was seeing and feeling.

"Sam?"

He dragged his eyes back up to her face. He was miserable. He was filled with shame. He was torn in two. "Heather, it's not only over. It never began."

Her arms were around him, her heartbreaking scar pressed against his chest, her lips against his ear by the time he realized that he hadn't said which girl he was talking about.

"**Why** are you like this?"

That is a question I've heard from a lot of adults in my life. Some of them related to me, some not. If they don't ask it out-right, I see the question in their eyes. And I'm not being paranoid. Trust me.

"Like this" in my case means loud, impulsive, messed up, combative, undisciplined, annoying. Other stuff, too.

The reason the question gets asked so often, with such impatience, is because there's no easy explaining when it comes to me.

I come from a nice family. Two parents, not one. We're rich, not poor. We're well educated. Or I should say, they're well educated. They pay lots of attention to me. They read me books when I was little. They made me drink my milk. It's really not their fault.

I have two nice brothers. They both go to good colleges now.

MARY MOSS

Growing up, they only teased me and beat me up the normal amount.

Why am I like this?

I don't know. Some people have a lot of space between thinking and saying or thinking and doing. I don't have any. Some people look at themselves from the out-side and try really hard to make what they see look good. I stay on the inside. I'd rather feel good than seem it.

Sometimes I love that about myself. Sometimes I hate it.

Why am I like this?

I don't know. I have a couple of theories, though.

It was not
of "utmost
importance"
that the . . . **like**
"subject" be **a**
kept alive.
That had **woman**
been **scorned**
their
mistake from
day one.

# GAIA RESTED HER HEAD IN HER

hand, staring at what remained of her frozen pizza, trying to fight off a terrible wave of loneliness. It seemed mean-spirited of biology to have left fear out of her DNA but to have made her feel loneliness so acutely.

# Worse Than Stupid

The Nivens' brownstone was empty and quiet except for the odd siren or car alarm blasting from Bleecker Street. Those were sounds you stopped hearing when you lived in New York City. Like a buzzing refrigerator or the hum of an air conditioner. You incorporated them into your ears.

The kitchen was sparse and orderly as usual. There was no sign, other than her plate on the faux-country wooden table, that a seventeen-year-old girl had just prepared and eaten her dinner there. Gaia was camping at the Nivens' more than actually *living* there. Low-impact camping. After five years in foster homes she'd learned never to settle in too much, never to get comfortable.

George had been called away on business just before the Thanksgiving holiday. She liked George. He was awkward with her, but sweet and well meaning. He had known her father. She would even feel disappointed by his absence, but like the sirens on Bleecker

Street, disappointment was something so customary, Gaia hardly felt it anymore.

On the plus side, when George was gone, Ella was usually gone, too. And Ella was most nearly likable when she was gone.

Gaia washed her plate, dried it, and returned it to the cabinet. No trace.

Thanksgiving wasn't Gaia's favorite holiday. The day was designed around warm family get-togethers, parents, grandparents, uncles, aunts, cousins. Blitzing yourself on great food. Thinking about all the wonderful things your life had brought you and feeling grateful for it.

Gaia had no family anymore (save one recently discovered man claiming to be her uncle, whose name she didn't even know). On account of that, she had trouble feeling grateful. Instead it brought to mind the wonderful things that life had taken away from her, which sent her down the spiral of thanklessness. And that didn't require a special day. That was every day.

Gaia peered into the fridge. She was still hungry, craving something sweet.

Apparently George had done the shopping for Thanksgiving before he'd been called away. The refrigerator was crammed with food, including a massive raw turkey on the bottom shelf.

It was a little depressing, seeing all the food that George had bought and now wouldn't get to cook.

43

Depressing but not exactly tragic. Although George could find his way through a tuna casserole, Gaia suspected his culinary talents `fell a few drumsticks short of turkey with all the trimmings`.

Ella certainly wasn't going to do it. Gaia doubted George's dumb wife could figure out the recipe for ice. The only way Ella would put her hands in a turkey was if her `Celine Dion CD` had been shoved inside.

It was revolting how tightly Ella had George wrapped around her finger. For a person who made a living in the intelligence community, George Niven was pretty moronic when it came to matters in his own home. You didn't have to be in the CIA to see that Ella was playing him.

No, the only way that bird was getting cooked was if Gaia did it herself.

Without warning, Gaia's mind was flooded with a rush of overlapping images. Memories of another time, another place.

*Chestnut stuffing . . . cranberry relish . . . a fire in a stone hearth . . . an ivory chess set, the pieces carved to look like Norse gods: Odin, Frigg, Thor, Loki . . . a man's sudden, shocked laughter: "My God, she just beat me, Kat!" . . . a gravy boat shaped like a swan and a woman's accented voice, saying: "It's lovely, isn't it? It was my grandmother's. Her name was Gaia, too. . . ."*

The mental pictures evaporated at the sound of the

front door being unlocked, followed by the sharp, staccato click of high heels on the marble entranceway. The hall light snapped on.

Gaia glanced over at the wall clock. 9:51.

Great. Apparently Ella's coven decided to wrap things up early tonight.

Quickly Gaia reached across the counter and flicked off the light. She closed the refrigerator, not hungry anymore.

It was uncanny: No matter how hungry Gaia was, whenever Ella approached, appetite retreated. Maybe it was an allergic reaction to Ella's unique combination of silicone, hair spray, suffocating perfume, and spandex microminis.

With the refrigerator door closed, the kitchen was swallowed up in shadow. The only light now came from the hallway and the faint red glow cast by the microwave's digital display.

Gaia stood silently in the reddish gloom, mentally urging Ella to stay away from the kitchen. She was hoping to hit the park this evening, maybe see if she could lure a mugger or two. A run-in with Ella would put a damper on that plan. Ella would pull the Carol Brady routine, and Gaia was in no mood to answer stupid, pointless questions at ten o'clock at night. "How was school?" "Great! I purposely blew my history exam and scammed sixty bucks at the chess tables before dinner, and now I'm gonna go to the park to kick some punk ass clear into tomorrow. Thanks for asking!"

She had the sneaking feeling Ella would *not* be amused.

Gaia listened closely for signs of life, but all she could hear was the loud ticking of the grandfather clock in the hall. When Ella still hadn't appeared after sixty more ticks, Gaia stepped cautiously into the corridor.

Maybe this was her lucky night. Maybe Ella had gone upstairs already, sparing Gaia the scary sight of a grown woman who still looked to Barbie for fashion cues.

No such luck.

Ella was standing smack-dab in the middle of the foyer. True to form, she was sporting a metallic turquoise miniskirt with matching pumps, topped off with a fuzzy pink angora sweater that had probably been too tight on the baby she stole it off of.

Gaia's luck hadn't completely abandoned her: Ella was faced away from her and hadn't heard her approaching. Gaia could still avoid detection. In fact, she was all set to scurry back into the kitchen—until she saw what Ella was holding.

Avoiding detection suddenly stopped being important.

"What do you think you're doing?"

Ella spun around, one hand still buried deep in the pocket of Gaia's electric yellow-green Polartec coat. For a second she just stood there—frozen, guilty—then she narrowed her eyes, jutting out her chin in defiance. "What does it look like? I'm searching for drugs." She started rifling through the pockets once again, as if daring Gaia to stop her.

Gaia was across the foyer in three swift strides. "Let me save you some trouble, Ella. There aren't any." Grabbing hold of her coat, she yanked it hard out of Ella's manicured clutches.

Ella reacted as if she'd been slapped, her hands recoiling like two wounded pink spiders.

Gaia stared her flatly in the eyes. "And for future reference? I don't do drugs." Then, just in case Ella still didn't understand, she added: "Leave my stuff alone."

Ella's nostrils flared. "You think I don't know what you do?" she accused. "You think I don't see you sneaking out of here at night, heading to the park? I know what goes on out there." She jabbed her finger at the front door, tossing her copper-colored hair indignantly.

Gaia rolled her eyes. "*Please.*" To Ella's blow-dried mind, the only reason Gaia might possibly want to go to Washington Square Park was to do drugs. Well, if that's what she wanted to believe, let her. There was no way Ella would buy the truth, even if Gaia had the patience to tell it to her. Which she didn't.

Besides, how did you explain that your hobbies

included luring out and beating up would-be felons for sport?

Hell, even someone with a measurable IQ would have a hard time believing that one.

Gaia turned to leave, but Ella suddenly seized her sharply by the arm, spinning her around.

"*I know what you are.*"

Ella's press-on nails felt like five plastic knives gouging through the flannel of Gaia's sleeve.

Gaia jerked out of the woman's grasp. "Trust me, Ella. You don't know the first thing about me."

Ella was physically shorter than Gaia, but her stiletto pumps put them at roughly the same eye level. Idly Gaia found herself wondering just what color Ella's eyes would appear to the color-blind Ed Fargo. To her they were the ugly, radioactive green of mint jelly. Did that mean they would look *red* to him? Or would Ella's *hair* look *green*? Somehow the mental image of a red-eyed, green-haired Ella wasn't too hard to conjure.

Ella's lips curled into a sneer. "I knew you'd be trouble the minute you set foot in this house. George wouldn't listen to me, of course. 'Poor little Gaia, she's had such a hard life. She needs our help.'"

Gaia was impressed. For a bimbo with no discernable skill as a photographer, Ella could do a pretty mean impression of her husband's voice. She'd obviously missed her calling in life.

Ella continued tauntingly: "Well, I got news for you. Maybe that wounded-bird routine works on George, but it never fooled me. Not for *one minute.*" She punctuated the last two words with two sharp pokes to Gaia's shoulder.

Gaia glanced down at the spot where Ella had touched her. "Are you through?"

"Not quite. I also know you're doing everything in your power to flunk out of school."

Gaia raised an eyebrow. "Really?" *And what was your first clue, Nancy Drew? The string of F's, maybe?*

"That's right. Your principal called to say that you're officially on academic probation." Ella smiled smugly. "Congratulations, Gaia. And after only three months. I hear at your last school, it took you a whole semester."

Whoa. This was definitely *not* the Carol Brady moment Gaia had anticipated five minutes ago. Gaia didn't know *what* role Ella thought she was playing tonight, but if the woman was hoping to get some kind of reaction from her, she'd have to keep on hoping. Gaia wasn't going to give her any satisfaction.

Ella crossed her arms and shook her head in mock pity. "Poor George. He still has some misguided notion that you're intelligent—that we'll actually get rid of you in a couple of years when you go to college. Ha!" She made an ugly snorting sound. "*That's* a joke. Do you think colleges would even *touch* a person with your grades? Do you?" Ella leaned forward, lowering her voice to a whisper. "Or do you think colleges simply let in little blond girls who can beat old drunks at chess and are friends with cripples?"

Gaia's hands involuntarily curled into fists. Her heartbeat accelerated. But she kept her voice remarkably cool and collected as she warned: "You should watch what you're saying, Ella."

"*This is my house!*"

Ella's voice exploded with such raw, unbridled rage that Gaia found herself backing away defensively. "In *my* house *I* say what *I* want *and you listen!*" Her breath was hot on Gaia's face.

My God, Gaia thought, who *is* this person? This wasn't the old Ella who Gaia knew and disliked. She had seen that Ella angry before, and it had never been anything even remotely close to this. *This* person . . . this was someone different. Someone wholly unfamiliar.

The woman's face was contorted in a mask of fury. Her pupils were mere pinpricks in two poisonous green irises. Her lips were curled away from her teeth.

"Things are going to change around here, *starting now!* From now on, you come straight home from school. No stops in the park, no chess games. *Understand?* You're going to go to your room and you're going to do your homework. No phone, no TV.

And at night you're going to stay in this house if I have to nail every damn window shut myself. You're going to stay in this house if I have to nail your *goddamn feet to the floor!*"

Whoever this person was—Ella or her more evil twin—Gaia had finally had enough.

"I don't have to take this from you," she informed the crazy woman standing before her. "You're not my mother."

"I'm *not?*" Ella reared back, slapping her left breast in a truly third-rate imitation of shocked dismay. "No, I suppose I'm not," she continued, leaning forward again, green eyes narrowing into slits. "*My* heart's still *beating.*"

Gaia watched her fist smash into Ella's face before her brain even knew she was throwing the punch. It was that automatic. That impulsive. As uncontrollable as a sneeze and (good thing for Ella) about as sloppy as one, too. Unlike her more thought-out punches, this one barely connected with its mark, catching the underside of the woman's jaw.

Not that it made a big difference.

Ella spun, crumpling to the marble floor like a sack of bricks, landing on her hands and knees.

Everything was suddenly deathly quiet.

For the next fifteen seconds there was nothing but the sound of Ella's steady, heavy breathing and the slow, rhythmic ticking of the grandfather clock in the hall: *Ticktock. Ticktock. Ticktock.*

Gaia felt like she should do something—*say* something—but she didn't know what. "Sorry" didn't seem right. For one thing, she wasn't sorry. Not yet, anyway. Maybe later she would be.

Instead she just stood there, frozen in place, absently rubbing the knuckles of her right hand, watching Ella's shoulders rise and fall, rise and fall, inside the tight angora sweater.

*Ticktock. Ticktock. Ticktock.*

After another fifteen seconds Ella slowly crawled away from Gaia toward the foot of the stairs. Once there, she reached up and grabbed hold of the banister, then hoisted herself to her feet. Her spandex skirt had bunched up around her waist, and she took a moment to pull it back down. She smoothed down her sweater. Then, squaring her shoulders, she started slowly up the stairs.

She was halfway to the second floor when Gaia found her voice.

"Ella . . ."

Above her, Ella paused but didn't turn around. Tilting her head slightly, like a sleepwalker hearing her name being called, she said softly: "Wait there." Her voice sounded strange. Thick.

She continued up the stairs.

Gaia watched as Ella's legs disappeared from view.

Listened as the click of Ella's heels faded away, drowned out by the clock in the hall.

*Ticktock. Ticktock. Ticktock.*

It sounded remarkably like a time bomb.

# Dissolving

BLOOD. SHE WAS TASTING HER OWN goddamn blood.

Once she was out of Gaia's sight, Ella moved more quickly. Around to the next flight of stairs. Eighteen steps to the third floor. Right foot, left foot, right foot. Up, up, up.

Her tongue felt too large for her mouth. It was too wide, too thick. As she mounted the stairs, she explored her tongue's surface with her teeth, wincing as her incisors sank into the gash she'd bitten into it when the little bitch had punched her.

*When the little bitch had punched her.*

The cut felt deep.

*The little bitch had punched her.*

Despite the pain she bit down harder now, feeling oddly energized as more blood welled into her mouth. It tasted sharp and bitter, like acid.

*Punched her. Her.*

It *was* acid, she decided, stepping swiftly onto the

53

third floor. Acid, pumping through her heart, coursing through her veins. She could feel it—couldn't she?—burning in her cheeks, raging in her ears. It would dissolve her. It *was* dissolving her. Eating her from the inside out. She had to hurry. There was no time to lose.

Ten feet down the hall to her dressing room.

Her gun was in the dressing room.

She didn't care what Loki would say. Didn't care what he would do.

*She was tasting her own goddamn blood!*

Besides, she knew what had to be done now. It was obvious.

Loki had been wrong. Loki *was* wrong.

It was *not* of "utmost importance" that the "subject" be kept alive. That had been their mistake from day one.

As long as his daughter was alive, Tom Moore wasn't going to risk her life by showing his face anywhere near her.

But the bastard *might* come to her funeral.

## TICKTOCK. TICKTOCK. TICKTOCK.

Gaia stood in the foyer. Watching the stairs. Waiting for Ella to return.

Should she stay? Try to fix this gaping

rupture? Was there any point? Could she make herself apologize for George's sake?

Stay or go?

Ella was insane. This night was insane.

Stay or go?

She could hear Ella's footsteps again. She was coming back down the stairs now, rounding the landing one floor above.

Without realizing she'd made a decision, Gaia let her long strides carry her down the hallway. Numbly she pulled on her coat and threw her bag over her shoulder. The cold doorknob filled her hand, and she turned it with a click.

"Good-bye, house. Good-bye, George," she whispered. "Sorry about this."

She had a feeling as she stepped out the door that she wouldn't be coming back.

I remember the summer I started carrying pennies.

I was five years old, and we were living in our Manhattan apartment. My mom's dad got sick late that spring. He was dying, it turns out. Every weekend when we'd drive my mother to visit him in his hospital in New Jersey, my dad would take me to the Jersey shore.

You see, when you're driving back into Manhattan from the Jersey side, you have to go through a tollbooth. Nowadays things are pretty high-tech, with laser scanners and special stickers you can get for your car, but back then my dad would pay using tokens.

Of course, to a five-year-old, a coin's a coin. And to me, those tokens looked just like pennies.

Somehow, in my little-kid brain, I concluded that in order to get back home, you needed pennies for the tolls. From that

moment on, I started carrying
extra pennies with me. Just in
case.

For some reason, I had this
silly notion that my parents
could somehow lose me. You know—
just take their eyes off me
around a corner or something and
not be able to find me again.
Maybe all kids think like that
when they're small. Anyway, I
wanted to make sure that if I
ever got separated from my
folks, I'd have enough money to
pay the toll and get back home
on my own.

Later on, when I was older and
knew better, I still carried pennies. By then it had just become
this sort of superstitious habit
of mine. My talisman. My good
luck charm.

It wasn't until I was in sixth
grade that my father finally noticed
and asked me about it. When I explained the whole tollbooth story to
him, he laughed. Told me I always
worried about the wrong things.

A year later my mother was
killed and my father took off,
leaving me behind.

So I guess it wasn't such a
silly notion after all.

I don't carry pennies for good
luck anymore. They don't work all
that well, as it turns out.

Mary attached herself to Gaia by the hand, and Gaia let herself be pulled toward a waiting group that for the moment at least, could pass as friends.

a reason to stay

THERE WERE TIMES WHEN A
four-dollar vanilla latte
with an extra dollop of
foam seemed like the
answer to every single
one of life's problems.

# Red Light, Green Light

Tonight it just seemed
like an overpriced cup of
coffee.

Sitting at one of the window seats at the Starbucks
on Astor Place, Gaia forced herself to take another slug
of the sickly sweet concoction. It wasn't easy. Ten minutes ago it had been lukewarm. Now it was closer to
cold. It reminded her of the milk left over from a bowl
of sugar cereal.

Outside, across Fourth Avenue, the giant clock face
on the side of the Carl Fischer building showed that it
was almost eleven.

God, what a night. Living with George and Ella
had never been great, but it was a place to be. A place
to keep what little stuff she had. And her tenuous toe-
hold in their house had made her a New Yorker. She
liked that.

Now it was gone, and she had that slightly
metallic, nauseating taste in her throat
that came with running away. Or drinking
syrup-sweet coffee soup. Or the combination.

She knew the taste because she'd run away before.

Never successfully, though. She always ended up back where she started or in a different foster home, facing even greater doubt and suspicion from her newest "family."

This time would be different. Packed into the various zippered compartments of her messenger bag and parka were bills totaling over eight hundred dollars—three months of chess winnings. She carried it on her all the time. It was ironic. She used to carry pennies for luck. Now she kept twenties for when her luck turned sour.

It was a lot of money, but it wouldn't last long in New York City. She would be smart to leave town.

With that thought, a picture bloomed in her mind. The face of Sam Moon, sitting across the chess table from her, drenched by rain, staring directly into her heart as no one, man or woman, ever had.

It would be hard to leave him. It would be crazy to stay for him.

Then there was Ed. Her first real friend since . . . forever. She was addicted to Ed.

And to the park. And the action. The density of criminals. The number of places where you could buy doughnuts at 2 A.M. The sirens.

But tonight Ed had taken off with his family to drive to Pennsylvania for a classic Thanksgiving with bickering parents and adoring grandparents. He wouldn't be back until Sunday. It just pointed out how different they really were. How different they would always be.

Sam belonged to somebody else (whom she incidentally hated). Ed was a decent, good person with a family who loved him. Far too decent for her.

There was nothing for her here.

She tipped her head and rested it against the cold glass window. The pale, late November color of her hands picked up a green glow from the traffic light at the intersection just beyond the window. Go.

Predictably, a minute later, her hands were bathed in red. Stop.

For minutes at a time she watched hypnotically as her hands changed from green to red.

Go. Stop.

Walk. Don't walk.

She'd let the traffic light decide her fate.

Behind her, there was a complaint of hinges and an inrush of street noise as someone pushed into the Starbucks through the side entrance. A second later Gaia was assaulted by a blast of arctic air. She felt its icy fingers snake around her neck and trickle down her spine and watched in morbid fascination as the skin of her arms pebbled into gooseflesh.

The sight transfixed her. It always did.

She traced a fingertip along the surface of her forearm—slowly, exploringly—from the crook of her elbow to her wrist. Every tiny, raised bump gave her a tiny, perverse thrill.

Gooseflesh. A symptom of fear.

Of course, in Gaia's case, it was just hair follicles reacting to an extreme change of temperature. That's all it would *ever* be with her. Still, she liked to believe that in some small, weird way, getting goose bumps was like getting a tiny glimpse into what fear felt like. The simple fact that she could experience one of fear's physical manifestations made her feel less . . . different, somehow. Less freakish. More . . . human.

The goose bumps were beginning to fade.

Gaia sighed. Who was she trying to kid? She would *never* know what fear was like. No more than Ed could know what it was like to tell red from green.

Red and green. Gaia suddenly remembered her appointment with Destiny. Would she stay or would she go? Taking a breath, she raised her eyes and looked out the window.

The light was yellow.

*Gee, thanks, Destiny. You sure know how to toy with a girl's emo—*

Gaia's thoughts were interrupted by something reflected in the plate glass window. Someone was rushing up behind her. Someone with red hair.

Before she could turn around, something cold and metallic was pressed against the back of her neck. "Don't make a move," a female voice warned.

Gaia didn't move. She just sat there, staring down at her arms.

There wasn't a single damn goose bump in sight.

# MARY MOSS WAS EXPECTING THE

girl's shoulders to jump or at least her muscles to tense. They didn't, although Gaia did turn her head quickly. "Your money or your life," Mary growled, pressing the metal tube of lipstick into Gaia's back.

**No Folks**

Mary snarled menacingly, waiting for a reaction.

Gaia didn't look scared, but she didn't look quite tuned in, either. She was glowing red from a traffic light outside, and her eyes were wide and confused.

Mary softened her expression and produced the tube of lipstick for Gaia to see. "Gaia, it's me. Mary. Are you okay?"

Gaia seemed to pull her eyes into focus. She took the lipstick and examined it.

"It's called Bruise," Mary offered. "Great color, poor firearm."

Now Gaia was green. She handed the lipstick back.

"How's it going?" Mary asked, taking the seat across the little table from Gaia and tucking the lipstick tube in the outside pocket of her backpack.

Gaia looked pretty out of it. Her light hair was gathered in a messy wad at the back of her head. Her acid green jacket was half inside out, hanging untidily over the back of the chair, and her messenger bag was clamped between her feet on the floor. On the table before her was the better part of a once frothy coffee substance.

Gaia rubbed her eyes. "Sorry. You surprised me. I'm—I'm . . . all right. How 'bout you?" she answered vaguely.

Mary studied the girl's face, wondering what was really up, knowing she'd probably never know. That was part of what made Gaia fascinating to her.

"Great. I'm not going to sleep tonight," Mary announced.

Gaia was paying attention now. "Oh, yeah?"

"Yeah. The night before Thanksgiving is one of the great nights in New York. It's a night for locals."

Gaia looked puzzled. "As opposed to . . ."

"Tourists. Gawkers. The bridge-and-tunnel crowd. Hardly anything that New York is famous for is actually happening for the locals. Broadway shows. Carriage rides through Central Park. Those dumb theme restaurants. The stores on Columbus Avenue."

"Um. Okay," Gaia said, not caring enough to argue if she did happen to disagree.

"Obviously the parade tomorrow is a major gawk

fest. But tonight, right outside the park, they blow up the floats for the parade. That part is still fun. It doesn't really get good until after midnight, so I'm going to a club first to hear this very cool neighborhood band. You want to go?"

Gaia just looked at her, waiting for her to finish, clearly not feeling a big need to act friendly. That was another thing Mary liked about her. "Well. Thanks and all," Gaia said distractedly, tapping her fingers against the table. "But—"

"You have other plans," Mary finished for her.

Gaia cocked her head. "It's not that. It's—"

"So come," Mary said.

Still there was hesitation in Gaia's face.

"You've got a curfew?" Mary tried.

Gaia shook her head.

"Your folks wouldn't be into it?" Mary suggested.

Gaia shook her head. "No folks."

"No folks?"

"I don't have any," Gaia said. Just a statement of fact.

"Jesus. I wasn't expecting that answer. God. Sorry."

Gaia's eyebrows collided over her nose. She was angry. "Sorry for asking me a perfectly normal question? Why do people say that? Why do they always flip out and apologize for no reason?" Her eyes were intense, challenging.

Mary's own anger reared up instantly. "I'm not

sorry I asked you the question, you idiot," she snapped. "I'm sorry your parents are dead."

Gaia's eyes widened, then her face got calm. "Oh."

"Fine," Mary said. She got up to order a triple espresso from the lone counter person. Starbucks sucked, but her favorite café had just changed management and installed computers every five feet. She turned back to Gaia, pleased to see the girl had gotten over her anger just as quickly as Mary had. "So, you coming?"

Gaia looked somewhat `bamboozled`. "I guess. Sure."

## Just Like Sam

". . . I'M BLIND. I'M EMPTY. I'M *stupid. I'm wrong. . . .*"

Gaia wasn't quite sure how this had happened.

She'd gone from being a bleak New York casualty, a teenage runaway, to being a frivolous club kid. Here she was, sitting in a round, red velvet booth at a downtown club surrounded by New York's young indulgents, listening to a band, Fearless, whose name and lyrics dogged her life in the creepiest way.

*". . . I need you to tell me I'm not what I am. . . ."*

The singer was ranting. Gaia stared into her vodka and tonic and tried not to think about it too much.

Most of the people at the table, including Mary, were on their third drinks before Gaia had drunk a third of her first. She didn't like alcohol very much. For one thing, it didn't taste good. Maybe that was babyish of her, but it was true. Besides, from what she could tell, the real reason people drank was to dull their fear. Not what Gaia needed. What if alcohol consumption pushed her from zero fear into negative fear? Gaia slid the sweaty glass a few inches toward the center of the table. That didn't seem like a good idea.

She turned her head as Mary tugged on a piece of her hair and then glided toward the dance floor. "You're having fun," Mary shouted over the din. It was more command than question. "Want to dance with us?"

"No," Gaia mouthed. It did actually look like fun, but somehow it didn't seem right, punching Ella out cold and hitting the dance floor in the same two-hour period. She felt obligated to remain dysfunctional and sullen for at least another hour.

Still, she couldn't help smiling at Mary, who was whirling like a dervish through the crowds. Mary was a wild dancer, not surprisingly, and her hair paid no attention to gravity. Gaia couldn't help admiring her. Mary had none of the self-consciousness that sometimes made it embarrassing to watch a person dance.

Gaia glanced at her watch. If she was leaving town, she needed to get going. Traveling on Thanksgiving was notoriously bad. It would be smarter to catch a train or a bus tonight. That way she could sleep in transit and not have to pay for a place to stay.

All of Mary's friends were dancing now. Gaia was alone in the booth. The place was packed, and she felt a bit self-conscious taking up this seating area for eight. She realized a guy standing by the bar was looking at her. No, make that staring. He appeared to be at least thirty. Ick.

Oh, shit, he was coming toward her. She directed an intensely unfriendly expression at him. *Go away now. I do not like you.*

He turned back to the bar. Ahhh. Good. Gaia had to hand it to herself. She could give a mean look like nobody.

Gaia gazed around the club. She'd never been to a place like this before. It was loud. It was dark. People were having fun. It seemed like a great place to go if you were a bored New York City kid looking to hook up. It was a weird place to go shortly after you'd decked your so-called foster mother, on a night you were running away for good.

But what if she *were* just a regular kid, stressed out

and angst ridden in a contained, urbane, happy kind of way, looking to hook up? It was a fun game to play sometimes.

She scanned the bar. There was a guy near the front windows who was sort of cute. He had hair the same color as Sam's. His nose and chin couldn't compare, though. And he appeared to be at least five inches shorter than Sam.

Another guy in a booth two away from hers had a good smile. Nice teeth. A little crooked. His eyes were nice, too. Not like Sam's, of course. Not turn-your-world-over nice. Besides, he was wearing one of those big, fancy metal watches. She hated those.

She slid her drink around in its little puddle on the glass table. The volume in the place notched up even higher. She turned to the entrance and saw another cluster of people packing themselves in. Her eyes froze. Oh, wow. There. That guy was beautiful, Gaia thought distantly. Tall, perfectly built. He had gorgeous red-brown-blond hair, neither wavy nor curly but somewhere in between. Just like Sam, her mind informed her dreamily.

Holy shit. Gaia sat up very straight. He wasn't *like* Sam. He *was* Sam. Her mind raced. Her heartbeat quickened. Goose bumps sprouted on her arms. *Almost like fear.* But not fear. Something else.

Gaia's eyes darted to the faces of Sam's nearest companions.

`Clunk.` Down slid her hopes.

Yes, indeed. The good-news, bad-news duo. Hateful Heather was in her usual spot right there beside him. Why *shouldn't* Sam and Heather make an appearance on this night from hell? How could it be otherwise?

Gaia averted her gaze. She pointed her face at the tabletop. She really didn't want them to see her. A word from Heather might just throw her over the edge.

Suddenly she felt terribly conspicuous in the booth by herself. Where were Mary and all her friends? `Why couldn't they park their damn butts in the booth for five minutes and stop having so much fun?` Grrrr.

Gaia rested her face in her hand, using her fingers to cover up almost the entire part of her face that Sam and Heather could feasibly see from their angle. She would just stay like that until they got busy dancing or went to the back, and then she'd leave. She'd head for the bus station. Fine.

*Oh, no.* She couldn't actually look up to confirm her suspicion, but she had a terrible feeling that the group, which included her favorite couple, was heading straight toward her booth. There was definitely a shadow moving in. No. Go! Go!

"Excuse me? Would you mind if we shared your booth?" It wasn't a voice she recognized. Could she get away with not looking up?

"Excuse me!"

Go away, she urged silently.

*"Excuse me!"*

All right, that was annoying. She snapped her head up just as Heather and Sam registered the reality of whom they were about to share a booth with.

Who looked least happy? Sam? Heather? Gaia?

Hard to say.

Gaia thought she gave a mean look, but Heather's was better.

Gaia shot to her feet. "All yours. I was just going."

Six pairs of eyes stuck on Gaia as she fumbled to put on her parka. It seemed to take two hours. First it was inside out. Then she couldn't get her hand through the sleeve. As she grabbed for her bag, she knocked over her drink and spritzed the group with watery vodka and dead tonic. Why couldn't she keep her beverages to herself?

She couldn't bring herself to look at Sam. This wasn't happening.

"Gaia, wait." It was Mary, suddenly positioning herself as a bulwark between Gaia and the booth stealers. "Where are you going?"

"I—I gotta go. Now."

Mary looked around. She took in the presence of Heather. A light dawned in her eyes. "Hey, if it isn't the charming Ms. Gannis. Gosh, I remember the last time we were all at a party together. You were riding quite the welcome wagon that night."

Heather was silent.

Mary gave Gaia a confident smile and spoke loudly enough for Heather's benefit. "Don't worry, Gaia. If Heather treats you like that again, I'll smack her."

Heather looked stunned. A couple of Heather's friends seemed to think Mary was kidding around. Gaia didn't look at Sam to gauge his reaction.

Mary attached herself to Gaia by the hand, and Gaia let herself be pulled toward a waiting group that, for the moment at least, could pass as friends.

"Bitch," Mary mumbled to Gaia, not letting go of her hand. "Let's get out of here."

Gaia felt like crying as she bobbed along after Mary. Nobody ever took care of her like that. Gaia was so taken aback, she didn't know how to feel.

Following the electrified red hair, she experienced a rush of real warmth in spite of the stiff, late-autumn breeze.

Maybe there *was* a reason to stay in New York for a while longer.

## HEATHER FELT LIKE SHE WAS CHEWING

on a lemon. She couldn't seem to get the sour taste out of her mouth or remove the pinched expression from her face.

Sam sat down next to her, stiff as a two-by-four, saying nothing.

That was the best strategy. They would just let this pass and get on with their night. No need to talk about it.

"Who is that girl?" Sam's friend Christian Pavel wanted to know.

"You mean Mary Moss? The redhead?" Heather heard her friend Jonathan Singer respond.

"No, the blond one."

Heather waited numbly for the conversation to be over. She tried to think of some effective way to change tracks.

"That's Gaia Moore," Jonathan said flatly.

"She's unbelievable," Christian said.

Every person at the table waited in uncomfortable suspense to hear the precise way in which Christian Pavel found Gaia Moore unbelievable.

"She's gorgeous. A total goddess. Do you know her? Can you introduce me?"

No one said a word. Heather's mouth was drawn up like a twist tie. She felt like crushing all ten of Christian's toes under the table.

Sam cleared his throat. "H-H-Have you all seen this band before?" he asked the group gallantly, putting a wooden arm around Heather's shoulders.

Conversation resumed. Heather watched Gaia's back disappear through the door. She wished she could give Gaia a poisonous cloak.

Then again, Gaia's phlegm-colored jacket was pretty poisonous as it was.

# SAM SAT IN THE BOOTH, AS CROSS

## Lustful Looks

and sullen as a sleep-deprived toddler. Too sullen to drink. Or dance. Or make small talk.

He was annoyed at Heather for being his girlfriend. He was annoyed at Christian for looking lustfully at Gaia. (That was *his* department.) He was annoyed at Gaia for a whole list of things:

1. Not being his girlfriend;
2. Looking so spectacularly beautiful;
3. Ruining his life;
4. Ruining his relationship;
5. Not meeting his eyes for a single second tonight;
6. Not being his girlfriend.

Mostly he was annoyed at himself. For blundering deeper into the thing with Heather. For being so goddamned stiff and awkward tonight. For not talking honestly with Heather about what was really going on. For having blown a perfectly good chance to do so.

For still staring at the door fully forty-five minutes after Gaia had walked through it.

*My Dear Gaia,*

*Having seen you so recently (though you did not see me), my pain at being apart from you is only stronger. You have grown into a formidable woman, Gaia, as your mother and I knew you would. Your strength and intensity still astound me. I see now that you have the spirit to fight fiercely for your life, and that is a great comfort to me.*

*My other comfort is the knowledge that at last you have a good home with my kind old friend George. It's a safe place. I trust George will do his very best by you. I'm glad to know you'll have Thanksgiving there, with someone who truly cares for you.*

*Each year at Thanksgiving, I write to tell you that you are my reason for thanks, my reason for living. Each year, with my heart full of hope, I pray that next year we'll spend this holiday together. And though realism chips away at my hope, I'm still praying.*

*Know that I love you, Gaia. That you are always in my heart.*

Tom Moore signed the letter and thought about Katia. Twice a year he allowed himself to cry for her, and this was one of those times.

When he was done, he walked to the file cabinet.

The top drawer was stuffed full of letters like this one. He found the manila folder labeled Thanksgiving Letters and dropped it in.

He dug his hand in the pocket of his corduroy trousers and felt the penny that lay in the bottom. Perhaps, with luck, this would be the last time he would need to write to Gaia on Thanksgiving.

Gaia clutched
the stretchy
plastic in
her fist as
they rose
under a
cloud of
helium,
higher
and higher.

**fun,**

**for**

**a**

**change**

**"WHAT *THE DEVIL* WENT ON THERE** tonight?" Loki's voice thundered.

Ella stood before him, heavy with a strange mixture of shame, pride, and frustration. Her jaw throbbed, and her tongue felt like it belonged

# The Good Uncle

to somebody else. "We fought. She punched me. She left." Ella didn't bother to mention the part where she got out her gun and went after Gaia, fully intending to blow her brains out. Luckily that part didn't appear on the surveillance tape.

"Stupid woman, have you lost your mind?"

Ella cupped her jaw tenderly. There would be no sympathy from him. That was certain. "The girl hit me."

"I would have hit you, too, the way you carried on," Loki said sharply.

Ella held her painful tongue. It was as expected.

"Absurd self-indulgence," he spat, pacing across the soft, honey-colored herringbone floorboards. Last month he had a vast loft above the Hudson River. Tonight she'd been ordered to meet him in a starkly modern apartment building on Central Park South. He'd only be there so long as he kept perfect anonymity. Then he'd relocate again. "Why I put up with you, I do not know."

Ella remained quiet. He'd get bored of the tirade eventually. The greatest mistake would be to attempt to defend herself. That would only inject a surge of energy into the project. Where Loki was concerned, what the world gained in a terrorist, it had lost in a lawyer.

His angry voice faded into a dull roar. Ella stared out the large picture windows, waiting for him to be done. Three-quarters of a mile uptown, the enormous helium balloons for the Thanksgiving Day parade were rising to life from the lawns of the Museum of Natural History on Seventy-seventh Street. Long ago, in her other life, she'd gone with friends to watch.

That was before Ella had been "discovered." Well before Gaia had come into their lives, a much more perfect fulfillment of Ella's early promise. Ella felt a wave of nausea climbing her chest.

*"Ella!"*

She turned to him. Oh. He was finished, then. He'd asked her a question of the nonrhetorical variety. "I'm sorry?"

"You are sorry. A truly sorry creature. I asked you why you were caught with your arm in Gaia's coat."

"I was planting the tracking device," Ella replied.

"And were you able to complete that *onerous* task?" His voice was laced with sarcasm.

"I was."

"Fine. And I gather you've chosen someone to perform the job?"

"Yes." Ella fiercely hoped he would not ask who that was.

"Well, then. With any luck we'll be done with Tom shortly." He smiled the least cheerful smile Ella had ever witnessed. "That should be fun. And then the real plans begin."

# "SO WHO DO YOU LIKE?" MARY

asked. "Clifford, the big red dog? Random Rugrat? Snoopy?"

The night was misty. The octagonal stones around the beautiful, castlelike Museum of Natural History were slick with yellow and brown leaves.

## A Big, Red M&M

Gaia and Mary were still clutching hands like kindergarten best friends, running through the crowds, watching the enormous balloons come to life.

"Spiderman is cool," Gaia observed, gazing at the balloon reaching four stories into the sky. A net above them kept the balloons on good behavior until the parade began in the morning.

"Spiderman is already up, up, and away," Mary said somewhat breathlessly, pulling Gaia along. "We need to pick one that's only partway blown up."

"We do?" Gaia asked.

Mary raised her eyebrows mischievously. "We do."

Gaia caught up even with her. "What exactly are you planning?"

"Something fun. You'll see." She glanced over at Gaia. "You scared?"

"Uh-uh," Gaia replied.

"Here." Mary yanked her to a stop. "These ones are good. Shhh. Stay still a minute."

The ones Mary was referring to were huge ponds of half-inflated plastic, one red, the other green. Gaia couldn't tell what they were.

Mary looked around. "Okay, follow me. Move quickly, before anybody sees us."

Gaia nodded, intensely curious.

Mary paused in thought. "Hang on. Which one? Red or green?"

"I don't care," Gaia said.

"Pick!" Mary ordered.

Gaia rolled her eyes. "They're the same. It doesn't matter. I don't even know what we're doing."

Mary was still glaring at her expectantly.

"All right, fine. Red," Gaia said.

"Go," Mary hissed.

She darted around the growing balloon to the side

that was closest to the museum fence and used the fence for a boost. She transferred her weight from the fence to the balloon, clamored up the soft, loose plastic, then rolled down into the sagging middle. Gaia followed close behind. When they settled in the middle, they had to cling to the plastic to keep from rolling on top of each other.

"This is cozy," Mary said, laughter in her voice.

"I still don't know what we're doing," Gaia said.

"Shhh. Stay still. We have to keep quiet."

Mary's excitement was contagious. "Why?" Gaia asked.

"'Cause the last time I did this, I got arrested," Mary explained happily.

"Oh," Gaia said.

"Scared yet?" Mary asked.

"Not yet," Gaia replied.

Gaia heard the rush of helium into the balloon get louder.

"Cool," Mary whispered. "They're turning it up."

"They?"

"The inflators," Mary said.

"Is that a word?" Gaia asked.

Mary's giggle came out like a snort. "I think so."

Gaia felt the helium filling the space under them. They were rising appreciably. "Now what?" she whispered.

"We wait," Mary said. She reached for Gaia's hand and held it again. Gaia was so unaccustomed to physical contact (apart from punching people) that it felt weird to her. Weird, but nice, too.

As the minutes passed, the plastic began to fill and grow around them. Soon the thin, rubbery plastic was puffing up all around them, becoming more and more taut.

"What is this balloon, anyway?" Gaia asked.

Mary lifted her head and looked behind her. "Judging from the green one next door, I think it's an M&M."

"An M&M?"

"Yeah, look." Mary rolled partly onto her side and pointed at the green twin.

"We're on a giant red M&M?" Gaia realized she was getting punchy because for some reason, this seemed hilarious.

"Okay. This is where it starts to get fun." Mary's face was flushed with anticipation. "Hold on tight, okay? I think we've got a facial feature of some kind here."

It was thrilling. Gaia clutched the stretchy plastic in her fist as they rose under a cloud of helium, higher and higher. She was amazed nobody had seen them yet. She twisted her head and saw the buildings above. The ritzy apartment buildings on one side, the museum on the other. They were rising faster now, above the streetlights, nearing the tops of the trees.

Closer and closer to the gauzy, dark purple night sky. She looked ahead to the ever improving view of Central Park with its dark carpet of trees and the twinkly lights along Fifth Avenue.

Gaia felt her own breath swelling inside her chest. It was magical. "Beautiful," she whispered to Mary.

Mary squeezed her hand.

Gaia tried to stamp this feeling, these sights, into her brain so she could remember them later, when she needed to convince herself there was happiness in the world.

"Oh, shit!" Mary suddenly cried, puncturing Gaia's reverie. Mary yanked her hand from Gaia's, pinching wildly at the plastic of the balloon to steady herself. "I'm losing it, Gaia!"

The plastic had grown so taut under their hands, it was hard to keep holding. Mary's grip was slipping fast.

Gaia turned to her new friend, expecting to see fear in the girl's eyes. Instead she saw wide-eyed thrill.

"Gaiaaaa!" Mary was yelling. "Eeeeeee! This is where it gets *really* fun! When I say go, let go!"

A laugh erupted from Gaia's throat. This was crazy. It *was* fun.

"Go!" Mary screamed.

"Ahhhhhhhhh!" The two girls' voices mingled in a

scream as they slid on their stomachs all the way down the growing mountain of balloon and landed hard on the ground.

They lay there for a moment in a tangled clump.

"Are you okay?" Mary asked, pushing her hair out of her face, trying to organize her limbs.

"Okay? That was awesome!" Gaia jumped to her feet and pulled her friend beside her. "Let's do it again."

Mary laughed and swatted Gaia on the shoulder. "I *knew* we were gonna get along."

## TWO HOURS LATER GAIA LAY BESIDE

### Extra Love

Mary on the grassy part of Strawberry Fields and watched the first light of sun spread across the sky. The air felt damp and surprisingly mild.

Gaia fell in love with the place on first sight. She loved the curving pathways and the odd accumulation of humanity gathered on the handsome benches. She loved the white-and-black mosaic that said "Imagine" in the middle.

"This is my favorite place," Mary said, grabbing the sentiment right from Gaia's mind.

"I see why." Gaia turned her head to see Mary's face.

Mary yawned and raised her arms, stretching long fingers toward the sky. Gaia caught the yawn from her.

"Hey, Mary?"

"Yeah."

"Thanks for inviting me along on this night. It's been great."

Mary turned to her and smiled. "It wouldn't have been great without you."

Gaia must have been very tired because she was saying things she would never normally say. She was forgetting to censor her feelings and words, forgetting what the consequences could be. "And thanks a lot for looking after me at that bar."

"No prob," Mary said to the sky. "I always take care of my friends."

Gaia thought for a few moments. "Why is that?" she asked. Her voice was so quiet, she wasn't sure it would carry to Mary, two feet away.

Mary yawned again. She put her fingers into her fiery hair. "Because I can afford to."

Gaia squinted at her. "What do you mean?"

"I get a lot of love. From my folks, my brothers. I have extra."

In the pale morning light, that seemed to Gaia both a totally unexpected and beautiful thing to say. She tried to imagine what kind of parents would love Mary so well *and* let her stay out all night, doing whatever she pleased. "Why not keep it for yourself?" Gaia heard herself asking. It was unusual for her brain to connect to her mouth so directly. "That's what most people would do."

Mary considered this. "I have trouble holding on to it."

Silence enveloped them again.

After a long time Mary turned on her side and propped herself up on her elbow. "So, what are you doing for Thanksgiving dinner?"

Gaia hesitated. She couldn't say she was doing nothing. It was too pathetic. It was begging for sympathy and an invitation. But she couldn't lie, either. She had a feeling Mary wouldn't buy a lie very easily. "Oh. Well. I was thinking I might—"

"Wait a minute," Mary broke in. "Why am I asking? I know what you're doing."

Gaia furrowed her brow. "You do?"

"Yeah."

"Okay. So?"

"You're eating with my family."

"I am?"

"You are. You definitely are."

"Are you sure?"

"Completely, one hundred percent sure."

Gaia couldn't help but let a smile out. "Great. I'll let myself know."

**THE DOCTOR TIED THE BELT OF**
his nondescript and greatly
despised tan trench coat. In
recent years he'd become attached to very fine clothes.
But this coat continued to
be useful to him when he
was conducting his "side

# A Crowded Thursday

business." It was not only too boring to warrant notice, but of such an inferior material that it was machine washable. That part was important.

Pausing briefly at the corner of Fifty-fifth Street
and Fifth Avenue, he studied the information stored in
the tracking device. Now, this was a very busy
girl. First the West Village, then Astor Place. Then
the remote East Village, then West Seventy-seventh
Street, Central Park, and what appeared to be a high
floor of an apartment building on Central Park West
and Sixty-fifth Street. Did teenagers no longer find
sleep necessary at all?

He would need to follow her carefully. He wanted
this job done by midnight, and her current location—
no doubt in a private home—was far less than ideal.
That whorish woman—what was her less than amus-
ing alias? Travesura?—had assured him this girl spent
a lot of time on the streets and in public places. It had
better be so.

He touched his trusted knives, tied up in

felt casing in his roomy pocket. This girl was reported to be quite beautiful and exceptionally strong. That was enticing to him. That's why he'd taken on the job.

"Excuse me!" he snapped, nearly colliding with a shabby-looking woman pushing a stroller containing a shabby-looking infant.

He tried to remember why there were so many people—so many children—milling around the streets of New York City on a Thursday morning at nine o'clock.

For me, Thanksgiving is a mixed bag. On the one hand, there's turkey with stuffing and my grandfather's apple pie. I love that. On the other hand, there are turnips and pumpkin pie. I'd like to know: Who really likes pumpkin pie? Let's all be honest.

On the one hand, there are people like me, hanging out with my grandparents. I love them. On the other hand, there are people like Gaia, who have nobody. That's heartbreaking.

If you think about it, even the first Thanksgiving was in no way a cause for bilateral cheer. I mean, sure, the Native Americans had shown the Pilgrims how to farm the land, and they were psyched about their first harvest. But what did the Native Americans have to celebrate? Alcoholism, VD, and blankets infected with smallpox.

One arm. Two arms. The fab-ric settled with unexpected ease over her stomach and butt, the skirt grazing a few inches above her knees.

**too nice**

**"THIS IS TOO NICE."** GAIA SAID
it out loud to the Victorian-
colored glass chandelier that
hung over the vast, pillow-laden
guest bed in Mary's family's
apartment.

# The Red Dress

Being friends with Mary was
too nice. Mary's unbelievably
huge and fantastic apartment on Central Park
West was way too nice. The smell of roasting
turkey and buttery stuffing was too nice. The
thought of spending Thanksgiving with a real family for the first time in five years . . . too nice to
think about.

Gaia tried to remind herself to keep her suspicions
close around her, but Mary, this place . . . it was
dazzling. Can't you just enjoy something? she
asked herself impatiently. Accept that some places,
some people are purely nice?

She didn't have time to answer herself. There was a
knock on the door, and seconds later, Mary opened it
partially and poked her head in. "Hi."

"Hi."

"Did you sleep?"

"Like a vegetable."

"Me too. Guess what time it is?"

Gaia shrugged. She wasn't used to having someone
talk to her while she was lying in bed. She wasn't a

slumber-party kind of girl. She sat up and hugged a pillow on her lap.

"One o'clock. P.M. Big meal is in one hour."

Gaia cleared her throat. What exactly had she'd gotten herself into here? "Is it a dressed-up sort of thing?" Her voice came out squeaky. She didn't want to bring up the fact that she had no home, no possessions, and certainly no Central Park West party clothes at the moment.

Mary had a knack for coming to Gaia's rescue without Gaia even having to ask. "Just a little. I've been laying out stuff in my room. I have the most fabulous dress for you. Come on."

Gaia sat on the edge of the bed. She was wearing a big gray T-shirt she'd worn under her flannel shirt last night. Her legs were bare, her feet covered by white cotton socks. "Like this?" she asked.

"Sure," Mary said. "It's just down the hall. No brothers in sight. I mean, in case you care."

Mary was under the mistaken impression that Gaia was a normal human being who did things like this. The easiest thing would be to play along, to pretend she had comfy pals whose clothes she borrowed, in whose homes she felt perfectly fine wandering around in a T-shirt and socks.

Gaia was a terrible actress. She skulked down the hall and darted into Mary's room like an escapee from Attica.

Once the door was shut, she made herself relax. Mary wasn't kidding about laying out clothes. If there was a carpet in the spacious room, it would have taken an archaeologist to find it. Only the rough shapes of the various pieces of furniture were apparent under thick piles of clothes.

Mary was unapologetic about her colossal slobbiness. Gaia liked that in a person.

"Okay, you ready for the perfect dress?" Mary asked.

Gaia nodded.

"Tra la." Mary held up a tiny, red, crushed velvet dress with a plunging neckline.

Gaia stared. "Are you kidding? I couldn't fit my left foot into that dress."

Mary frowned. "Have you tried it? No. Shut up until you try it."

Gaia held out her hand for it. It weighed about three ounces. "Yes, ma'am. I've never been dressed by a fascist before." Feeling large and self-conscious, Gaia pulled the T-shirt over her head and quickly yanked the dress over her head and shoulders. One arm. Two arms. The fabric settled with unexpected ease over her stomach and butt, the skirt grazing a few inches above her knees.

Mary was surveying the progress with her hands on her hips. When Gaia turned around, her frown blossomed into a smile. "Wow! See?" She took Gaia's hand and pulled her in front of the full-length mirror on the back of her closet.

Gaia gazed at herself in genuine surprise. The dress actually fit. Granted, it was made of stretchy stuff. And it did cling to her gigantic muscles in an unforgiving manner.

"I look like Arnold Schwarzenegger in a dress," Gaia mumbled.

"*What?*" Mary demanded. "I'm going to smack you, girl. You look incredible."

Gaia turned around to examine her backside. "I have incredibly huge muscles."

Mary blew out her breath in frustration. "Guy-aaaaa," she scolded. "You have the body every woman would die to have. You have the long, defined muscles that keep the rest of us slogging it out in overpriced gyms around the country. You have to see that."

"I see Mr. Universe."

"Shut *up!*" Mary roared. Now she was mad. She held out her hand. "So give it back. Seriously. I mean it. If you can't appreciate that it looks beautiful, you don't deserve to borrow my goddamned dress."

Gaia cast her a pleading gaze. "Look, I'm trying. I really am." She studied herself in the mirror for another minute, trying to see herself through other eyes.

The dress really was extraordinary. Gaia loved the too long sleeves and the way they flared at the wrist. "Please let me borrow it?" Gaia asked, weirded out by hearing those words in her voice. "I'll say anything, true or untrue. I am Kate Moss. I am a waif. I can't do a single push-up."

Mary laughed. "Fine. It's yours. In fact, you can have it for keeps. After seeing you in it, I won't be able to stand the sight of me."

Now it was Gaia's turn to glare. "Hang on. *You're* allowed the exaggeratedly negative body image, but not me? Who made these rules?"

Mary waved a hand in the air. "Point taken. Never mind. But keep the stupid dress." She gestured at the snowstorm of clothes. "I have others, as you may have noticed." She rooted around the bottom of her closet and threw Gaia a pair of black cotton tights.

"Thanks," Gaia said.

"Oh, and here."

"Ouch." A dark red, forties-style pump flew out of the closet and hit Gaia on the shin. Thankfully, she dodged its mate.

"Sorry," Mary murmured. Now she was gathering jewelry for Gaia.

"What size are your feet?" Gaia asked, staring suspiciously at the shoe.

"Eight."

"I wear eight and a half," Gaia said.

Mary was busy untangling a clump of necklaces. "So? Close enough."

Apparently Mary didn't get hung up on little matters like housing all five toes.

Again, though, Mary was right. The shoe was close enough to fitting. Gaia put on the second one and stomped around the room, trying to get used to the heels.

Mary spent the next twenty minutes coaxing Gaia into the makeup chair, and the twenty minutes after that brushing Gaia's hair, spangling her with jewelry, and hunting down the exact right shade of lip gloss. At last she was done. "Oh my God, my brothers are going to be drooling," she announced, nodding at her finished work.

Gaia did feel prettier, but she also felt like someone else.

"Are you ready to meet the clan?"

If Gaia had the potential to feel nervous, now would have been an obvious time. "I guess so." She looked at Mary. Mary was still wearing blue nylon warm-up pants and a wife-beater tank top. Light freckles stood out on her thin shoulders and arms. Her hair was possibly the craziest mess Gaia had ever seen.

"Oh, I'm fine," Mary claimed. Her eyes darted around the room, and she picked up the first thing in her path, a blue chenille sweater, and stuck her head through. "All set," she confirmed.

Gaia was speechless as she followed Mary out of

the room. She remembered what Mary had said about not holding on to love very well.

**"HOW ARE THE POTATOES COMING,** Sam?" Mrs. Gannis's voice floated into the kitchen.

**Potato Physics**

Sam looked up from the huge aluminum pot. He felt like a wolf with its leg caught in a trap. He finally understood the wolf's perverse temptation to chew off its own leg.

Why had he insisted, in that breezy, thoughtless way, that he would take care of the mashed potatoes? At the time, mashed potatoes seemed like the simplest thing on earth. You get potatoes; you mash them.

Besides, he'd figured this important job in the kitchen would keep him out of the fray of tense Gannis-family relations. It would give him a little breathing room from Heather, too, which they both needed. It had gotten to the point where every single thing brought them right back into the danger zone. A casual question from Heather's mother about what they'd done the previous night, an innocent reference to chess, a song on the radio about a girl with blond hair. Not being in the same room with Heather or talking about anything at all seemed the safest bet.

But Sam now understood that making mashed potatoes belonged in a category with particle physics, only harder. Before you mashed them, you had to cook them to make them soft, it turned out. How were you supposed to do that? First he'd thrown the whole pile in the oven, but what was the right temperature, and how long would it take? Then he took a cue from the one meal he'd ever made successfully—spaghetti. You made hard noodles soft by boiling them. So he boiled up the potatoes. It seemed to take hours before they were soft.

Now he was beating the crap out of those poor, boiled potatoes, working up a sweat. On the table was a whole tool kit of discarded instruments. The dinner fork was too small, obviously. The plastic whisk was wimpy. The metal slotted spoon made a tremendous racket. At last Mr. Gannis had acquainted him with a tool called a masher. A masher! A holiday miracle. Who could have guessed there'd be an implement built for this exact purpose?

Now he was madly mashing. Only the potatoes still didn't look right. Mashed potatoes were supposed to be smooth and pale yellow in color. These were lumpy and riddled with brown skin. Oh. Something occurred to him. You were supposed to take the skin off first, weren't you? He tried to fish out the bigger pieces of skin. It was hopeless.

Well, maybe they tasted good. He took a taste.

They tasted slightly more flavorful than air. All right, well, that's what salt was for. He shook in a small blizzard of salt.

He cast an eye at the fridge. Hmmm. He took out a box of butter. He remembered his mom once saying that her motto for cooking was, When in doubt, add butter. He threw in a stick. He threw in another stick. He was still in doubt. He threw in a third.

He stirred, hoping his mother hadn't just been being witty.

## "SO, GAIA, HOW LONG HAVE YOU

lived in New York?"

Now Gaia remembered

# Disappointment

the problem with meeting strangers, particularly the parents-of-friends variety of strangers. They asked you things.

Gaia chewed a piece of turkey breast and tried to look agreeably at Mary's mother. She swallowed it with effort. "Well, I guess I—"

"No questions," Mary interrupted, coming to Gaia's rescue yet again. "No interrogating Mary's new friend, Mom."

Mary's mom laughed, which Gaia thought was pretty sporting of her. She gave Gaia a conspiratorial look. "My daughter is very bossy. You may have noticed this."

Gaia liked Mary's mom so far. She had dark red hair, sort of like Mary's but far better behaved. She wore cropped black wool pants and a bright orange velvet button-down shirt that clashed mightily with her hair. It wasn't standard middle-aged mom apparel, but it wasn't a grown-up person trying too hard to be cool, either.

The family's cook, Olga, appeared at Gaia's elbow with a steaming silver serving dish of baby vegetables. They were tidy and beautiful, not the creamed vegetable slop that usually showed up on Thanksgiving. Gaia guessed from Olga's accent that she was Russian and that she hadn't been speaking English for long. "Thank you," she murmured, trying to serve herself without bouncing baby potatoes into her lap. Or Mary's dress's lap.

"The food's fantastic," Mary's brother said to Olga.

Was he Paul or Brendan? Gaia couldn't remember. He was the cuter one, though, with light blue eyes and a quarter-inch of stubble on his chin.

"Absolutely," Mary's father agreed. He raised his glass for at least the fourth time in the meal. "Let's give thanks for Olga, a godsend." They all clinked glasses and agreed yet again. Gaia noted that there was sparkling water in his glass and not wine.

Olga seemed pleased with the attention. "Stop eet, Meester Moss," she ordered coyly.

Out of the corner of her eye, Gaia saw Mary stand up.

"I gotta pee. I'll be back in a minute," Mary announced to the table at large.

Mary's mom smiled in her forbearing way, and Gaia saw an emotion she wasn't sure how to analyze. There was something in the woman's face that struck Gaia as both worried and apologetic at the same time.

Suddenly Olga was back at Gaia's elbow, this time holding a basket of corn bread. It smelled like happiness. "Would you like some?" Olga asked.

Remotely, without really thinking about it, Gaia registered that Olga's words came out clear and crisp, without an accent.

"Of course. It smells delicious. Did you make this, too?" Gaia asked politely.

She served herself a fat piece of corn bread, and when she looked up, the entire Moss family, minus Mary, was staring at her. Olga was staring, too.

Gaia glanced from face to face. Oh, shit. What had she done now? These stares were too extreme to signify she'd used the wrong fork. She felt her mouth to see if she was wearing a mustache of cranberry sauce or anything.

"You speak Russian," Mr. Moss declared.

"I do?" Gaia found herself asking dumbly. She looked back at Olga and realized what must have happened. Olga must have murmured to her in Russian, and she must have answered in Russian without thinking. "I—I guess I do. Some, anyway," Gaia said, her fingers pinching and pulling at the napkin under the table.

Gaia felt badly thrown by this. Her mother spoke Russian to her from the time she was a baby, and Gaia grew accustomed to switching back and forth between languages hundreds of times a day. But those words gave her a feeling on her tongue that she associated purely with her mother. She hadn't spoken Russian in five years.

The table was still silent. Gaia felt her vision blurring. She stood up, keeping her gaze down. "Excuse me for just a moment," she mumbled.

"Of course," Mrs. Moss said.

Gaia walked blindly from the dining room and down the hallway. She hadn't meant to go to Mary's room, exactly. She just wasn't thinking.

The moment she opened the door to Mary's room, Mary froze. Gaia took two steps forward and froze, too.

Mary was bent far over her dressing table. Her eyes, turned now to Gaia, were large. In her hand was a rolled-up tube of paper. On the tabletop was a mirror, and on the mirror were several skinny rows of white powder cut from a tiny white hill. A razor blade winked at her in the light.

Gaia was naive and inexperienced, but she wasn't stupid. She knew what Mary was doing, and it made her feel sick.

She stared at Mary for another moment before she turned and left the room. She strode to the guest room and gathered her bag and coat.

She forced herself to take a detour on the way to the elevator.

"Mr. and Mrs. Moss," she announced from the entrance to the dining room. "I'm so sorry, but I have to go. Thank you very sincerely for letting me come."

She made her way to the elevator vestibule without a backward glance. She shrugged on her coat as the car descended. Yellow-green jacket. Red dress. She thought of Ed.

Outside on the street a siren blared, surprising her with its jarring unpleasantness.

**"MY GOD, SAM, THESE ARE THE** best potatoes I've ever eaten," Mr. Gannis said heartily, serving up his fourth helping. Sam hoped he wasn't going to be responsible for putting the man in the hospital with a heart attack.

He looked at the other plates around the table.

Each of the four underfed Gannis women still had on her plate an untouched pile of potatoes so calorie packed, they were bleeding butter. Heather met his eyes apologetically. "They're awfully, um . . . rich."

*Dear Ed,*

*I'm sorry not to be saying this to you in person, but good-bye. I have to leave New York for a while. Things got out of hand with Ella, and, well . . . hopefully I'll get the chance to tell you about it someday.*

*It's time for me to set up a new life. I'm almost of legal age to be on my own now. And with all of my useful skills and abilities—not to mention my sunny temperament—I should have all kinds of great job possibilities:*

> *Waitress*
> *Counter-person at 7-Eleven*
> *Tollbooth attendant*
> *Dishwasher*

*So before I go, I just wanted to tell you this one thing, and I hope you'll forgive me for being sappy. But as I wracked my brains to think of stuff to be thankful for, the only thing I felt sure of is you. You are a much better friend than I've ever deserved.*

*I will never ever forget you for as long (or short) as I live.*

*Gaia*

He wheeled back
and opened the
door just wide
enough so that

# pennsylvania

he could **station**

toss the

bloody scalpel

into the trash

can.

GAIA LOOKED UP AT THE BIG destination board that hung above the expansive waiting area of Penn Station. The board operated like the tote board on **One Way** *Family Feud*—its tiles turning to reveal all the destinations. "Survey says . . . Trenton—Northeast Corridor—track 12—5:09." "Survey says . . . Boston—New England Express—track 9—5:42."

The place was ugly and crowded, and it smelled bad. And by the way, she wondered sourly, whose brilliant idea was it to call the train station smack-dab in the middle of New York City Pennsylvania Station? Hello? Ever take a geography class?

She felt tired and sad and cranky, no longer riding the powerful surge of anger and indignation that made it much more satisfying to run away.

She eyed the different cities, having absolutely no idea where she wanted to go. If she could go anywhere, she'd choose Paris. The Latin Quarter. She'd sit at the terrace of a quaint café across from the Notre Dame cathedral. Sip a double espresso as she read some poems from Baudelaire's *Fleurs du mal*. But that wasn't going to happen. Not today, anyway. She didn't have a passport, let alone money for the flight.

Hmmm. Maybe Chicago. She'd always wanted to visit the museum there. If she couldn't go to Paris, she could at least sit for an hour in front of Gustave

Caillebotte's wall-sized painting, *Paris Street, Rainy Day*. She first saw it in an art magazine she was flipping through while waiting to have a wisdom tooth pulled. The dreary scene spoke to her. Ambling along a cobblestone street on a gray, rainy day. That was her.

*Engine, engine, number 9, going down the Chicago line. If the train falls off the track, do you want your money back? Yes.* Y-e-s *spells yes, you dirty, dirty dishrag—you.*

She waited in the Amtrak ticket line behind a twenty-something couple from Jersey who—Gaia gathered from overhearing—had met the night before in an East Village club. They couldn't keep their hands off each other. Pinching, groping, giggling. It took everything Gaia had not to gag before she finally reached the window, where she came face-to-face with Ned, the ticket vendor.

She leaned forward to speak into the round voice amplifier.

"Chicago. One way."

He visibly perked up at the sight of her. His eyes leered at her from behind the thick Plexiglas.

"Going all by yourself?"

"Yeah. Is that a problem?"

"No . . . I just thought . . ." He raised his eyebrows suggestively.

"Thought what?"

"I don't know, a girl as pretty as yourself. Just seems like you'd have a . . . companion."

She sighed. "Well, I'm alone. Is there a sleeping car on that train going to Chicago?"

He swiveled on his seat and clacked a succession of keys at his computer. "Not until nine-thirty tonight."

"How about another train, then? Is there any train with a sleeping car leaving soon? Doesn't matter where it's going."

He looked at her. Then back at his screen. Ten more seconds of clacking. "There's a train to Orlando leaving in about an hour."

Gaia took a moment to ponder Orlando. It was a light-year away from this rainy day. It was an artificial city populated by tourists and the people who served the tourists. It was the land of water slides and theme parks, of Mickey Mouse and Jaws: The Ride.

"There's definitely a sleeper car?" Gaia wanted to confirm.

"There is a sleeping compartment, yes," Ned replied.

"I'll take it."

What the hell. She needed a vacation. And a little sun never hurt anybody. If it was warm enough, maybe she'd even buy a bikini. Hit the beach.

But she still had a whole hour to kill. After Ned slid her ticket under the window, she leaned a final time into the voice amplifier.

"Is there someplace that sells stamps around here?"

# THE DOCTOR QUICKENED HIS STEPS

## Getting Acquainted

as he approached the escalator that would carry him down into the bowels of Penn Station, unquestionably the most hideous train station in the country. But he was pleased to be here. He was downright overjoyed that his target had abandoned her safe perch up on Central Park West and come down here.

The ugly, subterranean corridors of this station were hardly fit for any human pursuit, but the place fit his needs quite perfectly.

According to his device, she was less than two hundred feet away. He began scanning the crowds in the hope of identifying her, acquainting himself a little with her face before he went to work.

# GAIA REREAD HER LETTER TO Ed.

## Out of Order

She was seated at the counter of a small coffee-and-muffin place in the train station's row of shops and eateries. What a stupid letter.

She went to crumple the letter, then stopped herself. She needed to say something to him. She thought of him calling her on Friday night at eleven o'clock, expecting another of their ricocheting, sleepy, oddly intimate conversations. He'd call her and find out she wasn't there. Really, really wasn't there.

Gaia sighed. She propped her chin in her hand. This was harder than leaving had ever been before. None of the other places had Ed.

Or Sam.

She folded her letter carefully and put it in the envelope. She wrote out Ed's address and placed the stamp in the corner so it wasn't crooked.

She felt the eyes of a man slumped at the next table over, hovering on her legs. She turned to him.

"Letter to Mom and Dad, sweetheart?" he asked. The smell of stale alcohol on his breath made Gaia wince.

Okay, she thought. That's it. She was sick of being leered at. Time to lose the dress. First the smarmy ticket vendor, now this loser.

"That's right. *Honey*," she said. Turning her attention back to the envelope, she licked the inside edge of the flap and sealed it.

"I like to watch you do that."

Gaia narrowed her eyes at the old pervert. Blech. As she got up, she knocked over her half-filled paper cup of coffee so that it spilled into the man's lap.

"Oh, I'm sorry," she lied. Then she swung her bag over her shoulder and took off.

A minute later she arrived at the women's rest room. A hand-scrawled sign taped to the door read Out of Order.

Perfect. She didn't need to pee. She could change her clothes in peace. But pushing open the door, she was immediately struck by the most powerful stench this side of the Hudson. She wanted to bolt, get out of there, but the room was empty—it would take her only a minute. Slip off the dress; pull on the jeans and sweatshirt. Off. On. Go. Like a pit stop at the Indy 500.

Just as long as no one lit a match.

She hurried to a stall. Holding her breath, she quickly slipped off Mary's shoes. She was peeling off the tights when all of a sudden she heard the door fly open.

"Let go of me!" a young female voice demanded.

Gaia looked through the crack of her stall: Two thugs had just entered, dragging behind them a teenage girl, dressed in a Nike sports bra, a leopard-print skirt, and just one stiletto heel. The other one must've been out there somewhere, floating among the sea of arrivals and departures. Quickly Gaia pulled the tights back up over her waist.

"Let's have it, bitch," ordered the shorter of the two, the one with the New Jersey Devils baseball cap.

"I don't got it. I swear," the girl cried.

The girl's hair was blond and tangled. She looked no older than Gaia—maybe sixteen or seventeen. Like Gaia, she'd probably done the rounds in foster care. Like Gaia, she'd probably run away at least once. Gaia suspected she was a prostitute and that the bigger guy was her pimp.

Each of the men grabbed one of the girl's pale arms, and together they shoved her into the dirty, white-tiled wall. She cried out in pain but managed to protect her head.

Gaia watched from the stall, letting her anger grow inside her chest. She hadn't had any real release in days. The anger was right there, so easy to call upon. There was her rage at Ella. Her fury at crazy, misguided Mary who had everything in the world and chose to screw it up.

"We're not playing games this time, sunshine," said the big, bearlike thug, whose belly hung out from a black T-shirt that asked, Got Milk?

Gaia saw his big, paw hands fumbling, then heard a noise. Flick. The Bear underlined his threat by holding up a fierce-looking switchblade that gleamed under the fluorescent light. "Now, let's see it, or you'll have a brand-new face to look at in the mirror." He held the knife against her cheek.

Gaia threw open the door of her stall.

The two men turned to stare at her.

Gaia forgot until she read the particular looks in their eyes that she was still wearing Mary's clingy, short red dress.

"Check you out," the man in the Devils hat said, studying her appreciatively. "We've got a regular party happening in here."

"Get off her," Gaia said.

"Pardon?" the big one asked, curiosity and amusement flashing in his eyes.

Gaia came closer. She spoke loudly and enunciated her words clearly. "Get off the girl. Let her go."

The Bear shook his head. "Is this your business? I don't think so. Why don't you stand aside, sweetheart? It'll be your turn next."

Gaia liked to protect her conscience by being absolutely clear about her intentions before she did harm. "I'm warning you. I'll kick your ass if you don't lay off her."

They both guffawed at her. "Len, grab her," the big one instructed the smaller guy. "This is gonna be fun."

Len did as he was told. When he reached for Gaia's arm, she backhanded him hard against the side of his neck. She caught him by surprise. He staggered sideways. Gaia kicked him hard in the chest and watched him slam into the hand-drying machine and slide to the floor. Len was disappointingly easy.

"Holy shit."

Gaia turned her head to see the Bear staring at her

with astonishment. She'd talked enough. She went after him.

The Bear was holding that blade, which made her approach trickier. She didn't hesitate, though. He stood to confront her, as she gambled he would, and she grabbed the knife-wielding arm by the wrist and bent it sharply behind him. She wrenched the other arm back to join the first and pulled him down so she could lodge her knee in his back.

The Bear groaned in pain. `The blade clattered to the ground.` The girl backed off into the corner, shivering.

Gaia let his arms go. Now that the blade was out of the way, she could give him some room.

He literally growled as he turned on her. He raised his arm to punch her in the jaw, but she caught it long before it landed and took the force of his own sloppy effort to flip him onto the linoleum. It was kind of a trademark move of hers. Effortless. Fairly graceful. Totally satisfying.

She backed up a few steps and let him get up. She hated herself for enjoying it, but she did. The Bear deserved anything she gave him and much more. He'd obviously spent too long believing that women could be intimidated. Let him remember this.

It was all he could do to get himself back on his feet. He staggered toward Gaia, swinging at her. His lack of skill was pitiful. There wasn't much point in trying to make it a real contest. She clipped his jaw with her right fist. She very likely broke his nose with her left. She wanted to leave him a memento.

His eyes displayed real fear now. Although Gaia couldn't feel fear, she was astute at recognizing its signs. Wild, darting eyes, rapid, shallow breaths. Gaia took that as her cue to finish him. She landed a hard, fast blow to a calculated spot under his ear. As expected, he crumpled to the floor, unconscious. Gaia knew he'd feel like shit when he came to. But he *would* come to and not much worse for the wear, either.

Suddenly the girl was shrieking. Gaia heard movement behind her. Much closer than she was expecting. Before she could regroup, the smaller guy appeared in the corner of her eye and shoved her hard in the back, sending her sprawling across the floor. Gaia got up fast, but he was barreling toward her.

Gaia turned, smashing his face with a roundhouse kick so powerful, she was sure she'd knocked him out. But she rushed the kick and threw herself badly off balance. She lost her footing, and her head came down hard against the corner of the porcelain sink.

Gaia groaned, holding the side of her head. She put both of her hands on the side of the sink for support and swayed back up to her feet.

At last the wretched-smelling room was quiet. The girl was backed against the tiled wall, gazing at Gaia with a stunned expression. "Are you okay?"

Gaia nodded. "I think so."

The girl put her hands up to her cheeks. "God, I

don't know what to say. Thank you. I never had anyone stick up for me before. Is there anything I can do for you? Buy you a coffee?

Gaia shook her head, then leaned herself up against the wall for support. Her eyes closed. Her head was pounding ferociously. She'd hit it hard.

"Hey," the girl said, reaching out to her.

"I'll be fine," Gaia tried to assure her. "Just give me a minute." She shielded her eyes with her hand. Her pupils were reacting sluggishly to the bright, fluorescent light above.

Gaia started to slide down along the wall until she ended sitting up on the floor. Right next to the girl.

"I'm gonna call 911."

"No!" Gaia ordered. "I just need to rest." She started to drift, to give in. "Rest," she murmured again. And then she blacked out.

"ALL ABOARD FOR THE SOUTHERN Star, now boarding on track 12. All aboard!"

A large segment of the Penn Station crowd shuffled in unison toward the steps that led down to the waiting train.

# Unholy Moment

120

He shuffled right along with them, his yellow-green eyes darting wildly. Searching for his target. His tracking device told him he was at point-blank range.

He reached the platform and caught a glimpse of her—a blond in a yellow-green Polartec jacket, carrying a black messenger bag. She was just stepping into one of the train's sleeper cars. He calmly made his way through the frantic human herd and boarded the same car, but at the other end. He walked with haste and purpose through the car, noticing the blond up ahead. She was scanning the compartment numbers as she advanced, finally entering one near the middle—on his left. Number 33A.

He arrived there not more than ten seconds later, pausing a moment to close his trench coat over his tie—a Salvatore Ferragamo yellow silk, dotted with little teddy bears. A client had given it to him a few years back to thank him for the perfect cheekbones he had given her. And they were perfect. He had truly outdone himself. So in the name of mastery and precision, he always wore the tie for these unholy moments. It had become part of the ceremony. Priests wear their robes; he wore his Ferragamo teddy bear tie under his cheap, washable trench coat.

He slowly, silently turned the brass handle of the compartment door and entered.

"Hey!" the blond snarled. "This one's taken."

"Is that right?" he replied with `zero inflection` in his voice. Then he grinned like a used car salesman as he stepped inside.

"Hey!" she repeated. "What do you think you're doing?"

He just kept smiling and closed the door behind him, pulling down the shade to cover the small window.

# FIVE MINUTES LATER, HE STEPPED

off the train. One of the conductors, doing some final work on the platform, gave him a curious look.

"Wrong train." The doctor tossed him a shrug, pretending to be embarrassed. "I must be blind."

He made his way back up the steps, back to the vast waiting room with the giant destination board. On the way he couldn't help thinking that the redheaded woman was a little off in her assessment. The girl was hardly "tough." Annoying, maybe, but tough? And her face wasn't so pretty, either. He imagined a little sculpting work on that nose would make for a significant improvement. . . . Perhaps a little Gore-Tex in those thin lips. An injection for those premature lines in her forehead. Under different circumstances he would have certainly left his card.

*Oh, well . . .*

He stopped at the rest room, whose door had a crude Out of Order sign taped to it. A perfect place to get rid of the instrument. But when he opened the door, the stench that hit him was so overwhelming, he had to quickly close it. He started off, then changed his mind. He wheeled back and opened the door just wide enough so that he could toss the bloody scalpel into the trash can.

A few feet to the left of the trash can he saw the prostrate body of a teenage girl. She was graceful, blond, quite pretty, in fact. Probably strung out on drugs. From the bruise on her face it looked like somebody had beaten her up. Her pimp, no doubt. It was pitiful, really.

He tossed the scalpel and watched it sink cleanly to the bottom of the trash can.

Too bad, he thought as he was making his exit. It had been such a trusty tool. Why, he had used it just that morning on Mrs. Gardner. Carved her the best-looking chin money could buy.

**After** I hit my head in the train station, I saw red and green sparklers bursting in front of my eyes. I must have passed out after that because I had this weird, dreamlike reverie about Ed and his being color-blind. Don't ask me why.

In my dream I was color-blind, too. I couldn't see green, which my whacked-out mind was convinced was the color of fear. Green looked the same as red, but red wasn't the color of fear, according to my dream self. What was red the color of?

It became this desperate, urgent thing I needed to figure out. What was red the color of? Green was fear; what was red?

*What was red?*

Well, red is the color of tomatoes, you might say sensibly, and shut up already. But you know how dreams are.

Anyway, I guess it was around then that I came to.

Heather was too hurt to feel it. Her heart was on autopilot once more. "You've fallen for **not a penny** her, haven't you?"

# HER VISION AND AWARENESS CAME

back slowly. She blinked open her eyes and then closed them again. Then came the smell.

# A Freaking Mess

What the hell was that? Where was she?

Gaia forced open her eyes. Oh God. The bathroom. The awful bathroom in the train station.

She sat up and looked around her. The thugs she'd fought were still passed out on the other side of the room. One of them was breathing loudly, fitfully. The other was clutching his jaw and moaning. They'd be up and at it soon enough.

And the girl. Where had the girl gone? Suddenly Gaia froze. She clambered to her feet, ignoring the searing pain in her temple. She checked the floor around her. She checked the stall where she'd begun to change. Mary's shoes were just where she'd kicked them off, but her bag was gone. Her bag with her wallet and her money and her clothes and shoes. Oh Christ, and where was her coat? Her coat with the train ticket to Orlando inside the pocket.

It was gone. All of it. Shit.

Well, that was gratitude for you. Save somebody's ass, and they'll rob you blind. Give a lot, and they'll take a lot more.

*Shit!*

She moved to the sink, splashed cold water on her badly bruised face. When she looked in the mirror, she got a shock. The left side of her face, her cheekbone all the way up to her temple, was already covered by an ugly purple bruise. The corner of her lip was bleeding, not to mention her mascara. Mary's velvet dress was ripped in two places. She was a freaking mess.

She retrieved the shoes and squeezed them on her sore feet, trying not to let herself cry. Now what? She'd arrived at the station full of cash and ready to start a new life.

She'd be leaving it broke and broken.

# Hunted Prey

"WHERE IS GAIA? I THOUGHT SHE'D be joining us."

Ella took a protracted sip of her third glass of merlot, letting the velvety nectar wash over her tongue. Then she made a whole show of sliding back the sleeve of her blouse to glance at her watch.

"Oh, my, it is getting late, isn't it?" she said, wondering just how Gaia was doing. Although the obnoxious girl had run, she had certainly not gotten away. It was helpful that Gaia had taken off *after* Ella had slipped the tracking device into her coat pocket.

Ella sat with two of George's old agency friends and their wives. They were gathered at a table for six in the opulent dining room of La Bijou, an haute-cuisine restaurant on West Sixty-fourth Street, off Broadway. Most of the patrons here were silver-haired, silver-spooned socialites who just an hour earlier had been watching the new opera across the street at Lincoln Center. The waiters were French to a fault.

And then there was the menu. A menagerie of hunted prey, ranging from roasted duck to wild Scottish hare to rock Cornish hen with the word of caution to be careful of possible bird shot.

This was George's consolation prize to Ella for his being called away on Thanksgiving. The restaurant was fine with her; the company, a bore.

"I would so like to see Gaia, that poor thing," Mrs. Bessemer agreed. "Her parents were such lovely people."

Ella stifled a yawn. She shrugged daintily. "Gaia is a teenager, as you know. Her appearances are difficult to predict. I told her of course how much you'd all like to see her, but . . . Gaia has a mind and a schedule of her own." Ella lied effortlessly, without even needing to listen to herself.

Besides, she has an appointment with a doctor, Ella added silently. She tapped her menu. "Listen, why don't we just go ahead and order? I'll order a little something extra for Gaia so when—if—she comes, she can join right in. I'm sure she won't mind."

That said, her beeper went off. She opened her purse, extracted the beeper, and looked at the number. "That's probably her now. If you'll excuse me, I'll be back in a moment."

# THE DOCTOR STOOD INSIDE THE

# Insult and Injury

phone booth just outside Penn Station's southwest entrance, annoyed at this particular aspect of his written instructions. Who used a phone booth anymore? It was rather galling. He'd punched in the beeper number as instructed, and now he waited for the ring. There it was.

"Mrs. Travesura, I presume?"

"Yes, Doctor. Is it done?"

"Of course."

"Excellent. And in what condition is our patient?"

The woman could barely contain the pleasure in her voice.

"Alive, as promised," the doctor responded. "Though not likely to recount her experiences anytime soon." He wouldn't reward her with the graphic details.

"No one saw you?"

The doctor sighed impatiently. "Absolutely not."

"I'm sure. Now, did you remove the bug from the pocket of her coat?"

This had grown annoying, verging on insulting. "Mrs. Travesura. I am a professional. You need not grill me on these absurd details."

"I apologize . . . *Doctor*. If you'll permit me one last question?"

He sighed again. "Yes."

"Are you holding the tracking device in your hand?"

"I am."

"Good. Good-bye, then, you disgusting, evil bastard."

The doctor was blinking in fury, barely able to process the childish affront, when the device began beeping in his hand. He held the readout close to his face, trying to discern the message in the darkness of the booth.

He could make out numbers scrolling across the screen. 5 . . . 4 . . . 3 . . . 2 . . . 1 . . .

The explosion ripped the tiny booth apart.

GAIA TURNED AT THE SOUND OF

**No Refunds**

the explosion. Virtually everyone in the station jumped at the noise. Within a minute she heard a symphony of sirens.

She glanced ahead of her in frustration at the single open ticket booth. She glanced behind her at the ten or so people who continued the line, all of whom looked as cranky as she felt. She didn't care if her own feet exploded. There was no way she was losing her place in this line.

Scores of policemen were zipping in and out the south doors of the station. Many civilians were running around, too, wanting a piece of the action.

"There was a bomb!" she heard somebody shouting. "Right out front. Blew up a phone booth!"

There were lots of oohs and ahs and murmurs throughout the station, but Gaia was morbidly amused to see that not a single person left her line.

Just wait until the camera crews from the local news get here—then it will really be a circus, Gaia found herself thinking.

Another ticket salesperson opened a second window. That would speed things up. Minutes later, Gaia was waved forward. Before she reached the window, she realized she was being reunited with her old friend Ned.

"How can I help you?" His eyes showed not a flicker of recognition. Apparently she was a lot less attractive battered and bruised.

"Remember me? I bought a ticket to Orlando from you about an hour and a half ago. The sleeper car?"

His face was blank.

"Well, listen, my ticket got stolen. I need to get a refund."

Ned shrugged. "Sorry. Train 404 to Orlando is long gone. Unless you can produce the ticket, I can't give you a refund."

Gaia rolled her eyes. "How can I produce a ticket if it got stolen?"

Ned's face was devoid of interest or sympathy. "No ticket, no refund."

Gaia was starting to feel desperate. If she couldn't get a refund, she'd have no money. Not a cent. Nothing. How long could she last on the streets of New York flat broke? Even the flophouses cost a few dollars. "Ned, please. We're . . . *friends,* practically. Can't you help me out here? I really, really need the cash."

Ned shook his head. He wouldn't look anywhere near her eyes. A pretty, confident, sexily clad girl with a wallet full of cash was interesting to Ned. A bruised, desperate, penniless girl was not. He focused his gaze over her head. "Next?" he called to the person at the front of the line.

Suddenly Gaia felt overcome by a wave of dizziness so powerful, it almost made her sick to her stomach. She grabbed the edge of the high counter to steady herself. "Ned! Ned. Please. Don't be an asshole. Just listen to me for a minute, okay?" Gaia could hear her voice rising in her ears. "Ned! *Ned!*" God, if he weren't enclosed in the bullet-proof booth, she'd love to belt him. "Ned!"

The next thing Gaia knew, there was a police officer, a young Hispanic man with a crew cut, grabbing her by the arm. "Come on, miss," he said. "There's a long line here, okay? Gotta keep it moving."

"But I—" Gaia grabbed her arm back. "My ticket got stolen. And all my money. And I really need—"

Gaia stopped. He wasn't listening. It was hopeless. She could tell the policeman was looking her over, and she could tell exactly what he was thinking, too. Gaia was wearing a shredded, clingy minidress, high heels, and a big bruise on her head.

"Come on, miss," he said again. His voice was patient, tired, pitying. "Do you want to step out of the way, or do you want me to arrest you? I'd think a girl like you would have good reason to stay out of the way if you can help it."

*A girl like you.* It was obvious he thought she was a hooker. A hooker addicted to drugs who'd just been shaken up by her pimp. It was ironic, but that was exactly what she looked like. While the *actual* drug-addicted hooker who'd been shaken up by her pimp was zipping off to Orlando in a pair of jeans and a fluorescent yellow-green Polartec jacket, carrying almost 450 bucks in her pockets.

Gaia wondered if her luck could be any worse.

## HEATHER LAY BACK ON THE COUCH

# The (Other) Magic Word

and rested her head on Sam's lap as he flipped channels with the remote control. Without looking at her, he rested his hand on her stomach. She felt her iridescent pink silk blouse riding up over her belly button. She studied his face above her. It was so unbelievably handsome. His strong jaw was smooth and clean shaven for this event. His brownish gold hair had gotten long and was curling around the collar of his cobalt blue oxford shirt. His complicated hazel eyes were framed by long black lashes. She wanted those eyes on her. On her face, her hair, her breasts, the bare swath of skin above her skirt.

But at the moment his eyes were riveted on the television screen as he burned through almost a hundred channels' worth of programming. It was hopeless sitting in a room with a boy, a television, and a remote control. You never got any attention or even the pleasure of watching any one show for longer than three minutes.

She smiled up at him. She didn't mind. This was the kind of relationship problem she enjoyed having.

She heard clinking sounds from the kitchen. Her parents cleaning up the last of the dishes. She heard the faint sound of laughter—Lauren talking on the phone. From her and Phoebe's room she heard the inevitable hum of the stair-climbing machine, Phoebe's most prized possession. God forbid an ounce of turkey should stick to her hips.

"Having a nice Thanksgiving?" she asked Sam.

"Hmmm," he said, his eyes not flickering from the screen.

"My dad loved your potatoes."

"Mmmm."

Sam wasn't going to talk, obviously. But he did move the remote control to the hand that rested on her stomach. He used his free hand to caress her forehead, softly pushing her hair back from her face. She breathed in deeply and let out a sigh of pleasure. It felt so nice, she wished they could just stay like that forever.

For the first time in weeks she felt truly relaxed. The dinner had gone fairly well. No hysterics or anything.

She was relieved to have finally confronted Sam with the Gaia issue and gotten the answer she wanted.

"Hey, wait, hold it there a minute," she ordered. The local news was showing footage of the Thanksgiving parade. She used to love that when she was a kid. The camera zoomed in on one enormous balloon after another: `Barney`, `some pig or other`, `a Rugrat`, two gigantic M&M's. She remembered sitting on her dad's shoulders for hours—so long that both her feet would fall asleep—and watching the floats and marching bands go by.

The report on the parade ended abruptly, and the picture changed to show a gloomy-looking Penn Station lit up by dozens of red flashing lights.

"God, what happened there?" Heather mumbled.

"Shhh," Sam ordered, leaning in to listen.

". . . Two mysterious tragedies here in one evening," the telegenic special reporter was saying into the camera. "Are they related, and if so, how? That is what detectives are asking tonight as they start a two-pronged investigation here in Penn Station."

The camera moved to show a phone booth that had been blown to bits. Twisted metal and glass were everywhere. "A bomb was detonated here, outside of New York City's busy Penn Station, less than an hour ago. . . . One person dead, not yet identified . . ."

The camera moved to show a stretcher carrying a

girl. ". . . And in a second calamity, a young girl, not yet identified, was brutally slashed and disfigured in her sleeping compartment in a train pulling out of Penn Station at 6:47 P.M. She remains in a coma at Roosevelt Hospital . . ."

Beneath her, Heather felt Sam's legs go rigid. "Oh my God," he whispered. "Jesus."

Suddenly Sam was on his feet, dumping Heather's head rudely onto the couch. She sat herself upright quickly. "Sam, what's your problem?"

Sam was stammering, pointing at the TV. "Th-That's—could that be? I think that might be Gaia's coat! That green coat? Oh my God."

Sam was pacing, holding his head, unable to watch the screen and then watching it again. "Her hair. Do you see her hair? It's blond. Is that Gaia? Could that be her?"

Heather glared at him in disbelief. He was *freaking*. Absolutely freaking. She'd never seen him anything like this. She wanted to slap him.

She went closer to the TV and studied the picture. Yes, she recognized that hideous jacket. She squinted and tried to get a look at the face, a crazy mixture of emotions swarming around her heart.

Just before the camera switched back to a shot of the shattered phone booth, Heather caught a glimpse of the girl's face. It was heavily bandaged, but she could see enough to know it wasn't Gaia.

Sam paced. His face was the color of skim milk.

Heather angrily snatched the remote control from his hand and used it to switch off the TV.

"What are you doing?" Sam demanded fiercely. He tried to take the remote back. His eyes were wild.

"Calm down!" she shouted at him.

"Heather! Please!" He made another grab.

"Calm down, you idiot! It *wasn't her!*" she screamed at him.

Those were the magic words. Sam stopped moving finally. In his beautiful hazel eyes Heather saw so much hope and relief, she thought she might throw up.

Sam took a breath. "What did you say?"

Heather didn't try to hide the disgust in her face. And Sam was so far away, he didn't seem to see it or care. "I said, it wasn't her. It wasn't Gaia," Heather repeated flatly.

"Are you sure?" Sam asked, his eyes too vulnerable for words.

Heather couldn't help wondering, in a profoundly awful way, whether anybody, *anybody* would ever care about her as much as Sam seemed to care for Gaia right now.

Real rage began smoldering in her stomach. Couldn't he at least *pretend* he didn't adore Gaia so deeply? Couldn't he consider

Heather for *one single second* and attempt to spare her feelings? "I'm sure," she spat out bitterly.

"Oh," he said.

Finally he brought his eyes back to Heather. He seemed to remember she was in the room with him. He took another few breaths. He looked tentative. He was ashamed. But more than that, more than anything, he was relieved that cut-up girl wasn't his beloved Gaia.

In one quiet moment everything was clear. They'd both known the truth long before this. Sam was obsessed with Gaia.

Heather was too hurt to feel it. Her heart was on autopilot once more. "You've fallen for her, haven't you?" Her voice was empty.

Sam ran a hand through his hair, leaving most of it standing straight up. He looked down at the floor, then back to Heather's eyes. "I guess I have." His voice was so quiet, he mouthed the words as much as said them.

At least he didn't lie or try to bullshit her, she told herself. His honesty made for cold comfort, though.

"I don't know why. I'm so sorry," he finished earnestly.

She hated him.

"Don't apologize," she snapped icily. "Just . . . get out of here. I don't want to see you right now. We'll talk about it some other time." Anger was accessible to her right now. Pain was not.

Numbly she strode to the coat closet and grabbed his corduroy jacket. She practically threw it at him. "Please go!"

He looked sorry, all right. Sorry and regretful, but also relieved. So relieved, he was ashamed of himself. He was happy to be getting out of there and away from her.

She hated him.

"I'm sorry, Heather," he said again as he walked out of the apartment. "I'm really sorry."

She hardly waited until he was clear of the door before she slammed it with all her might.

She wheeled around. "I hate you!" she shouted at the empty living room.

For some reason the story of Medea invaded her head again. The bitter, scorned, miserable woman.

Heather went back to the couch and threw all the pillows on the floor. It was lucky for Sam that they didn't have any children.

# GRANDPA FARGO'S FAMOUS APPLE PIE

## Ingredients:

>          8 red Rome apples
>          1 recipe pie crust
>          $\frac{1}{2}$ cup sugar
>          $\frac{1}{2}$ teaspoon cinnamon
>          2 tablespoons flour
>          pinch of nutmeg
>          pinch of salt
>          1 tablespoon butter
>          1 well-beaten egg

## Filling:

Peel and core apples and slice into $\frac{1}{2}$"
wedges. Place in large mixing bowl. Add
sugar, cinnamon, flour, nutmeg, and salt.
Toss until thoroughly blended.

Roll $\frac{1}{2}$ pie crust dough to $\frac{1}{8}$-inch thickness.
Line 9-inch pie plate with dough, allowing $\frac{1}{2}$
inch to extend over edge. Add filling. Dot
with 1 tablespoon butter. Roll out rest of
dough and lay over pie plate, tucking excess
dough along pie-plate edge. Crimp along edge
with knife handle to create a wavy pattern.
Use fork to puncture a few holes into top of
crust in pattern of your choice. Brush top of
pie with 1 well-beaten egg.

Bake at 425 degrees for 15 minutes. Turn
down heat to 350 degrees and bake for $\frac{1}{2}$
hour.

Without
thinking,
she threw
herself on
his **freedom/**
**nothingness**
bed. It was
sick, but so
delicious.

GREEN. RED. GREEN. RED. OUT
the front window of the diner on
University Place, Gaia watched the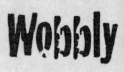
traffic light run its cycle again and
again. She thought of Ed.

She'd meant to go, she really had. But
here she was again.

She realized she was still shivering. She put her
hand to her throbbing head. God, what she would do
for a dollar to buy a hot cup of coffee.

"Excuse me, sweetheart, but if you're not going to
order anything, I'm going to have to ask you to leave."
The waitress wasn't mean. She was old and tired. She
had turned a blind eye to Gaia for the last forty-five
minutes. Now she was doing her job.

"But it's so cold out," Gaia said, mostly to herself.

"What's that, hon?" The waitress leaned in.

"Nothing, I'm going." It took all of Gaia's strength
to climb out of the booth and balance herself on her
feet. The room spun around her. She closed her eyes,
trying not to be sick.

"Are you okay?" the woman asked.

Gaia opened her eyes. She steadied herself against
the top of the vinyl seats. "Yes, I'll be fine," she said.
She walked as steadily as she could to the door and
steeled herself for the cold blast of wind.

Back out on the street she hugged herself for
warmth. She wished she had her coat. She wished

she had a blanket. She wished she had anything heavier than this skimpy red dress. And Mary was wrong. These shoes were too small. Her feet ached.

She made herself walk. What now? Where could she go? The light to cross Thirteenth Street was red. To cross to the west side of University was green. She crossed.

She kept walking west. Her teeth chattered uncontrollably. When she got to Fifth Avenue, the light to cross was red. The light to cross Thirteenth to the south was green. She crossed.

The wind that whipped up Fifth Avenue seemed to find its way into her skin—into every muscle and nerve and tendon. It chilled her blood in her veins, and her veins circulated that chilled blood all through her body and into her heart.

The light to cross Twelfth Street was red. The light to cross to the west side of Fifth was green. She crossed. Without instructions her feet were taking her to her home in New York City—Washington Square Park. She crossed Twelfth Street and got another green signal to cross Eleventh. The miniature Arc de Triomphe that marked the northern entrance to the park was in full view now.

She glanced up and stopped. The building to her right was familiar. Familiar mostly in a painful way. It was Sam's dormitory, the place where she'd walked in on Sam and Heather having sex.

She started walking and stopped again. Another image appeared in her mind. The broken doorknob. Too well she remembered the wobbly brass sphere almost falling off in her hand, giving her access to one of the worst sights a person could see. But right now, from where she stood, the broken doorknob held a certain appeal.

SAM FELT DISGUSTINGLY LIGHT ON his feet as he walked down Third Avenue. He should have been miserable or at least heavyhearted. But he wasn't. His muscles were buzzing with life. The world looked new to him. Clean and fresh and in excellent focus.

He looked at the shops on either side of the avenue, closed up for the holiday, with their iron safety gates pulled down and locked. It was the kind of sight that had depressed him when he'd first moved to New York. Tonight he liked it.

He was sorry about Heather. He was sorry *for* Heather. He genuinely was. She didn't deserve to be treated the way she'd been treated. But nor did she deserve to have a boyfriend who thought so constantly of someone else.

And now, for the first time in months, he felt free. Free for the moment, anyway.

Free to be with Gaia, a voice in his mind added.

Hold up, he ordered that voice. He wasn't sure about anything yet. He wasn't sure what the real status was between him and Heather. He wasn't sure whether Gaia had ever looked at him the way he looked at her.

Most importantly, Gaia was a major proposition. For him, he knew, she represented a love-of-his-life possibility. He had to be slow. He had to be careful. He had to make sure he didn't somehow get killed in the process.

He stopped at a red light. His happy legs had covered a lot of ground without him even knowing it. Now where?

He imagined his dorm room. It would be so lonely tonight. The place would be absolutely deserted. But where else could he go? All his friends were back home or visiting relatives. He imagined his family back in Maryland. His older brother was bringing his new girlfriend home to meet the folks. His parents were sorry that he wasn't there, and now, the way things had turned out, so was he.

His mind turned to Gaia, as it often did. Where was she spending Thanksgiving? She didn't have parents; that was one of the few things he knew about her. A very sad circumstance on a day like this. Did she like the Nivens, those people she lived with? Was she in their house on Perry Street right now? Was she happy? On some level he knew she wasn't, and that gave him a deep, achy feeling he didn't often feel for another person.

Why did he care for her like this? How had it happened?

He saw the lights of an all-night diner burning up ahead. It was one of the few establishments open along the whole avenue. Maybe he'd duck in there. Find himself a copy of *The New York Times* and while away the evening with a couple of cups of coffee.

## THERE IS NO WAY SAM COULD BE

here, Gaia told herself for the tenth time. She was certain of it. Sam was the kind of guy who had a loving family and scores of other

# The Key

good backup options for Thanksgiving in case the family thing wasn't happening. In fact, he was probably sharing warm food and feelings with the she-wolf.

Still, Gaia felt self-conscious as she stepped into the

entrance of the NYU dorm. She was tired of looking like a prostitute in this awful dress. The place was nearly deserted but for the omnipresent security guard at a table a few yards into the lobby. Shit, she'd forgotten about him. He was absorbed in a noisy hockey game playing on the tiny TV perched on the table less than a foot from his eyes.

The warm air felt so good. If she could just manage to stay in here for a few minutes, maybe she'd be okay. Now that she'd finally slowed her pace, the dizziness was coming back.

The guard and his TV were in their own little world. Maybe she could just . . .

"Excuse me? Uh, miss? Can I help you?" Damn. There must have been a time-out in the game or something. The security guard was now staring at her with his full attention.

"H-Hi. I j-just. Um. My f-f-friend lives here, and he inv-v-vited me over," Gaia said. She was shivering so hard, it was difficult to talk.

The security guard got a knowing look in his eyes. "Hey, I'm sorry, sweetheart, but we can't have none of that here." He took in her slinky, ripped dress, her heels, what was left of her makeup. "This is a college building, you know? You oughtta get out of here." He kept jingling his keys in one hand. It seemed like a nervous habit. She noticed that the key ring said Mustang and showed the black silhouette of a horse bucking against a blue background.

"B-B-But I—" Gaia knew there was really no point in arguing. There was no way he was letting her past his table unless she clobbered him, and she simply didn't have the strength. She just wanted to use up a little more time inside. She couldn't face the cold again. What could she talk about with him? The New York Rangers? Cars? Guns?

"Look, kid, I'm sorry. I really am. You look like hell"—he shook his head with a mix of sympathy and disgust—"but you can't stay here."

## SAM TOOK OUT HIS WALLET SOON

after he'd sat down at a table to see how much cash he had. He rifled through every compartment. Unfortunately, he had none. He checked the pockets of his jacket. He had no money. Not one red cent.

# Moving Right Along

He remembered now that he'd given Heather two twenties to buy pies for dessert from an overpriced Upper East Side gourmet shop.

He flagged down a waiter. "Excuse me, do you take credit cards?"

The surly waiter fixed him with a look that clearly meant no.

"Do you know if there's a bank or an ATM around here?" he asked.

The waiter looked like Sam had burned his house down. "Twenty-theerd," the man replied in a clipped, Eastern European accent.

"But this is Thirty-first Street," Sam said, wondering why he bothered.

"Twenty-theerd," the waiter said, louder.

Sam blew out his breath. "Okay, thanks." He headed toward the door. It looked like he was going to end up in his dorm room after all.

# Moony

AS SHE LEFT THE DORMITORY, THE cold practically knocked Gaia senseless. She was covered head to toe in goose bumps, only they didn't seem the least bit compelling.

Suddenly, a few yards from the building, she stopped. Her eye caught on a logo on the hood of a car parked directly outside the dorm's entrance.

So she wasn't totally senseless. She walked slowly

around the car, studying it for another moment. Then she saw the vanity license plate. RANGER-FAN, it read. Oh God. Could it be? Could there actually be a small piece of good luck in all of this blackness?

Gaia put her hands to her head. She needed to expel the dizziness, to gather her wits and her physical capabilities if she had any left.

Okay, now. She raised her foot to the side of the hood and shoved it hard. The car rocked violently, and a car alarm blasted through the silent night air. Perfect.

She ran to the side of the building and backed herself up against the wall, a few feet beyond the front awning.

Exactly as she'd hoped, the security guard dashed out of the building to check on his precious vehicle. Thank God.

Gaia found enough speed left in her legs to carry her into the building, undetected. With excitement fizzing in her veins she sprinted into the stairwell and up four flights to the door of Sam's suite.

She slowed down. Okay, this was starting to bring back some bad memories. Still, it was warm. There was a bed. She had to put her emotions on ice for a while.

Slowly she opened the door to the common room of the suite, blanking out her mind. Good, it was empty. The door to room B5, with its infamous doorknob, was just ahead.

Please be broken still, she begged of the doorknob. She closed her eyes and closed her hand around it at the same time.

Yes. She let out a breath. It jiggled brokenly in its socket, and she was able to push open the door.

Icy as her emotions—and the rest of her—were, she wasn't prepared for the effect of the smell. The tiny dorm room smelled like Sam. In a good way. In an aching, moony, grab-you-by-the-heart way. The smell intoxicated her. It gave her shivers. Why was it that a smell could evoke a person more powerfully than a million pictures could?

This, she realized, was what people meant when they talked about chemistry.

Without thinking, she threw herself on his bed. It was sick, but so delicious. His bed. Where he slept. She imagined him in his boxers, tangled in the sheets. His shoulders, his torso, his stomach, his . . . God, what heady torture.

She sat up. She had to pull herself together. She was semidemented from bashing her head and from cold and exhaustion. Time to act like a sane person.

First thing was to get out of this dress. She pulled it over her head in one swift move. She pulled the shoes off her miserable feet and stripped off the tights. She wound up the dress, the shoes, and the tights in a ball and sank them into the wastebasket next to Sam's nightstand.

Shower. She needed a shower. She wanted a boiling hot shower so bad, she could feel it.

Aha. There was a towel hanging over the door of Sam's closet. On his bureau were a bar of soap and a bottle of shampoo. Eureka. She had to hope that this dorm really was as empty as it appeared.

She cast off her bra and panties, feeling an unfamiliar and lustful pleasure at seeing them strewn about on Sam's bed. She wrapped herself in the towel and set off in search of the bathroom.

She listened for the sound of the germs, and they led her to a totally filthy and wonderful bathroom off the common room. What could you ask from a bathroom shared by four college students? She didn't care. She loved every microbe.

She blasted the shower as hot and strong as it would go and climbed in.

She gathered sex felt pretty good, but she couldn't imagine it felt much better than hot jets of water pounding against her frozen flesh. Ahhhhhhh.

Suddenly the tiles were starting a slow spin around her. She pressed her palms into her eyeballs. It didn't help. She sat right down on the floor of the shower and let the water beat down on her head. She would wait for the dizziness to pass.

When her body finally felt warm from the outside in, she got back to her feet and scrubbed her hair and face and body and rinsed for ages. She had to force herself to turn off the water.

She wrapped herself in Sam's towel and crept back into his room. Now what? Should she sleep naked or should she . . . hmmm. She went over to Sam's bureau and opened the top drawer. Waiting for her there were a soft, clean, ribbed white tank top undershirt and a pair of well-worn cotton boxers in a faded plaid of blues and greens. Yum.

This night had turned from sheer torment to the most sensual and thrilling experience of her life. She felt a bit like a stalker, but she wasn't doing any harm, was she? She'd put everything back in order before Sam returned. He'd never even guess she was there.

On the floor at the foot of his bed she suddenly spied his shoes, the scuffed leather, lace-up shoes he'd been wearing the day they played chess. For some reason, the sight of them stole her breath. Though empty, the shoes sat in a pose that was strongly suggestive of Sam—of exactly how he stood and walked. It was crazy that a pair of uninhabited shoes could carry so much subtle information about him. But they did. They brought him right into the room with her.

The aching feeling was back in force. She shivered again. An army of goose bumps invaded her arms and legs and back. *Almost like fear.*

It was like fear, but it wasn't fear.

Maybe it was . . . love.

*Dear Gaia,*

*I made a decision today, a few hours after you left. I'm going straight—I'm giving up drugs. Not "one day at a time" or any of that crap. I'm giving it up for good. Right now. When you saw me snorting coke today, I saw myself through your eyes, and I hated what I saw. If I keep going like this, I'm going to die. Yeah, it's that bad. And I don't want to die yet.*

*You probably wish I'd just leave you alone. You're wondering why I'm dragging you into my problems. I'm not sure, exactly. I'm not a very reflective person. But for some reason, I really do want to be friends with you. I want to be close. (Don't worry. Not in* that *way. I'm not a lesbian.) I've made a specialty out of not caring what other people think. But I do care what you think. I want you to think I'm a good person.*

*I have this idea about you and me. I have everything—parents, money, friends, a lot of love. You have nothing. I get so much, and the thing that sucks is, my heart is like a sieve. I want you to have some of what I have. You deserve it, not me.*

*That's weird, right? Sorry, it's just how I am.*

*So, anyway, I'm kicking the drugs whether I ever see you again or not.*

*But I just wanted you to know that wherever you are,*

*however you feel, you always have a friend out there in the world. Not a perfect friend or anything, but one who's trying to do better.*

*Mary*

Mary finished the letter and stuck it in an envelope. She'd get a stamp from her mom later. Then she got an idea. She went to her desk drawer, where she'd had a one-pound bag of M&M's ever since Halloween. She dumped the entire contents on her floor and picked out every last one of the red ones. She transferred the letter into a bigger, sturdier envelope and threw in all of the red M&M's to keep it company. She threw in a few green ones, too.

Now she'd need a whole bunch of stamps.

He was
leaning
forward,
leaning
over her. So
close now.
So real.
"Can I?" he
whispered.

**the**

**color**

**of**

**love**

**"HEY, BAUMAN, WHAT'S UP?" SAM** said to the security guard. "How're the Rangers?"

Bauman grimaced. "Down by two in the third. How's your holiday, Moon?"

# Something Sublime

Sam actually thought about his answer. "Good," he said. "Surprisingly good." Except for the fact that all twenty digits had lost feeling about a mile ago. He rubbed his hands together. "Quiet here tonight, huh?"

"Yes, it is," Bauman answered vaguely, his attention back on the game.

"Later. Happy Thanksgiving," Sam called over his shoulder as he entered the stairwell. Not that he expected his bland sign-off to compete with the Rangers. `He was pathologically polite.` He couldn't help himself.

He took the stairs slowly. Was he the only student in the entire building? It felt almost eerie.

None of his suite mates were around, that much he knew. He swung open the door of the common room. The place was exactly the pigsty he'd left it. He didn't even bother to turn on a light. He'd so completely frozen himself, walking almost seventy blocks, he was eager to strip down and climb under his down comforter.

He took out his key and had started to fit it in the

lock when the doorknob fell off in his hand. "Shit. Gotta get that fixed," he cursed under his breath, as he did two out of three times he entered his room.

A warm, reddish light from the street was filtering through the small window, lighting the bed. . . .

Oh. Jesus. Sam stepped backward. He was suddenly transported to a Three Little Bears moment. There was someone sleeping in his bed.

He stepped forward and froze. His heart stopped beating. He stopped breathing. Brain function shut down.

Could that someone be . . . ?

He turned his eyes to the door and then back to the bed again, sure that the mirage would be gone. It wasn't. There was still a sublimely beautiful blond girl in his bed who looked very much like Gaia.

He'd heard that people hallucinated in the happiest way just before they died of exposure. He hadn't chilled himself that badly, had he?

Now. Time to breathe, lungs. Time to beat, heart. His vital organs appeared to need a little coaching. There. Better. Okay, deep breaths. Yes.

He would just calm down, slow down, and think a minute.

He crept a little closer, terrified that this magnificent vision would disappear if he disturbed the air the slightest bit.

Still there. Please stay, he begged it. If this was a

figment of his imagination, then he prayed his imagination would keep it up.

He would just look at her. That would be okay, wouldn't it? Even if it was an imagined version of her, he still wanted to look. The few interactions he and Gaia'd had were so charged or awkward or plain antagonistic that he never got to study her, to see how her face looked in repose.

Her head was turned to the side, and her silken yellow hair—hair he'd fantasized about more times than was good for him—was splayed out on the pillow, leaving a shadow of dampness on the white cotton. Her bewitching eyes were closed in sleep. Her face was serene and lovely beyond description—light freckles over her cheeks. He drew closer. Palest, finest down along her jawline. Her eyelids flickered. He drew back.

She was still again. He came closer. His eyes moved down her neck.

Oh Christ! She was wearing his T-shirt. He felt the blood churning in his ears, gathering in other parts of his body. His T-shirt, which had spent its long, dutiful life covering large, rough stretches of masculine skin, now had the exquisite experience of gracing skin so delicate and fine, it was almost transparent. He envied it.

He saw that the too large shirt had gotten pulled around under her, revealing the sloping side and top of her breast.

He had to look away. Partly because it was too much to take and partly because he felt wrong seeing her like this, without her knowing he was seeing her. Without her wanting him to.

He made himself take a few steps backward and put his hands over his face to regain his composure.

He knew now, more than ever before, that he loved her. He loved her deeply and urgently, with a fierceness that made him know he'd never grasped, even grazed, the concept of love before. But he couldn't go on like this, without knowing how she really felt.

And what if she wasn't real at all but a figment of his fevered, lustful mind?

Well, then she'd be more likely to tell him what he dreamed of hearing.

## GAIA WAS DREAMING A BLISSFUL

## A Real Kiss

dream. Surrounded as she was by the smell and feel of Sam, by his place and his things, it was natural that she should dream of him vividly.

In the dream he was there beside her, sitting on the edge of the bed. He was so close, she could feel his warmth and smell his smell more intensely. An alive smell now.

He took her hand so gently and held it. Just held it. Making her safe.

Consciousness was tickling her eyelids, summoning her. *Please, sleep, stay with me. Don't make me go back yet.*

But it was happening. She couldn't help it. She was waking up in spite of every effort to fight it. She flicked open her eyes.

*No.*

She closed them again.

*How could it be?*

She opened them again. Was the dream still with her? . . . Or was it . . .

"Sam?" she whispered, her heart filled with awe.

He was still holding her hand. In the dream and . . . here. He was still holding it, one of his hands cupping her fingers, the other holding her wrist. His beautiful hands with the wide nails and fraying cuticles. The ones he'd used to stomp all over her chess pieces that day in the park when this had started.

"Gaia," he said. She'd never heard her name sound just that way before.

He was leaning forward, leaning over her. So close now. So real. "Can I?" he whispered.

"Please," she said.

He took his hand from her wrist and touched his first two fingers to her elbow, then drew them in an air-light caress up to her shoulder. "Mmmm," she sighed.

As his head hovered over her she looked up at his neck and chin, touching her finger to the place where his whiskers started, moving them up over his jaw, feeling the slight hollow of his cheek, the strong bones that came together at the corner of his eye. He gazed down at her, his eyes voracious and questioning. She turned her head to face him straight on.

"Oh," he said, drawing in his breath. He touched his fingers to the ugly bruise along the side of her cheek and forehead. His face showed real worry. "Are you okay?"

She felt like crying just then. She'd forgotten about everything that had happened. Now she remembered, and she felt ashamed of it and of all the ugliness and violence she represented in Sam's good, peaceful life. "I'm sorry," she said randomly, her eyes filling with tears.

"No, Gaia," he whispered. "Don't. Just . . . be with me."

The feelings inside her were too round and full. She couldn't hold them. Her chest was bursting, and her head was spinning.

He pulled her up so she was sitting beside him and gently held her face in her hands. He put his lips, gentle as sunlight, to the wound on her forehead, then dotted her cheekbone with kisses.

Please, please, please, she begged silently. Wishing.

Oh God. And then he found it, and her wish happened. His lips found her mouth, and the gentleness gave way to intensity. A kiss. A real kiss more perfect than any imagined. She was kissing him back, hungrily, pressing herself against him.

A thought came to her as his lips melted into hers. *This,* she thought, *is the mouth that I was meant to kiss. This is the mouth I will always kiss, and no other.* And blending into that thought was another thought. More a feeling than a thought, because there were no words to it at all. But the feeling was that her lips and her hands had found a home. The one safe, healing place on earth. And that maybe, maybe . . . who could ever say? But maybe she really would have kids someday. (Not just one.) Because there was somebody in the world for her. She knew that now, from this kiss, and nobody could take that away.

His hands held the back of her head now; they were buried in her hair. His lips explored hers. She tasted him and felt him and smelled him all at once. Her senses mixed and blurred. Her blood roared in her ears.

He stood up and pulled her with him. He pressed the entire length of his body against her. She tilted back her head, not wanting to break the kiss. She let her hands explore his graceful, muscular back, his wide, sturdy shoulders. She touched his neck and felt the way his hair curled sweetly around his ears. Digging her fingers into his hair, she pushed him deeper, harder into the kiss.

He moaned. His arms were around her now, gathering her up, holding her as tight and close against him as she could be and still remain a separate person. His lips left hers, landing under her jaw, down her neck, her collarbone.

"Aaaaaah." A breathy sound escaped her lips. The dizziness was overpowering; it was shutting her in. These feelings were too fragile and beautiful to be held, the love too big to fit into her scarred, shrunken heart.

"I love you." Did she think it, or did she say it? Or did he say it? Or did she imagine he said it? Were the words in the air or just in her mind?

Before she could be sure, the darkness engulfed her, and she released herself to the sureness of Sam's arms.

# "I LOVE YOU," SAM WHISPERED

**Siren Song**

against her neck. "I love you."

He'd always wondered what it would take to say those words, how much he'd have to push and prompt and coach himself to utter them. He didn't realize it wouldn't require any intention at all—that the words could come without thought or plan, as naturally and passionately and irreversibly as a kiss, without waiting for his consent.

Suddenly he felt her weight sink into his arms.

"Gaia." He pulled her up to him, finding her face with his lips, kissing her eyelids. They were closed. "Gaia?"

Her eyes didn't open. She breathed a sigh. Her head fell forward, resting against his chest. "Gaia?"

He cradled her head in the crook of his elbow and tipped her back gently. "Gaia? Are you all right? Gaia?"

She had fainted. She was motionless in his arms. All the feelings whirring in his chest changed directions, from pure exultation to surprise and fear.

He picked her up in his arms, cradling her against him. "Gaia. Gaia!" He jostled her, hoping to rouse her. Her head fell back, `exposing her delicate throat.`

"Gaia, please? What happened? Are you okay?" Panic was building. His eyes found the terrible bruise on the side of her head. Could it be . . . ? What if . . . ?

"Gaia, come on. Stay with me here, would you? Please, Gaia." The fear was talking. He was listening only distractedly.

He managed to support her weight with one arm and with the other plucked the phone from his nightstand. He dialed 911.

"Thirty-two Fifth!" he blared into the phone as soon as he heard a voice pick up. "Fourth floor. Send an ambulance."

"Sir, can you tell me what has happened?" the voice urged calmly.

"M-My . . . girlfriend." (Girlfriend?) "She's fainted. I can't rouse her. She hurt her head. Maybe—"

"All right, sir, we'll send the ambulance immediately."

Sam's heart was slamming in his rib cage. Thoughts were careening around his brain like a million errant Ping-Pong balls. "Oh, Gaia, please be okay," he begged her still body.

He laid her down as gingerly as he could on his bed. It was cold out. He needed to cover her. Did she have clothes or . . . ? No time.

He grabbed his thick, terry cloth robe from his closet and wrapped her in it. It was a strange set of circumstances that would force him to willingly cover her magnificent body, not to let his eyes linger over her exquisite stomach and hips and legs.

He found a wool blanket on the shelf and bundled her in that, too. Then he scooped her lifeless body up and strode out into the hallway. He punched the button for the elevator, his ears pricked for the sound of a siren. It was the one time he invited that sound, desperately wanted to hear it.

The elevator came. Sam stabbed at the lobby button.

There it was! The siren! Thank the Lord for a quick response. He raced past a stunned-looking Bauman and met the ambulance just as it was pulling up outside.

Fear blended with appreciation as Sam watched

the emergency medical team burst into action, their limbs and instruments a blur of confidence and precision. He loved them in that moment as much as he loved his parents and friends.

Before a minute had passed, Gaia was bound in a stretcher, hooked up to various medical gadgets, tucked into the back of the vehicle with Sam beside her. The engine roared, the siren kicked in again, and they were off to St. Vincent's, just a few blocks away.

Sam held her hand tight, never wanting to let it go.

"I love you," he whispered to her again, pleading with his crazed heart to stay in his chest for a while longer.

He considered it for a moment, his newly awakened heart. He remembered the puzzling conflict between heart and mind. Well, it was settled now.

In case there was any mystery, he now knew who was in charge.

GAIA WAS FLOATING. SAM WAS there, holding her hand. There were unfamiliar people, sounds, words, things she couldn't make sense of, but there was always Sam. He held her. He gave her his warmth.

# Heaven

"I love you." The words came to her in Sam's voice. She wanted very much to open her eyes and see if it really was Sam, and if so, to see if he was talking to her when he said them, as she fervently hoped he was. And if he was saying those words to her, and maybe even if he wasn't, she wanted to say the same words to him.

But she couldn't. She couldn't open her eyes or make words.

Was she alive anymore? Was Sam real? Was he really there with her?

Maybe it was him. More likely it was heaven.

But if this was heaven, if this was what death felt like, then it was okay with her.

I've been trying to figure out why I don't have any tears for Sam tonight.

I do hate him at the moment; that's true.

But I thought I loved him.

All this time I figured I haven't been able to cry over him because I'm too numb. I'm too bottled up and confused to feel things very well.

I never imagined the possibility that I didn't love him.

Because I do love him. I mean, I'm pretty sure I do.

I mean, I do. Don't I?

You know what's really retarded? An hour after Sam left, I called Ed Fargo.

Then I remembered he was in Pennsylvania. He was there for Thanksgiving with his weird, obese grandmother who called me Feather.

Then the
memories
fell into
fragments
and shards
that **hunger**
didn't make
any sense at
all.

ELLA ROLLED HER EYES AT THE
emergency-
room doctor
in St. Vincent's
Hospital. This
was a night of
highs and lows,
currently stuck
on low.

# More
# Disappointment

The doctor was talking about Gaia, bleating words like *concussion* and *subdural* something and *hematoma* something else. But he wasn't saying anything about "slashed to ribbons," which was what Ella really wanted to hear.

She was jubilant when she'd first gotten the call from the hospital, sure that her plans had gone off without a hitch. Then she entered a period of confusion after she arrived at the hospital, during which it appeared that Gaia *hadn't* been slashed at Penn Station. Gaia, she was told, had spent several semidelirious hours before a doting Sam Moon brought her to the hospital, unconscious, from his NYU dormitory. The girl who'd been slashed (Ella had followed the story excitedly on the eleven o'clock news) was *not* Gaia, and yet Gaia had found her way to the hospital with some grave problem nonetheless.

Ella perked up when she heard the doctor use the

word *coma*, hoping that her goal might be achieved even without the extra bonus of disfigurement. But wretched, impossible Gaia had miraculously managed to sidestep the coma, in spite of a serious head injury.

"Mrs. Niven, I'm sorry to bother you with all of this information. I'm sure you'd like to see her," Dr. Somethingorother was saying. He was Indian or maybe Pakistani and spoke precise, melodious English.

Ella sighed. She couldn't very well say no, could she? "Of course," she said.

"You'll be pleased to know she's already been moved out of ICU. Her condition is stable."

*Whoopee.*

Ella followed the white coat up an elevator and down a hallway, through a set of swinging doors, past a waiting room and a nurses' station.

Dr. Whatever turned around to talk some more. "She's not yet fully conscious. Still a bit bleary. Try not to be alarmed. We do expect her to make a quick recovery, but it's never as quick as all of us would like."

If Gaia woke up before she was thirty, it would be too quick. Ella nodded blandly. She hated doctors. Particularly the one she'd blown up earlier in the evening.

The doctor stopped in front of room 448. The

door was partially open. He gestured for her to enter first. She started into the room and quickly stepped backward. She backed out into the hallway.

"Excuse me, Doctor," she said. "But there's somebody else in the room."

The doctor's eyes lit up. "Yes, that's her friend who brought her here. His name is Sam, I think? He hasn't left her side in hours. He is quite devoted to her, no? He is the one who gave us the information to find you."

"Fine," she said. "Very nice. But would you mind asking him to leave? I really need some time alone with my . . . foster daughter." Sob, sob. "Besides," she added in a confidential tone, "if I can speak frankly, I don't like that young man. I wouldn't be surprised if he were part of the reason that Gaia is here in the first place. . . ." She let her voice float off enigmatically.

The doctor hesitated. Clearly he didn't know what to think, and yet he was too polite to question her. "Yes. As you wish," he said.

"I'll just use the bathroom and collect myself for a moment," Ella said, stepping down the hall. "I'll come back when I can see Gaia alone."

A strong instinct was telling Ella she didn't want to be introduced to Sam Moon. A somewhat twisted instinct, but those were the ones she'd learned to listen to.

# One Witness

SAM WATCHED GAIA'S EYELIDS for signs of her waking. Just in the last five minutes she'd opened and closed her eyes three times, once almost focusing on his face. His heart soared. Dr. Sengupta said she was going to be okay, and he was starting to believe it.

Sam ran his thumb from the tip of her index finger up her hand and wrist to the soft underside of her forearm. Her eyes flickered.

He leaned over her and buried a gentle kiss on her neck. That was more for him than her. He hoped she didn't mind. The hint of a smile seemed to pull at the side of her mouth. Or did he just imagine that?

What he really wanted to do was to climb into the narrow bed and press her close to him, to hold her with his whole body until she woke up. And after she woke up, too. But you weren't really supposed to do that in a hospital, were you?

Most people hated hospitals, and in theory, Sam did, too. But this hospital, on two separate occasions, had brought him closer to Gaia. It was the site of some of his worst experiences and yet some of the happiest feelings he'd ever had.

"Sam?"

He glanced up. He saw Gaia's doctor and felt slightly abashed. "Yes?"

"I'm sorry to ask you because I can see how much you wish to stay with Gaia, but her guardian, Mrs. Niven, has asked for time alone with her."

Sam knew it was a reasonable request, but his heart was breaking nonetheless. "Maybe I'll just wait in the waiting room for a few minutes till she's done."

Dr. Sengupta took in the state of Sam's hair and clothing with kind eyes. "Why don't you get yourself home and have a rest? Perhaps you could come again tomorrow? Visiting hours, as you might imagine, are long over."

Visiting hours? Sam was no visitor! He was . . . what? Nothing. He was nothing. But Gaia was his life. Did that count for anything?

"But I—" He really, really didn't want to go yet. He wanted to help usher Gaia back into the land of consciousness, to be with her when she crossed over. He needed to make sure they both knew that what happened between them was real. "Please, could I just—"

"I'm sorry. I have to respect Mrs. Niven's request." The doctor did look truly sorry.

Sam turned back to Gaia. He took both of her hands and brought them to his heart. He leaned over and pressed his cheek against her good one. "I love you, Gaia," he whispered in her ear. "I can't help it anymore." It might not have been a classically romantic thing to say, but it was true. She'd understand, he knew. He kissed her ear, then straightened up.

Her eyelids were fluttering again. He saw her hands moving against the sheet as soon as he'd released them. Were her hands looking for his? Did he just hope so?

"Thank you, Doctor, for everything," he said, trying not to look as unhappy as he felt. "She's really going to be okay, right?"

"Yes, I believe she is."

Sam trudged out of the room and down the hallway.

"Good luck to you, Sam," the doctor called after him, and the words somehow sounded ominous.

Every cell in Sam's heart was telling him not to leave her now. He was afraid that once he was gone, their magical, frightening night together would be gone, too, with him left as its only witness.

And not the most reliable witness, either.

IT WAS HARD AND CRUEL. IT downright sucked. In her dream, hovering someplace beyond the

**Disappointment 1,000,000,000**

living, Gaia had Sam. He held her and told her he loved her.

Here, in reality, she had Ella.

She wished she could go back to being dead.

". . . You have quite a track record, Gaia. Twice in the hospital in two months," Ella was blathering. "You're going to send George's insurance premiums into the stratosphere."

Gaia exerted all her strength propping herself up in the hospital bed. It made her uncomfortable for Ella to see her lying down.

". . . And insurance only covers eighty percent of the bill, you know," Ella continued pettily.

Gaia looked down at her hands. They felt cold and lonely. "Thanks a lot, Ella," she said numbly. "That makes me feel a lot better. If the photography thing doesn't work out, maybe you could get a job with Hallmark in the get-well-card department."

Ella exhaled in annoyance. "And you're a rude ingrate as well."

Gaia closed her eyes, wrapping her misery around her like a blanket. She was right back where she started. She'd thought she'd made a new friend. She hadn't. She'd thought she'd run away. She hadn't.

She'd gotten nowhere, changed nothing.

Her mind summoned an image of Sam. She was kissing him, touching him, wrapping her body around his in his bed. The image brought a deep flush to her cheeks. But that hadn't really . . . They hadn't actually . . . had they?

She glanced at Ella.

What exactly *had* happened to her? How had she gotten here? She tried to piece together the endless, surreal day. She remembered being at Mary's house, of course. She remembered hitting her head on the sink in the bathroom at Penn Station. She remembered passing out—if you could call that remembering.

Things got fuzzier after that. She didn't remember coming to, but she did remember trying to get a refund for her stolen ticket. She vaguely remembered an explosion. She remembered walking outside and being cold.

Then the memories fell into fragments and shards that didn't make any sense at all.

She glanced at Ella again. She could hardly stomach the notion of needing information from the bitch goddess, but how else was she going to know?

Gaia took a breath. She needed to sound as disinterested as possible. "So, anyway, Ella. What happened to me? How did I get here? How did you get here?"

Ella opened her eyes wide in fake surprise. "Wait a minute. You are asking *me* questions about *your* life?"

Gaia shrugged. "You know, severe head wound and all." She touched her hand to her bruise. "I just wondered if the doctors told you anything about how I ended up here."

Ella studied her for a moment. "Actually, yes. Do you really not remember anything at all?"

Gaia shook her head. "Not much."

Ella nodded slowly. "Well, you made quite a little scene. The cops found you outside an NYU dormitory. You were delirious, totally out of it, raving endlessly about somebody named Sam."

Gaia felt her heart clench. The flush returned to her cheeks and deepened by one hundred times. If she'd really believed she'd made her heart tough enough to withstand disappointment, she'd been badly, profoundly mistaken.

"I was alone?" Gaia asked in a small voice, even though she knew she'd regret it. "I came here alone?" She was so far gone, she was giving evil Ella a straight shot at her vulnerability.

"Except for some freaked-out cops, yeah," Ella informed her.

So Gaia's fragments of memory weren't memory at all. They were fantasy. Sam hadn't kissed her, held her, told her he loved her. Those were the crazed delusions of her bashed-in head and her `pitiful, hungry heart`.

She was tempted to bash her head again, to return to the place where she'd had those feelings. Of course they didn't happen in reality. Not in her reality, anyway. It was too nice, too purely good to have happened in her life.

Gaia lay back again. Ella didn't matter. Nothing mattered.

Her misery wasn't a blanket. It was a `strait-jacket` fastened way too tight, threatening to squeeze out her last bit of hope.

I had a terrible thought when I woke up this morning in the bed that Gaia and I had shared, briefly, last night.

I had the thought that I dreamed the whole thing.

I would have stuck with the thought, but I smelled Gaia's faint, sweet smell in my bed. I found more than one long blond hair on my pillow. I found a somewhat tattered red dress and shoes balled up in my garbage can. I confirmed that my under-shirt and boxers were, in fact, missing.

Then I had a fear that was worse than the thought. I was afraid that it had actually hap-pened, but that Gaia wasn't there. I mean, her body was there. But she was so badly hurt and delirious, and practically comatose, that everything I imag-ined between us happened to me. Only to me.

This fear makes me physically sick because I hate the thought

**SAM**

of having taken advantage of her
in some way.

Selfishly, that's not even the
very worst part. Even worse, I
fear I've opened my stubborn,
tyrannical heart to an event—a
girl—so stunning and miraculous,
I've even gotten my brain to join
in on the thrill of it. Only to
discover that it never actually
happened.

Which could make a man feel
like a creep and a big, pathetic
fool.

My brain, not surprisingly, is
threatening a very sour "I told
you so."

That's the fear, anyway. I'm
not sure it's the truth.

But I can say this. I never
understood loneliness until I
woke up in my bed without her
this morning.

**Maybe** Ella was telling me the truth. Maybe I was discovered by the cops, raving outside of Sam's dormitory, and taken to the hospital alone.

But when I stepped out of the hospital bed after my night of observation and walked my bleary self into the bathroom, I discovered something peculiar. Under my hospital robe, I was wearing a man's undershirt and a man's boxers. These are things I know I do not own. I don't care how hard I banged my head.

At the back of the boxers, just under the waistband, scrawled in permanent black marker are two wonderful words. Can you guess them?

1. Sam
2. Moon

These pieces of physical evidence happen to fit with some memory shards I have—fuzzy, I'll admit. I have bits of memories of being in Sam's dorm room, and putting those things on.

GAIA

I'm not saying Sam definitely kissed me. I'm not saying he told me he loved me or anything like that.

I'm just saying, maybe Ella was wrong. Maybe she lied. Maybe.

In all honesty, I don't even want to find out for sure. I want to hold onto these pieces of memory—hopes, if you want to be a killjoy. I can't bear to discover these things didn't happen. I need to cling to the possibility that they did.

Because even the *possibility* of something so beautiful could sustain a heart as desolate as mine for a long, long time.

*LUST*

*To Colton and Gabrielle Bryan*

I guess the only time most people think about blood is when it's gushing out of their veins and they need to find a Band-Aid—or an emergency room—to keep it from messing up the white carpet. But I've been thinking about it a lot lately. Little red platelets and big white corpuscles rushing through everyone's veins. Keeping us alive as long as it stays on its dark little course—but signaling weakness or death when it wanders off the path, out into the light to spill on the ground.

Funny thing about blood: It also connects people. There it is, hidden inside your skin, yet it manages to call out to other blood, related blood, inside someone else's skin. You might have nothing else in common, but that red stuff really is thicker than water. There's nobody in the world I should have more cause to hate than Oliver. Or should I say, Loki. He has engineered more destruction—starting with that of

GAIA

my own mother, the woman who created the blood I'm talking about—
than anyone else in my life. So a
bout of postcoma confusion has
forced his pre-Loki, kinder and
gentler Oliver personality to
emerge, and suddenly he regrets
his evil ways.

At best I should feel indiffer-
ent toward him. But because we
share blood, I find myself drawn
to him. I find myself willing to
try to trust him—this new,
remorseful Oliver—because our DNA
matches up so nicely.

Am I just a sucker? A girl so
lonely she'll cling to any semblance of a family connection? Or
is this an instinct, speaking
through the bowels of primordial
history, telling me the tide has
turned for Oliver?

Let's hope it's the latter.

Let's hope it's the blood
that's letting me forgive him.
Anyone else would get nothing
from me but my everlasting hate.
Like Natasha and Tatiana, the
mother-daughter team from the

third ring of hell. A couple of lying, conniving females who took my dad from me and almost had me convinced he was dead. But he can't be dead. My blood would tell me if he was. They're still going to pay, though—maybe with their own blood. If I get half a chance, you can bet that'll be the case.

But that's so a priority. What's important now—what's got to happen before anything else—is I've got to find my dad. My real blood link. Even closer than Oliver. He's the one I owe my loyalty to. And I'm going to find him. Come hell or high water, the blood pumping in my veins is going to give me the strength to reach around the globe and find him. You can bet on that.

She had to

remember to

keep her

distance

**unfamiliar**

this

**terrain**

time.

Within her

heart, and

out in the

world.

# Dangerously Accurate

GAIA SAT SLUMPED IN AN UNFORGIVING wood-and-metal chair as she cycled through the seven local stations one more time, looking for something that would amuse her and Jake in his hospital room. The television, which looked about twenty years old, was bolted to the ceiling and made a disconcerting fuzzy noise between each channel, like the *cchk* sound at the beginning and end of a walkie-talkie broadcast. The static was only marginally less interesting than daytime TV.

"Is this *Judge Judy*?" Gaia wanted to know.

"No, that's a different show" Jake said, pointing to the screen. "I forget what this one's called. . . . It looks like a judge show, but then they bring in therapists and it turns into a corny love fest where everybody's hugging and crying, even though tomorrow they're going to go back to throwing chairs at each other."

"Well, there's nothing else on. You need better health insurance. This no-cable thing is a problem."

"Aren't you supposed to be in school?" Jake asked again. Gaia glared at him.

"Didn't I already sidestep that question?" she wanted to know.

"Yeah, that's why I have to ask it again. I'd think

you'd be more considerate—it's tiring, ya know? All this verbal back-and-forth. . ."

"Whatever. I skipped again," she admitted. "I can't sit still in school. I'm too agitated."

"What? Because of this?" Jake shrugged. Gaia tried not to think about the fact that he'd been shot when he'd been ambushed. *Because* of her. So what if it had turned out to be nothing more than a flesh wound? He was hurt because he'd gotten in the way of people after Gaia. And that made her feel ill.

He wasn't the first person to end up lying on a metal cot with a tube in his arm because of her. And she felt a leaden certainty that he wouldn't be the last.

"Please. Don't flatter yourself," she said sheepishly, glancing at the bandages enveloping his powerful shoulder.

"Well, whatever it is, why don't you just go to school and avoid getting in trouble?"

Gaia blinked at him. "What are you, a Boy Scout?" she asked.

Jake laughed. "No, I'm just saying, you could go to school to pass the time just as easily as you can sit here."

Gaia knew he was right. She didn't know why she had such an aversion to school. Maybe it was because she already knew everything that was being droned about in the front of the classroom. Her dad—her dad and her mom, actually—had made sure of that, having made her take advantage of her sharp intellect from the moment she could read, which had happened at around age three. Maybe she just couldn't stand being fenced in. Maybe she was worried that another strike would hurt the students around her.

Or maybe she just wanted to be here, at the hospital, with Jake.

"Oh, why start behaving now?" she muttered. "It would just confuse everyone."

"You know what I think?" Jake gave her a sidelong look.

"No, in fact, I don't possess that particular skill," Gaia responded dryly.

"I think you like putting one over on people," he said with a tiny nod. "You like being Invisible Girl, appearing in class at will, while everyone else sticks to the rules and studies and worries about the SATs. Because you know you can pull a passing grade out of your ass, and you like the challenge."

"Oh, really?" Gaia knew she was just being teased. But even being fake-dissected gave her an uneasy feeling.

"Yeah. Plus, now that I know how crazy your life has been, it makes even more sense. You'd hate to feel settled and centered, wouldn't you? That would just be too unfamiliar to stand." Jake was enjoying this, Gaia could see that. She was acting nonchalant, but inside she squirmed with discomfort under the probing spotlight of this much attention. Not to mention the fact that his theory sounded dangerously accurate.

"Hey, I have a great idea, Jake. Why don't you get out of my head and back into your hospital bed? I think it's time for your lower G.I. series."

"Oh, hoooo!" Jake laughed at the sharp tone in Gaia's voice. "Man, are you easy to tease!"

"You're annoying," Gaia told him. "I'm going to request that your next sponge bath be given by a male nurse."

As if Gaia's guilty feelings had taken human form, the door clunked open and Jake's father entered the room, along with a stout old woman. Gaia stood up as if she'd been caught pulling the wings off a fly. She couldn't help but worry that Mr. Montone would eventually come to his senses and hold her responsible for Jake's condition. There was no way he could believe it was pure coincidence that his golden boy had gotten shot while he was out with his mysterious new friend.

"Gaia!" Mr. Montone came straight for her and gave her a... hug? Gaia's nerve endings did a confused little dance; they'd been expecting a slap, or at least the cold shoulder.

"It's so good to see you," Mr. Montone said. "You've been such a good friend to Jake through all this. Ma, this is Jake's friend Gaia. The one who got him to the hospital."

"You do so good!" the old woman said, reaching up to grab Gaia by the cheeks and giving her an affectionate—and powerful—squeeze.

"A lot of girls your age are somewhat. . . flighty," Mr. Montone added. "Might have panicked and run home. You really kept a level head, and I appreciate what you did for my son."

Gaia sent a telepathic thank you to the CIA agents who'd talked to Mr. Montone after the shootout. Who knew what on earth they could have told him? But whatever it had been, it had evidently completely ruled out any possibility of Gaia's involvement.

"Oh, no," Gaia stammered. "I mean, I didn't really—" *Shut up and quit while you're ahead*, she muttered internally. *For once, someone thinks you did something right. You'd better enjoy it.*

"Dad, Nonna, what are you guys doing here?" Jake asked. "Is something wrong?"

The door opened again. A nervous-looking young doctor in a white coat shuffled in, eyeballing the visitors who already seemed intent on bossing him around.

"Excuse me—I understand you want to take Jake home?" he asked, with all the authority of a kid who'd missed his curfew.

"We don' just wanna," Jake's grandmother said. "We *gonna* take him home."

The doctor looked to Jake's dad for help, but he just shrugged and started packing Jake's things into a duffel.

"Mrs. Montone, I really must tell you, we'd prefer it if we could watch Jake for one more night."

"Watch him what, starve to death because of your hospital food? I need to get some braciola into him before he fades to nothing."

Gaia snorted with laughter. She couldn't help it. Jake was so huge and solid that the idea of him wasting away was ridiculous.

"We'd just like to observe. . . oh. . . fine," the doctor said resignedly.

"Good man," Mr. Montone said, patting him on the back. "Don't worry, I can watch him. I know what to look for: infection, gangrene. I work at Mount Sinai, you know."

"Yes, sir."

It was amazing. Gaia hadn't noticed it as much back at Jake's apartment, but for all intents and purposes, Mr. Montone looked like an older Jake, only with white hair and a bit of a belly. He peered at Jake over his half-glasses and said, "You. Up."

"Gaia, do you mind?" Jake asked.

"What? Oh! I'll wait in the hall." She caught a glimpse of him sitting up and shifting over in bed, preparing to take off his hospital gown. Flustered, she left the room.

Immediately she realized she should have just made

her excuses and left. Of course, she could still just leave, but she hadn't said good-bye, and Jake's family would think she was weird.

*And why do you care what Jake's family thinks?* she asked herself.

*I don't,* she answered. *Who cares? Just because his father fed me the best homemade dinner I've had since I was a kid and welcomed me into his home, and just because his son is basically my only friend? I don't give a hoot what they think of me.* But somehow she stood in the hallway, shifting her weight from one foot to the other with nervous energy until they emerged.

Jake was fully clothed, except he hadn't managed to get a T-shirt over his bandages, so his loose flannel button-down shirt fell open at the chest. His dad and grandma followed behind him, arguing over which one should carry the duffel bag.

"Gimme that. You've got the bad back," his grandmother ordered.

"I've got it. It's not heavy," his dad said.

"Sure, it's-a not heavy till you throw your back out again. Come on, give."

Jake slowed down so that they had to pass him, then let the elevator door close without him.

"See you downstairs," he called out as his grandmother tried to hit the door-open button and failed.

"The hospital would have been some welcome peace and quiet," Jake said, indicating with a nod

11

that he was referring to his father and grandmother.

"I think they're great," said Gaia.

"They are. But Nonna's a bit much." He sighed and hit the down button so they could get on the next elevator.

"Are you sure you should be going home?" Gaia asked.

"Oh, yeah," Jake said. "I fully expected my dad to show up and yank me out of here. He always says the best way to get sicker is to spend time in a hospital. This thing does ache, though."

"Yeek." Gaia peered at the big bandage. "I don't think you're going to be doing much intramural karate."

Jake groaned. "I know," he lamented. "You're off the hook, though. If I'm not competing, we won't win anyway."

"God, you've got the fattest head!" Gaia complained. "You think I couldn't beat everyone single-handedly?"

"You could, but you won't," he pointed out. "I was really looking forward to it, though. I was all revved up for the competition. Without it, the next few weeks are going to be so boring. And I'm going to get so out of shape."

Gaia felt the bud of an idea fatten in her head. "Hmm," she said.

"Hmm, what?" Jake asked, poking the button a few more times.

"Hmm, I was just thinking—when I was going

through my martial arts training, my dad showed me a bunch of techniques for working out that give various muscle groups a rest. I could teach them to you, just so your precious muscle mass doesn't evaporate during your recovery."

Gaia couldn't believe the words that were coming out of her mouth. Was she actually being forthcoming? This Jake guy had a very unusual effect on her.

"Gaia Moore, are you offering to be my personal trainer?"

She rolled her eyes. "Yeah, right. If you're going to be an idiot about it, I won't bother."

Jake smacked her lightly on the back of the head. "Cut it out," he said. "I'm sorry. I would be really grateful if you could show me your special commando workout."

"Fine. I will," Gaia said.

"But only if you go to school tomorrow."

"Fine."

"Of course, you're going to be gone within a day or two," Jake pointed out as the elevator finally arrived and the doors creaked open. "Some 911 situation will come up and you'll be out of here. I'll be left with atrophying muscles and a gunshot wound."

For a moment, Gaia had a vision of Sam Moon's scarred chest—another wounded friend, a romance destroyed by the life she was forced to lead. She had to

13

remember to keep her distance this time. She wouldn't let the same thing happen to Jake.

Gaia was silent, watching the numbers light up in descending order. This was the slowest elevator in the world. She noticed Jake giving her a look.

"What?" she snapped.

"I think it's funny," he said.

"*What*?"

"The way every single thought in your head goes walking across your face before you shove it back in its closet," Jake said. "You really think that because you don't say things out loud, you can deny they're there, don't you?"

"All right, smart guy—so what thoughts am I repressing?" she asked, crossing her arms and continuing to stare as nine flipped to eight with agonizing sluggishness.

"Oh, no. I'm not making things easier for you. You'll open your mouth when you're good and ready, and not before."

Gaia clamped her mouth tightly closed, tucking her lips inside it for extra emphasis, and refused to look at Jake. He was so close to her, she could feel the heat from his body making the left side of her face flush. Without her permission, her eyes flicked toward him, then away again. The expression in his eyes—he seemed to *know* her in a way she wasn't sure was either good or bad. He was teasing her, daring her to feel something for him. It was maddening, frustrating.

The doors finally opened. "Jake!" Mrs. Montone called out, her arms extended as if she were about to reach in and yank him out. "Why you sneak off like that? Come here."

Jake shot Gaia one last look and joined his father and grandmother, who draped a coat carefully over his shoulders.

"Gaia, can you get home all right?" Mr. Montone asked. "Should we drop you somewhere? We've got a car service waiting."

"Oh, no, it's all right," Gaia promised. "I can take the subway."

"Are you sure? It's no trouble."

Gaia was touched. If Mr. Montone knew what she'd been through in her life, the guy wouldn't have been concerned about her being inconvenienced by the midday subway.

"I promise. It was nice to see you again. And nice to meet you, Mrs. Montone."

"Yeah, I see you again," she said, nodding cheerfully.

"So I'll see you tomorrow after school?" Jake asked. "You'll show me that stuff we were talking about?"

Gaia felt herself nod. Maddening, yes. Frustrating, yes. But whether it was out of guilt or some kind of unexpected fascination, she'd have to see Jake again.

OLIVER SEARCHED THROUGH THE
databases he had found stored on his
computer—the ones that hadn't self-
destructed when he'd gotten his log-
in wrong the first time. It had taken
him half a day just to get access to
his own information. This was like
trying to put together one of those
all-black jigsaw puzzles. In the dark.
During a windstorm. If something
looked familiar, he had to then ask
himself why, and what it might connect to, and how he
should approach it. He felt like a blind man in a mael-
strom.

**Internal Hard Drive**

Finding this information required the highest level
of mental functioning. For someone so recently out of
a coma, it was exhausting. And there was something
else that was required: To access some of the memories
he needed—passwords, log-in names, locations of files,
meanings of notes—he had to force some of Loki's
memories to the surface. And Oliver was not a computer; he couldn't just pull up one file out of a folder
and leave the rest safely closed. If he exposed one
memory to the light, others would try to bubble to the
surface as well. And he could not afford to have that
happen.

He was dancing a dangerous tango with
his evil former self.

Oliver took a long drink of water and turned his eyes to the screen again. He had to secure transportation for them. Airline tickets. How did this work again? He had to get the passports in another name, the visas to match, enough tickets for everyone. . . . The screen began to swim in front of him. It seemed to morph into a television screen. On it he saw a man—a man dressed as a doctor—in an antiseptic room, a white room, but not a hospital. A loft of some kind. . . A young woman was there, a girl, a friend of Gaia's; something in him told him that. The scene was new but dripping with familiarity, like in dreams where some subconscious voice acts as a narrator for unfamiliar terrain.

The girl bent over and the doctor injected her with something. Oliver squinted to see more clearly. Then the screen split; on one side, he saw the beautiful young woman struck blind as a result of the injection. On the other side he saw the doctor raise his face. With horror, Oliver recognized his own eyes staring back at him from the television screen.

Jolted, he jumped back, knocking his chair to the floor with a clatter. The noise made him look down, and when he looked back up, the taunting television screen had become his computer again—his safe, familiar computer, quietly listing his old contacts for him to pore over.

"Loki," he said out loud. "It was Loki, and I have control over him."

He straightened the chair and placed it in front of his desk again, glanced nervously at the computer screen. But it was still covered in calm, static numbers. No more streaming video straight from his buried internal hard drive. Oliver took a deep breath and sat down again.

He needed to find a few contacts who would still do him favors. He needed to check those favors, to be sure he was not being scammed. He had to secure these passports and visas. His brother's life depended on it. Gaia's happiness depended on it.

He mustered his energy and forced himself back to work.

## "WELL, LOOK, WE'VE INTERVIEWED A

bunch of guys, but you're the only one who seems normal. If you want the place, it's yours."

Sam Moon took the hand extended to him and shook it. "That's great, man," he said. "I appreciate it. You want the check now?"

"Yeah, if you've got it."

# Outer-Borough Frat House

Sam nodded and went into the room that was going to be his. The two guys—his new roommates—who already lived here seemed cool. They were students, but not at NYU, so Sam didn't have to worry that they'd know of his strange past.

This room—something about an empty room made it full of possibilities. The wide wooden slats of the floor invited him to plop a futon down. The cavernous closet, with nothing but two wire hangers and a baseball cap inside, awaited his meager wardrobe. The pale walls, painted `an indiscriminate shade of greige`, were made for dorm-style décor—black-and-white art posters, an Escher print, maybe an Anna Kournikova calendar. It was like a blank canvas.

He strolled to the windows and looked out. The windows were old and heavy. They rolled up and down on thick chains, and he could feel a palpable breeze where the frames met the jambs. They looked out on a busy Queens boulevard, filled with at least six different international restaurants, based on a quick count. Afghan, Indian, Chinese, Mexican, Greek, and something in a language he didn't even recognize. So he didn't live in Manhattan anymore. So he was going to have to work for a while before he could get back to school. That was okay. Because he finally had some kind of control over his life.

Of course he was worried. Of course he knew he could still be a target. But living in hiding, in Chinatown with Dmitri, was no longer an option. He couldn't live like a caged animal anymore. Dmitri was great—it was a loan from him that was making this all possible, after all—but he was just one more reminder of that whole bizarre Gaia chapter of his life.

Gaia. She was the most fantastic, sexy, romantic, exciting person he'd ever known, but being with her had come with a price. Whatever mysterious forces she was connected to had destroyed Sam's life. Operatives bent on destroying Gaia had come after him, killing his roommate, framing him for the murder, and finally shooting and imprisoning Sam for months. He still wasn't fully recovered, physically or mentally. And Gaia hadn't come through for him. Yeah, she had rescued him, but when he'd tried to reconnect with her, she'd thrown up so many walls that he just hadn't been able to. Plus there was that boyfriend of hers. Obviously she was still stuck on him. There just wasn't room in her heart for Sam Moon.

That had been painful. So rather than be halfway in her life, he'd made the decision to cut himself off from her entirely. Make a fresh start. Hence the empty room in this outer-borough frat house.

Yeah, he was taking a chance. Whoever had hurt him the first time could be after him still. But he was as good as dead, hidden away in Dmitri's apartment. He had to take this chance.

"Dude, you okay in there? We were just going to get

some beers—you want to come with?"

"Yeah! I was just looking for my checkbook," Sam said, scribbling out a check for a ridiculous amount of money and taking it out to the living room. "Here you go. First and last month's rent, plus a security deposit."

The beers were going to cost Sam pretty much everything left in his account, but that was okay with him. Pretty much everything was okay with him right now. He was completely psyched to restart his life. All he had to do now was find a job.

So what could a guy with a back full of scar tissue and half a college education do to pull down some cash?

He followed his new friends to the dark Irish pub downstairs and watched three beers get ripped open in rapid succession. He took one and tipped it back, feeling the cool bubbles slip down his throat. Of course. Why hadn't he thought of it before? He had enough hard-luck stories of his own to know how to listen to everyone else's. He'd be a bartender.

I see mountains. Snowy mountains. They're beautiful, cold, remote. I'm not a fool. I recognize them. I am in Siberia.

Siberia. Like some kind of Soviet Union-era dissident. I suppose it has its own romantic appeal. Except, of course, that most of those dissidents ended up dying of consumption.

I'm amazed at how calm I'm remaining. I know that I'm infuriated enough to bang my head against the wall of my jail cell, to grab the bars of my cell and pull on them until my knuckles break. This is unbearable.

I'm in Siberia, a region so remote it doesn't even have regular telephones, let alone cell phones.

My cell is eight by eight. Too small for a primate at the Bronx Zoo.

I can see the other prisoners exercising in the courtyard. I'm not even allowed to socialize with them. I'm locked up here like Hannibal Lecter.

And who's to blame for all this?

TOM

Loki. Once again, Loki.

The human mind cannot bear this kind of cruelty. Mere days ago, I was in the arms of my soon-to-be wife, enjoying the rosy glow of my new family. Watching Gaia become close to her new stepsister, Tatiana. Eyeballing Gaia's boyfriend, Ed. What made me think I could be a normal father with a normal family? What made me consider the idea of taking Ed aside to make sure he had Gaia's best interests at heart? I'm no father. I couldn't even stay clear of the evil creature who was once my brother long enough to finish dinner. Before it was done, I remember coughing. . . then choking. . . then blackness. Until I woke up here.

He did it to me again.

Perhaps my calm comes from the knowledge that this time I will destroy him. This time I will make Loki pay for the pain he has caused me, by eradicating him from the earth altogether. No matter what.

Even if it costs me my own life.

A week ago
she'd been
wishing
Oliver dead— **the**

now she was **old**

bantering

over **psycho-**

cell phone **killer**

etiquette

with him.

# "OW. OKAY, THAT HURTS."

## Dripping With Nostalgia

"It's supposed to."

"Yeah, but it really hurts."

"No pain, no gain, Jake."

"No gain, then! *Ack!*" Jake dropped the bulbous kettle-drum he had been holding up with his foot. It hit the floor with a crash, which was immediately followed by three thudding sounds from the floor below.

"That's old lady Teverasky," Jake said. "I think you made her week. She loves hitting her ceiling with her broomstick—it reminds her of the old country, where they do that for sport."

"Don't try to distract me," Gaia said, crossing her arms. "I'm supposed to be keeping you in shape."

"What shape? A rectangle?" Jake flopped backward on the couch.

"A rectangle? Why a rectangle?"

"Because that's what I feel like: a wreck and a tangle." He looked up at Gaia, who was trying to be really firm and drill-sergeanty.

"That's it, I give up," she said, flopping down next to him on the couch. "Your bad jokes are draining me."

"Oh, good, I give up, too," Jake said.

"You know, you're not going to get any stronger if you don't keep working out," she scolded him.

"You know what? Forget it," he said. "I've been on a workout regimen since I was, like, twelve years old. I think a couple of weeks off is just what I need."

"Whatever. Just don't come crying to me when you wake up and realize you're Mister Flabby."

"And what'll you be, Miss Crabby?"

Gaia snorted. Actually, that stung a little. She knew she was hard to get along with. Lord knew she'd lost enough friends along the way—more than most people made in a lifetime. She wasn't sure—she was never sure—if Jake was just kidding. So far, he always was. But she'd seen Ed, good old best-friend-cum-boyfriend Ed, go from being an easy-going buddy to being a jaded, bitter ex in no time flat.

She had to admit, though, that being with Jake felt nice. Mellow, sort of.

"So are you still feeling. . . agitated?" he asked cautiously. Gaia suddenly felt the walls closing in on her.

"I don't want to talk about it," she said, standing up and walking to the window. She felt bad for snapping at him, but she had to be careful about telling him too much. At the same time, she knew that her evasiveness made her seem ungrateful.

"Hey, okay, we won't," he said, trying to play it off. "You don't have to tell me anything you don't want to," Jake said. "I was just asking so I wouldn't be a dick for not asking."

That evoked a small smile. "I know, Jake. I didn't mean to snap at you."

She turned back and looked at him. "I have to go to Urban Outfitters to get new sneakers," she said. "I've been putting it off, but when my old ones got melted—well, just look at them." She held up one foot and displayed the way her ancient Chuck Taylor sneaker had split where the rubber met the fabric. Her sock poked out of the hole, and the sole was a mushed-up, melted mess.

"Nice," Jake said. "But weren't you caught in that fire like a week ago?"

"Something like that. I'm having separation anxiety. I've had these sneakers forever."

"It's time to let them rest in peace," Jake said somberly. "They've done their job. They're tired."

"Want to come with?" she asked.

"Nah. I'm tired. I'm going to take full advantage of my gimpy state and rest up a little."

Gaia knew Jake's shoulder was still bothering him from the shooting. She also knew better than to ask him about it. He was as private as she was—another thing she liked about him. "All right, I'll see you later," she said. "Don't get up. I'll let myself out."

"I wasn't getting up," Jake called after her. Gaia gave him a smirk as she went through the door.

Urban Outfitters was on lower Broadway. The walk wasn't long, but Gaia's poor old sneakers kept ripping, so by the time she got inside they were like flip-flops.

Gaia strolled around the shoe section, immediately rejecting the sneakers that had sparkles or platform soles. All she wanted was to grab a pair of Chuck Taylors identical to the ones ruined in the fire and get out of the cavernous store. But they were nowhere to be found.

"Chuck Taylors?" she asked the nearest salesperson.

"Uh, yeah, maybe if you visited the time-machine section of our store," she said snottily. "Try the Pumas, I guess."

Gaia tried on a pair of the black suede sneakers, marveling at how big her feet were. They felt like two little comfortable homes. She eyeballed her old Chucks, sitting forlornly next to her spanking-new shoes.

"Sorry, guys," she told them. "It was great while it lasted, but we should have parted ways long ago."

Gaia strolled up the sidewalk at her usual rapid pace. Lower Broadway was jammed with people, as usual, and she was bumping through them, heading uptown, when one bumped her especially hard, knocking her backward slightly.

"Oof! Watch where you're—Sam!"

She had literally bumped into Sam Moon. She hadn't seen him since their final, melancholy conversation. The one where Sam had basically told her that even though they were practically soul mates who had been though hell together, he just couldn't deal with her weird, shut-down personality and never wanted to see her again. Sam, the guy who'd been the first to pitch his flag on the surface of her heart. Gaia looked up at him, seeing the uncertainty and discomfort on his face.

"Hey," he said. He didn't exactly look happy to see her. Then again, he didn't look unhappy, either.

"What are you up to?" Gaia asked.

"I had to come here to get my new uniform," he admitted, in a sheepish tone that made Gaia feel protective of him. "I'm working at a restaurant. As a bus boy, for now. But they say I can work my way up eventually."

"Oh, man, that's great," Gaia told him, but inside, her heart sank a bit.

"Well, not really," Sam admitted. "I walked in there thinking I was going to be a bartender. Do you know they actually ask for resumes now?"

"Did you tell them you were a premed at NYU?" Gaia asked. "I mean, if you can pass organic chemistry, I'm sure you can mix a cosmopolitan."

"I don't think they see it that way."

"So where are you working? Is it somewhere near Dmitri's?"

"I actually. . ." Sam looked down, as though he couldn't really stand to meet Gaia's gaze. Then he took a breath. "I don't want to tell you where I'm working," he blurted out. "And I'm not living with Dmitri anymore."

"Oh." Gaia didn't know what to say. For once she didn't have a wisecrack or a comeback.

"I just needed a change," he went on. "I—this whole thing, it's just too strange. I need to make a complete break."

"Okay."

"It's nothing personal. I thought we could remain friends, but. . ." He shrugged.

"No, that's cool. You need space," Gaia said. "Time to get used to the outside world. I think I know how that goes." *Besides,* she thought, *I've sworn off friends for good, so it wouldn't work out anyway.*

"Yeah, I guess." He still couldn't quite look at her. They were so near the NYU dorm where he'd lived when they were dating. The whole scene was dripping with nostalgia.

"Don't lose my phone number, okay?" Gaia pleaded. "You never know when you might need someone to talk to. Someone who knows what you went through."

"Uh-huh." Sam was turning into Mister One-Syllable. This was too strange, too different from the Sam she used to know. Gaia wanted to get away.

"I won't be isolated," he said finally. "I've got roommates and everything. And there's the job," he added, waving his black pants and white shirt halfheartedly.

"I'm sure you'll be a bartender in no time," Gaia said, trying to sound reassuring. "Or even maître d'.

Can you speak with a French acc-*sant*? Maybe grow a little pencil moustache?"

"I'll think about it." Sam finally looked at her, and Gaia felt a little wiggle in her heart.

"I'm really happy you're making a clean break," she told him. "I think this'll be good."

"Thanks. Well. So I'm gonna go," he said, giving her a small wave.

Gaia waved back and walked away. Then she realized she was walking the complete opposite direction of where she needed to go. She'd have to take a different train now, from the west side, and go crosstown on the shuttle. But that was infinitely more attractive than running into Sam again and repeating the awkward scene she'd just been through.

Seeing Sam could not have been more uncomfortable. They'd been completely in love not that long ago, and now he was like a total stranger. Worse than that—he was like an *acquaintance*, someone she barely knew and didn't care about. But she did care about him. She cared about him, but she was mad at him, sort of, for not understanding her better. And she was mad at herself—furious, in fact—for being the reason he was feeling so screwed up. If he'd never met her—if he had just kept dating Heather—well, they'd both have been okay. He wouldn't have been shot, and Heather wouldn't have been struck blind, and everything would have been hunky-dory. The only ruckus would have been Heather's search for a dress to wear to his winter formal. But because of her, because of Gaia Moore, they were both in their own total messes.

And then there was Ed. Ed had been her best friend. She could hang out with him from morning till night and never get sick of him. They could be silent together, or they could talk about nothing and everything. Then they'd started dating, and everything in Gaia's life had seemed to blow up at once. She'd seen Ed threatened. And she'd also gotten distracted. In the end, Ed had gotten hurt, too. Not physically, but hurt just the same—badly. And he seemed to absolutely hate her now.

And finally there was Jake, who she hadn't even gotten close to yet, but who had `already been shot`. What else did she want?

She had to cross through Washington Square Park to get to the train. There weren't many people around at this time of day. The late afternoon shadows slanted long across the concrete tiles, and an eerie silence hung over the park. Gaia tried to shake off a feeling that something was about to happen, but some kind of spider-sense prickled within her. This time of day was always a little spooky, but she did hear something—a struggle. Somebody fighting, being shushed, being told to keep quiet while somebody else...

Gaia sprang into action. The sound was coming from the bushes by the gross little concrete buildings that passed as public restrooms. As she raced toward them, she could see a man and a woman locked in some kind of scuffle. The woman was much smaller than the man; Gaia could see her thin white arms flailing at her sides.

Gaia leapt in the air and knocked the man straight to the ground. He was concentrating so hard on mugging his victim that she took him completely by surprise. He offered no resistance as she fell on top of him.

"Take off, punk!" she demanded, but the guy wouldn't leave. He seemed to be trying to reach for the woman, even now. God, what a persistent little pervert he was.

"Ohmigod! Ohmigod, Rob, *help*! We're being mugged!"

"Just run," Gaia told her, not stopping to ask why she'd said "we," when clearly she was the only one getting mugged.

"Don't touch me!" the woman screamed, reaching into her purse. Gaia turned to tell her more firmly to stop panicking and run her ass out of the park, when she felt her eyes explode with pain.

"*Agh!* Did you *mace* me?" she asked.

"Rob, come on, quick," the woman shrieked, and Rob—the mugger—got up and followed her, while Gaia staggered a few steps away. She could hear them talking to a policeman almost immediately.

"We were in the park, and this wild woman attacked us!" The woman was still shrieking.

"Where were you, exactly?" the officer wanted to know.

"Well, we were. . . standing by the public restroom," the woman said.

"*Standing*?" the officer asked suspiciously.

"Okay, more like standing and kissing. . . Maybe we got a little carried away with each other," the guy said.

"I sprayed her with my pepper spray!" the woman added proudly.

Oh. *Oh, crap.* Gaia had a feeling the cop wouldn't be in too big a hurry to find her, but she didn't want to wait to find out. Her eyes still burned, and she was sure they were bright red and puffy. And she was horribly, horribly embarrassed.

What was the matter with her? She couldn't tell the difference between a horny couple and a mugging in progress? Had she lost all common sense?

No, she'd just misread her instincts because she was distracted—again. The frustration of running into Sam had thrown her off. And she'd taken it out on this guy Rob.

She got to the subway and descended the stairs, blinking painfully. She felt so stupid. Worse than stupid—she felt like a total and complete asshole.

What was that Bob Marley song? Who the cap fit, let them wear it.

She *was* an asshole.

# A Complete Lack of Drama

**"YOU ASSHOLE!" KAI LAUGHED. SHE** tried to shoot Ed Fargo back, but her laser gun was disabled for fifteen seconds because he'd gotten her smack in the back. He took this chance to escape through a back alley into the main room.

That was when the kid got him.

He couldn't have been more than eight years old, but he was quick, and Ed suspected he had a little-kid crush on Kai. He couldn't blame the little guy. Kai was like a Japanese anime character come to life: baggy pants, half-shirt, pigtails, and a thousand-watt smile. Plus she had enough energy to light Manhattan. She was a great girl, tons of fun, and Ed was fully enjoying spending time with her. Which was why the kid must have decided to fry Ed.

*Pa-tchoo!*

The pack on Ed's chest made a *wee-wee-wee* noise and Ed was completely disabled. Kai could walk up to him and shoot his bull's-eye as much as she wanted, which was what she did. Knowing their ten minutes in the laser room were almost up, he let his arms flop to his sides and just surrendered. Right on cue, the buzzer signaled the end of the session.

"You got me," he admitted. "You win. But next time, no fair enlisting munchkins to help you."

"I'm not a munchkin," the kid said.

"No, you're my hero," Kai told him, and ruffled his hair. The kid gave Ed the finger and raced off to find his parents.

"What the—" Ed pulled off his laser backpack and strolled with Kai to the front entrance. "These kids today—I'm telling you, they've got no respect."

"Yeah," Kai responded.

"Want to go get some really cheap Chinese food? There's a place on Ninth Avenue that's got the biggest combination plate you ever saw."

"Sure! That's cool!"

*Sure! That's cool!* Ed savored the words as they danced around in his head. No sarcastic comments, no pointed references, no distractions or family emergencies or mysterious chokings. Just Kai. Ed reached over and took her hand, and she squeezed his back enthusiastically.

"So that was fun when we went to Chelsea Piers to go rock-climbing," he said.

"Totally!"

"And I didn't realize that crazy boat ride at the South Street Seaport was so high-octane."

"I know!"

"So what are we going to do next?"

"I've got a plan in the works. A friend of my dad's

works at a construction site, and I think he'll let us go up in one of his cranes."

"Agh!" Ed yelped. "Do you really want to do that?"

"Why not?" Kai shrugged. "If all those construction guys can do it, I'm sure we can. You're not scared of heights, are you?

*No, but. . . oh what the hell*, Ed thought. Kai was such a breath of fresh air, he'd pretty much follow her into the gates of hell at this point. After all the petty bitchery of Heather, the frustration of Gaia, the multiple-personality disorder of Tatiana, he was having the time of his life. And Kai seemed seriously into him.

Finally, he had figured out what he wanted from a woman. Fun, fun, and a complete lack of drama.

*You hear that, Gaia? A complete lack of drama!*

## A Good Anecdote

GAIA DIDN'T WANT TO GO HOME after all. Her run-in with Sam had rattled her, and her mistake in the park hadn't helped. Instead, she pulled out her cell phone and dialed Oliver's number.

"Gaia," he said, startling her.

"I hate that you have caller ID,"

she told him, laughing a little. "I've got to remember to block my number so you can't do that to me."

"Sorry. I'll play dumb when you call."

She was struck silent for a moment. A week ago she'd been wishing Oliver dead—now she was bantering over cell phone etiquette with him.

"I suppose you would have called if any of the deliveries had arrived," she said.

"That's true."

"So there's been no change?"

"I'm sorry, Gaia, there's been no change. I'm working on it."

"I know." She kicked the concrete curb. "Do you know when?"

"It could be in an hour, it could be next week," he said. "The wheels are in motion, and I'm keeping in contact with everyone. But it's a touchy situation. I don't have many friends left, it seems."

"It'll be okay," Gaia told him, then hung up the phone. Just as she had so many times these last few days, she found herself feeling sorry for the old psycho-killer.

This was frustrating. She had to stay off Oliver's back and let him do his job. But she was bored. School was out for the day, she'd already been to Jake's, and. . . well, she didn't have any other friends, not anymore. The afternoon and evening stretched out in front of her like. . . like a really long afternoon and evening. She was so bored, even clever metaphors escaped her.

*Saved by the bell*, she thought as her phone chirped. It was Jake. Gaia hated to admit how glad she was.

"Yeah?" she asked.

"I'm bored," he said.

"I thought you were tired."

"I *was* tired. Of working out. Now I'm bored and I'm going to go to the comic book store. You coming?"

"Yeah, but it might take a while. I have to take a roundabout route to the east side."

"What? Why?"

"Long, long story. I beat up the wrong person."

Jake laughed long and hard in her ear. Gaia grimaced.

"Do you mind?" she asked. "It's not that funny."

"Actually, it is," he told her. "See you when we get there."

Gaia hung up. This was humiliating. But when she thought about it, she realized that maybe it was sort of funny. Some day Attack of the Killer Kiss-Monster would make a good anecdote.

**Was** that a bad idea? I'm supposed to play it cool with girls,
not spend all my time with them
when they pique my interest. But
I *am* bored, and even though she
just left my apartment, I want to
see Gaia again. I'm not going to
play some stupid keep-my-distance
game just to prove something to
my testicles. Besides, she's
about to leave town to go on some
mysterious mission. If I stick to
the Cool Rule, I might not see
her at all before she goes. Then
I'd feel like a total idiot.

    What the hell.

    Anyway, Gaia's not a girl per
se. I mean, she is, but not like
any girl I've met before. She's
not into shopping, she's not into
gossip, but she's also not so
punk rock that she hates all
girlie things just to make a
statement. She seems to be above
it all—I mean, just outside of
everything that most kids in high
school think is dementedly important. It's like she's lived more

than she's supposed to already.
She's seen more of the world than
she has a right to at her age.
And something about that—I just
want to be near it. I want to
soak it up.

So she won't be my prom date. I
can't picture her in a dress,
anyway. But girls like that are a
dime a dozen. Gaia's mysterious.
She's got so much going on. She's
on a whole different level.

I had no idea, when I found out
I was switching schools, that I'd
find such a prize. It's like I'm
getting a taste of the real
world. And I just want more.

## "TRY IT ON."

"I'm not trying it on."

"Come on, just the hood."

"The hood is the worst part."

"The cape, then."

"Jake, you're going to have to fulfill your fantasies some other way. I am not putting on that ridiculous getup."

**Feeling of Foreboding**

"I'm going to have to ask you to put that down," the salesclerk said. Gaia was quick to oblige. Jake, on the other hand, was clearly offended by the clerk's request.

"Let's get out of here—I want to get some dinner, anyway," Gaia said, defusing any potential "situation." "C'mon, I'll buy you some rice and beans."

"That's a whole dollar fifty," Jake called after her as she strode out of the store. "I can't let you do that."

They went to Burritoville around the corner and ordered. But just as they were digging into their Mexican concoctions, Gaia's phone bleated.

"This has to be good news," she said. "Unless it's a wrong number."

But it wasn't a wrong number. It was Oliver. Gaia made a few grunts of agreement, then snapped her phone shut. Her eyes were shining as she turned back to Jake.

"I've got to go."

"But your food," Jake said, knowing it sounded

lame, but not quite ready to watch her walk away for a week—or for the rest of his life.

"I'm not hungry anymore. I gotta go."

"Let me come with you."

Gaia turned to him, her forehead wrinkling. "What, are you kidding me?"

"You may as well let me. I'm just going to follow you, anyway."

"Yeah, right. I could lose you in half a second."

Jake gave a frustrated sigh. "Just let me come with you."

"Jake, this has nothing to do with you!"

"I've got bullet holes in my arm that beg to differ." The veins in Jake's forehead were bulging. "I mean, the least you could do to show your gratitude is to condescend to let me follow you."

That shut Gaia right up. Her eyes narrowed. "I guess it's okay," she said, shrugging. "But we have to go all the way out to Brooklyn."

"That's cool."

"Just. . . be careful, okay?"

Jake followed Gaia up Third Avenue, toward the L train. Oliver lived on that line, past the hipster part of Williamsburg and deep in the no-man's-land of Greenpoint.

But as soon as they got on the train, Jake sensed something was wrong. He looked at Gaia, but she was hard to read. She seemed deep in concentration. He supposed he was just imagining things. Still, his uneasy feelings hovered like a cloud over his head as they passed stop after stop. The other people on the train seemed innocent enough. So why this `feeling of foreboding`?

Finally Gaia stirred as they pulled into a station. "Come on," she said in a low voice. "Stay close to me. Someone's been casing us."

"I knew it," Jake muttered. "Who?"

"The cop. He's not a real cop. The badge is fake."

Jake was astounded. He hadn't noticed that. The cop would have been the last person he'd have suspected. Sure enough, when they got off the train, the police officer followed them. He didn't say a word, just tailed them up the steps to the street, where the sky was darkening and `the air was purple with dusk`. Three other men stepped out of the shadows and stood around them, ranged like numbers on a clock face.

They came closer. Alarms went off in Jake's head.

It was go time.

He'd known better than to expect St. John's or Montego Bay to have any place on Gaia Moore's travel itinerary.

GAIA STEPPED BACK A PACE, AND
Jake instinctively turned his back to her. If they were going to be surrounded, they could at least guard their perimeter completely. He crouched slightly, ready to fight. Then he listened, tuning to Gaia, letting her take the lead.

**Fake Cop**

The moment Jake was in a fighting stance, Gaia struck. One of their attackers came too close and caught a foot in his gut. At the same time, she sent whirling fists to the other guy on her side, and Jake did his best to keep up his end of the fight. The pain in his shoulder felt like a tearing of muscle from bone, but he couldn't worry about that. Running on pure adrenaline, he mustered up all his fighting skills, combining every martial art he'd ever studied to confront the fists coming his way. He pulled the first guy toward him, using his momentum to yank him to the ground and stomp him with a kick to the head. That took care of him for the moment, anyway.

He couldn't see Gaia anymore; things were happening too fast. The "cop" was next, and to Jake's horror—especially since he now knew what a bullet wound felt like—he saw him draw the NYPD-issue pistol from its holster. He thought of Indiana Jones shooting the sword-fighter and threw himself headlong at the guy's waist, hoping he'd get there before the gun could be cocked and fired.

Somehow, he did. The guy had the flabby paunch of a cop, that was for sure—that was probably why he'd been so convincing—and Jake hit it full force, causing the guy to stumble backward. He heard the gun drop to the ground and kicked it, soccer-style, halfway down the block.

He turned and saw an amazing sight: Gaia was fully whipping the other *three* guys, all at the same time. It was like something out of a movie. Every time one got up, another seemed to fall so that she could keep fighting. He tried to join in, but wasn't sure where he'd fit. The fake cop stood up and Jake flattened him with a two-fisted punch that knocked his head against the hard wall of a brownstone. It was a lucky shot. Gaia kicked another assailant down the subway steps and turned to him.

"This is the best we're going to be able to do for now," she said. "Can you run?"

"If I have to," he told her. "I'd rather finish these guys off."

"No way. No time. This is good enough for now. Come on," she said in a hoarse staccato, and took off.

Jake had never seen anything like this. She ran like a wild animal, like she was in fast motion; it was all he could do to keep her in sight. Their attackers didn't seem to be behind him—he heard them start to give chase, but they soon stopped. Just to be safe, Gaia led them around a few extra turns, taking a long route to Oliver's brownstone. When they arrived, she buzzed frantically, leaning on the door till it opened; Jake followed and they both dropped to the floor in the foyer, waiting.

Nothing. No pounding footsteps following them up the steps. No smash as the glass of the door was broken. No innocent-sounding buzz from their assailants, hoping to gain access without attracting attention. There was nothing.

"Who the hell were they?" Jake wanted to know.

"Some men who don't want me to—," Gaia answered. But her voice dropped off. Jake turned, his face grazing the grimy black-and-white tiles of the floor, to see Gaia's eyes rolling back in her head as she blacked out.

"Gaia?" he said. "Did something happen? Did you get hit? Gaia!"

A door at the top of the stairway opened and Oliver came out.

"Something happened to Gaia," Jake said, frantic now. "She passed out or something. These guys attacked us, and—"

"It's all right," Oliver said, moving quickly but calmly down the stairs. "Come on, help me get her inside. This is what happens to her after a fight. Using all that strength saps her energy."

This was getting stranger and stranger. Jake grabbed Gaia's legs and helped carry her up the dingy staircase. "I'm not exactly full of energy myself," he admitted, feeling his shoulder start to ache painfully.

"Different for her," Oliver huffed. "Superstrength. Supertired." They plopped her gently on the couch and Oliver turned to Jake.

"I'm glad you were with her," he said.

"Do you know who those guys were?"

Oliver ignored Jake's question. "We need to go now."

Jake nodded. "I guess you do."

Oliver gave him a strange look, like he was afraid to say what was on his mind.

"What?" Jake asked.

"They've seen you," Oliver said. "Not once, but twice. They know who you are. It's unsafe for you here. Especially now that Gaia and I are leaving."

Something shifted in Jake. Some sense of inevitability dawned on him. Before, he'd sort of been flirting with the idea of getting involved in something larger than his own life, something mysterious and dangerous. Now it was as if he'd wandered too long in the jungle and couldn't get out.

"You mean I can't just walk away," Jake said. It wasn't really a question. It was more a statement of something he already understood.

Oliver shook his head slowly. "I don't think so," he said.

"What do I do?" Jake asked. He thought of going home, then imagined what would happen there if he were tailed by people like the fake cops from the L train. His dad. His grandma. He suddenly felt a wave of homesickness that was more about sickness than home. "I can't go back, can I?"

Oliver looked at him with a cool, steady gaze. "It would be best to lay low for a while," he said.

"What about. . . I don't know, what about school?"

"It would be safest if you didn't go for the time being," Oliver said. "If you made up a really good excuse, then disappeared for a while." Oliver clapped Jake on the shoulder and led him into the kitchen. "Think about it for a moment. I'll sit with Gaia until she wakes up. It won't be long. You can take the time to get used to all this information."

Jake nodded and went to the kitchen as ordered— another point in his favor. Oliver was interested. Very interested indeed.

He sat on the floor next to Gaia, watching her breathe as she fought off her exhaustion. After about ten minutes, she stirred and opened her eyes. She sat up like a shot, assessing her surroundings with micro-processorlike speed.

"Where's Jake?" she asked.

"He's fine. He's here."

She turned to Oliver. "We got tailed. They saw him," she told him. "He can't—"

"I know. I discussed it with him."

Gaia slumped back down on the couch, letting loose a frustrated sigh. "I should never have gotten him mixed up in this. He'll have to stay here while we're away."

"He could do that. Or. . ."

"What?" Gaia turned to Oliver.

"I got extra travel documents," Oliver said. "An old habit that might work in our favor. He has excellent instincts. Apparently he can hold up his end of a fight. I have a good feeling about him, and we can use an extra agent."

"I don't want him in any deeper than he is already." Gaia insisted. "I mean, I almost got him killed already. Isn't that enough?"

"What if he wants to come?" Oliver asked. "We could leave it up to him."

"Leave what up to me?" Jake appeared in the doorway.

"Forget it. Nothing," Gaia insisted. "Jake, I'm so sorry. I should never have let you come with me. Now you have to—"

"It's all right," Jake said. "I mean, I was the one who insisted on coming."

"What about the other thing? How you can't go home?"

"That sucks," he admitted. "But if you guys are talking about having me come along to. . . wherever it is you're going, I'm in."

"Jake, don't be stupid," Gaia seethed. "This isn't level three of Grand Theft Auto."

"Don't insult me," Jake snapped back. "I've been watching you deal with whatever's been going on for a week now. I'm well aware of how serious it is. But according to Oliver, I've got to sit around, anyway. I'll go nuts here. There's no way I'll stay inside the whole time, and without you here to watch my back, I'll get nabbed for sure. And Gaia—I really want to come with you."

"Even if I'm going to *Siberia*?" she asked.

*Siberia?*

Quite honestly, if he'd had his pick of locales, Siberia wouldn't have been first—or even ninety-first—on his list, but he'd known better than to expect St. John's or Montego Bay to have any place on Gaia Moore's travel itinerary.

"Look, I know Siberia won't be a picnic. And I think I understand the danger. But it's weird—I feel like this is what I was meant to do. Like this is why I met you—because I'm supposed to do stuff like this. I'll never know if I don't try."

While Gaia turned herself into a knot of deep sighs and fevered hand gestures, Oliver gave meditative consideration to Jake's response.

"You don't seem frightened by this," he said.

Jake looked at him. "I know, it's weird. I'm not."

"We'd be leaving within twelve hours," Oliver said. "You wouldn't be able to see your father again before you left." He shrugged. "That's the bottom line."

"I can do it."

"Jake!" Gaia was exasperated. "You don't know what you're saying. This is dangerous."

"More dangerous than getting shot at, or outrunning a fake police officer and his cronies?" Jake asked. "So far, I've been able to handle it."

"It's worse than all of that. Jake, I was thrown into this world. You don't have to be in it. Are you crazy?"

"I don't think so. Do you think I am, Oliver?"

"Not as far as I can tell."

Gaia gave an infuriated roar. "I've seen a lot of people I care about get destroyed by being close to me," she said. "I've seen them ruined by this life. I don't want you to do this."

"But I'm in it," Jake said. "Look, let me get fully informed. Then I'll make my decision. But it's *my* decision. You can't get pissed at me for being okay with this."

"Watch me," Gaia muttered, and left the room.

Jake turned to Oliver. "Is she right? Am I destroying myself without thinking this through?"

"I've had a lot of experience with a lot of different kinds of operatives," Oliver said. "I've seen men who trained for years fall apart under questioning, and I've seen the most unlikely people turn into heroes. I don't think anyone chooses this life consciously. I think it's something you're born to. And much as Gaia claims to hate it, I think she has grown to be comfortable with danger and chaos. You might be cut from the same cloth."

"Might be?"

"This trip will be sort of a test for you."

"And what if I fail?"

Oliver shrugged. "Then you might want to return to life the way it was. I think you'll be able to, despite Gaia's protestations to the contrary."

Jake thought it over. Between Gaia and Oliver, it was certainly Oliver who had the most experience. If Oliver felt confident in Jake, that was really all the information he needed. Well, that, and one other tiny detail.

"Well then, guys, there's only one other thing I need to know."

"What's that, son?" asked Oliver.

Jake paused dramatically. "What the hell are we going to Siberia for?"

I can't imagine what it feels like to be Gaia. I mean, everybody goes through life thinking they're the only person who feels the way they do. But in Gaia's case, she might be right. If my dad were in captivity in Siberia, I'm not sure I'd be prepared to go save him. I'm not sure I could keep it together, knowing that my father's very survival depended solely on my ability to pull off a great escape.

On the other hand, whether she admits it or not, I'm the perfect person to help Gaia rescue *her* father. Maybe it's being the son of a doctor who spent years in the ER. Or maybe it's all my martial arts training. But in all honesty, I always manage to keep a level head in situations that send other people into a panic.

Don't get me wrong: I'm not so naïve as to think that believing I'm good at something means that I actually am. Just look at *American Idol*. All those people think they're destined for stardom. Most aren't even destined for a gig at the Holiday Inn lounge.

I have no idea what's going to happen to me in Siberia. But I'm not that worried about it. Maybe that means I really am crazy. Or maybe it means I always knew this would happen to me. It's like in *The Matrix*: The blue pill is always the way to go. Maybe I should be frightened of the unknown, but I'm not. I'm psyched. This really is what I want. My life has always been stable. I think I need to shake things up and see if I'm right. If I've got what it takes.

Am I going to feel the same way tomorrow? Am I just being impulsive? Am I making a life-changing move based on overactive hormones? I don't think so.

Jeez, I hope not.

Guess there's only one way to find out.

And while I'm at it, maybe I'll find out why Gaia's father was taken to Siberia in the first place.

Maybe.

But probably not.

**This** couldn't have happened at a better time. My biggest worry over the past days—a worry that haunted me at every turn—was that we didn't have enough man-power to complete this mission. All I kept wishing for was an extra agent. Someone who'd watch Gaia's back just in case some-thing happened to me. Much as I would love to be alone with her, my instincts told me we needed someone else.

And now this boy shows up, as if my prayers had been heard and answered.

It seems foolhardy. I don't know this boy very well. I've got no reason to trust him, other than those same instincts. But Gaia found him. She brought him here. There must be a reason for that. She is careful and suspi-cious enough to avoid trusting anyone until he has fully proven himself. Nobody knows that better than I do. And she's impatient enough to avoid anyone foolish or frivolous. I have a very good feeling about this young man.

And what if something goes drastically wrong? What if he cracks under pressure, makes an impulsive mistake, turns into a blubbering fool halfway through the mission?

This is where my instincts disappear. My Loki instinct would be to neutralize him. And my Oliver instinct? I don't know how I'd handle the situation now.

I'll just have to hope that's not a problem I'll have to face. For his sake. And for Gaia's.

And let's face it: for mine, too.

# THE NEXT MORNING, GAIA AND JAKE

# A Gaia-Sized Gap

left Oliver's building separately, walking in different directions and meeting up only after their train had taken them into Manhattan. They'd woken in silence, sipping coffee in the kitchen with Oliver without speaking. Now Jake noticed that Gaia really didn't want to talk. The ease, the friendship that had only just developed between them, seemed gone already.

"You're mad at me," he said.

"No, I'm worried," Gaia answered.

"It's okay. I understand the risks. I'm not getting dragged into this against my will."

"I just hope you're doing it for the right reasons."

Jake was quiet for a moment. "I've never had a chance like this. To go somewhere crazy and do something so out of the ordinary. I'm really into it."

Gaia shook her head. "And you think you can deal with your dad?" she asked.

"Yeah, I'll come up with a good cover story," Jake reassured her.

"And what about last night? Don't you think he's wondering why you never came home?"

"Nah, he was on call. That's the advantage of having an ER doctor for a dad," Jake explained.

They were within a block of his house. Together with Oliver, they had mapped out the area as best they could from Jake's memory, noting adjacent buildings and points of access. A few blueprints, downloaded from a confidential site Oliver had gained access to, didn't hurt either. They found the building around the corner that they needed, and Gaia stepped back and took a look up.

"Hm. Pretty good security," she said.

"Too good?"

"Nah. I'd climb the outside if it weren't broad daylight. We're going in through the basement."

"But the bars. . ."

"Watch."

Gaia sprayed each end of one of the bars with a canister she took out of her pocket. Then she straightened up and hooked her thumbs into the belt loops of her jeans, waiting.

"That's your big trick?" Jake asked. "You're deodorizing the bars?"

"Just wait."

After a minute she brought her foot down on the bar and it snapped easily, leaving a `Gaia-sized gap` through which she could reach in and smash the basement window. She slipped through and vanished into the room below.

"Hey," Jake said in a stage whisper. "Hey! I can't fit in there!"

The spray-canister flew out the hole and landed on the sidewalk with a clatter. He picked it up and sprayed two more of the bars.

"Where did you get this stuff, anyway?" he asked, kneeling on the concrete while he waited for it to take effect and weaken the metal.

"Gift from my Uncle Oliver," her voice floated up through the gloom. "Guess it was left over from his secret agent days."

"That's a catalog I'd like to have a look at." He stood up and kicked the other two bars out of his way and shimmied into the basement.

He held onto the bars for a moment, then dropped to the ground, expecting to land on a dusty floor. He hit linoleum instead.

"What the—"

Gaia laughed and snapped the light on. "I guess someone uses this as an office or a classroom or something," she said. "'Always speak in your inside voice,'" Gaia said, mocking the poster that hung in front of the room.

"Very helpful. Now how do we get from here to my apartment?"

"The two buildings share an air shaft. We need to get in there and climb up."

Across the hall, in the interior of the building, another room had a painted-over window. "I'll bet that's where we want to be," Gaia said. She knocked against it a few times with her fist. When it wouldn't budge, she stood on a chair and scraped away the layers of paint. Then she wiggled the overpainted hasps until they gave. The window popped open with a creak.

She slid out the window easily and found herself in a gloomy area about the size of a studio apartment, cluttered with decades' worth of garbage. She heard something scuttling around her feet and willed herself not to look down. Jake joined her. They could see blue sky far above, but here, at the bottom of four flights of brick, the sun never shone.

"You had to live on the top floor?" Gaia asked.

"If I'd known, I would have moved into that basement," he said. "Would have made this a lot easier, I know. And it was pretty nice."

"Do you know how to rock-climb?"

"I think you know the answer to that. But our shoes are all wrong."

"I know—I think we have to do this barefoot."

"Okay, now that's gross."

"See? I knew you couldn't handle it."

Jake squinted at Gaia and pulled off his sneakers and socks. Then, without another word, he found a handhold between two loose bricks and began his journey upward.

"I wish we had some rappelling line," Gaia muttered, then tied her own sneakers around her neck and followed him up.

It took an amazing amount of concentration. Gaia was an expert climber, but finding impressions on a rock wall was a lot easier than dealing with the repetitive bricks and their limited shapes and sizes. It was even slower going for Jake.

"I don't think anyone would have spotted me going into the building," he said, as he wrestled his way toward the window of his apartment.

"Shows what you know," Gaia said. She was already up there and was giving the window frame a few exploratory thumps. "These aren't even locked," she scolded.

"Yeah, well, it's four flights up, over an air shaft," he pointed out. "How paranoid am I supposed to be?"

"Once again, shows what you know." Gaia's voice floated out through the open window; she had opened the window noiselessly and slipped inside in the space of a few seconds. Jake shook his head. Amazing.

A rope ladder—Jake recognized it as his family's never-used fire-escape plan—came tumbling down the wall, almost knocking Jake off balance.

"Hey!" he yelled. "What am I supposed to do with this?"

"I thought it would be good if you could get up here before the end of the year," Gaia suggested. "Just use it—you don't have to prove anything to me."

"I'm not trying to prove anything to you," he said. "I don't know how to use the rope."

Gaia's head appeared two stories above him, black against the bright sky and framed in hanks of hair. "Jake, just grab it with one hand. You won't fall." Her voice was so matter-of-fact, Jake felt she was acting as if she'd ordered the laws of gravity to suspend themselves. Any minute now, she'd lose her patience. Jake's slow climb obviously wasn't cutting the mustard. He was going to have to take the risk.

From now on, he was always going to have to take the risk—at least, for the next few days, if he wanted to keep up.

He let go with his left hand and felt his center of gravity shift. He was going to fall for sure. The lurch in his stomach told him so.

He grabbed a rung of the ladder.

He got it.

And he hung on for dear life.

"Okay, Montone." He was going to have to be his own cheering section. He tried to do it coolly, under his breath, but he heard it come out in a squeak.

"Jake!" Gaia hissed from above. There was no more time to be nervous. Jake clutched the ladder and swung his body completely onto it, letting go of the safety of his tiny foot- and handholds and making a huge leap of faith. He scrambled up the ladder as quickly as he could.

His apartment was silent. He hadn't lived here that long with his dad, but it was still home, still filled with stuff that had followed him wherever he'd lived. The rich wool Oriental rug that had been a wedding gift to his parents, the dark wood furniture and the photos of his family. But even in these familiar surroundings, Jake felt like he was trespassing. Why was that?

Well, because he was. He wasn't supposed to be here. He'd come to say good-bye.

"Come on," Gaia said quietly, like she could tell he was having a moment of strangeness. "Get whatever you need, and let's go."

Jake gathered some warm clothes, the bare minimum he'd need, and his toothbrush. His dad. It was time to make the call.

He sat down at the dining-room table and picked up the phone. His dad had given him a lot of freedom, so that he wouldn't have to lie. Now he was going to. He dialed the number at his dad's office and had the receptionist put him through.

"Dad, I got a call," he said. "Remember that tae kwan do competition in Montreal I went to last year? They had a last-minute emergency and they need me to be a judge."

Jake felt weird lying to his father in front of Gaia. He was revealing a side of himself that wasn't necessarily the most attractive.

"How'd that go?" Gaia asked when he hung up the phone.

Jake looked down for a long moment. He felt

exposed. "Fine," he finally said. "Let's get out of here. Back out the window, barefoot, right?"

"Right."

Back out the window, barefoot. That sounded like a recipe for disaster if there ever was one.

It also sounded like Gaia's life in a nutshell.

ED FARGO SPOTTED AN ENEMY AGENT stepping out from behind a column on the subway platform. He raised his gun and shot as fast as he could—but

**Ping-Pong**

the bullets wouldn't come out fast enough.

"Where's my Glock?" he shrieked. "Oh my God, I can't get to my Glock! What's going on?"

Somehow he fumbled. His fingers wouldn't go where he wanted them to, and he watched helplessly as the enemy agent fired again and again and again. His vision went red, and then he was dead.

"Dude," Kai said. "You are the worst Xbox player ever."

"Well, excuse me," he shot back. "I spent my childhood skateboarding, not getting fat on Nintendo."

Kai nodded in that way she had, where she kind of ducked her head twice and gave a slow blink. Ed snapped off the video game and Kai's living room flickered into darkness. The only light came from the neon restaurant sign outside the window. It buzzed a little. Somehow that made the silence a little more oppressive.

"So," he said. "You play that game a lot?"

"I guess, yeah."

"It's pretty good."

"Yeah, I like it."

"They uh. . . they got a lot of the New York details right. There's nothing weird, like all of a sudden the Brooklyn Bridge goes to Jersey."

"Yeah, right." Kai gave a laugh. But she didn't add to the thought. Ed didn't know what he wanted her to say. But *something* would have been nice.

"So."

"Yeah?"

"What do you want to do?"

Kai shrugged. "I don't know. What do you want to do?"

The dreaded ping-pong question of two bored people. Ed cringed. But he couldn't think of anything. They had seen every movie there was to see. They had done everything adventurous there was to do. There was no activity available to them besides hanging out, and that wasn't going too well.

"We could make out," Kai suggested.

Ed looked at her. She was adorable. Her shiny, sleek

black hair fell to her shoulders, with two pigtails at her temples held up with Hello Kitty clips. He could see that under her white baby tee and army pants she had a seriously smokin' body. Of course, as a red-blooded American male, he was completely willing to spend his hanging-out time tongue-wrestling with a cute skateboard girl.

"Okay," he said, and smooched her.

But there was something unelectric about the whole thing. Sure, her lips were soft. Yeah, his body responded to hers as they lay together on the plaid couch. And he liked Kai. This was fun and all, but something was missing from the whole equation.

Kai was great to do stuff with, but the minute there was a lull, Ed had to admit it: There just wasn't much of a spark.

*Oh, no.*

Heather. Gaia. Tatiana. What did they all have in common? They all drove him crazy with their various insane behaviors. Bitchy, moody, or just plain schizophrenic, each one of them had a serious personality disorder that gave him a constant case of acid reflux.

And now he was addicted to them. He knew it. He was addicted to the frustration. Ed Fargo had completely, utterly lost the ability to be with a regular girl.

He shifted positions so that he was on top of Kai. She moved along with him willingly and opened her eyes long enough to smile at him between kisses. She ran her hands up under his shirt and he tried to stay in the moment.

*Stop thinking about them,* he ordered himself. *You're making out with a cute girl. Who cares about them? Who cares about Gaia, especially? You are making out, Fargo. Come on!*

"Come on," Kai said, sitting up. "We can go in my room. My parents won't be home for hours."

Ed followed her into her room, decorated with standard-issue posters of Green Day and System of a Down.

"What's up?" Kai asked him. "You nervous?"

"No, it's cool," he said.

"Cool." She stripped off her top and sat on her bed. "Come on, then."

He followed her over to the bed, smiling reassuringly, but he felt like a jerk. This was the most uninspired he'd ever been. What they were doing felt mechanical, cold. All it did was remind him how great it had been with Gaia. He kissed Kai one last time, closing his eyes and trying to enjoy it, but it was no use. He sat up.

"Oh, man," Kai said. "Now what?"

"I just remembered, my mom needs me at home," he said. "I'm supposed to. . . do something."

"Ed, what's wrong?" Kai sat up. "Is something bothering you? Is it me?"

"No! No, it's most definitely not you. It's one

hundred percent me," Ed insisted. He shook his head. "You're perfect. You're awesome, you're a great girl. I just forgot about this thing. My mom really needs me at home."

Kai peered up at him as though she wasn't sure whether she should believe him. She seemed a little hurt. But she didn't hit him with a stormy accusation, which was a relief. It was also a little strange.

"Well, okay," she said, pulling her shirt back on. "I guess I'll see you tomorrow, right?"

"Right!" he said. "Tomorrow. Yes." Ed got up and grabbed his skateboard. "I'm really sorry I've got to go like this. That was really, you know. . ."

"Yeah! Totally!" Kai nodded. "Come on, I'll walk you out."

Ed kissed Kai and left her apartment. The fact that she hadn't started a big argument about his having to leave so unexpectedly—it sort of threw him. He wondered if she was supposed to get more upset. Or maybe she was just normal, and he was too screwed up to know the difference? That was what he was really worried about. What if his sense of normal had been warped by his history of nutty girlfriends?

He looked up and saw the lights of a plane shooting slowly across the sky. Gaia leapt into his consciousness again, for about the fortieth time that night. Maybe because that plane was a mile away, like she always was. Maybe it was the blinking of its lights, switching on and off like her feelings for him. Or maybe she'd been on his mind already, and anything he looked at was going to make him think of her.

Oh, man. When was he going to get Gaia Moore out of his system?

So Gaia's in my system, like a virus. She moves around inside me, popping up when I least expect her. And she's not showing any signs of leaving on her own.

I wonder how you get rid of something like this? I wonder how I'm supposed to track down all the little Gaia-modules among my platelets and obliterate them? Maybe I should just envision the process as a video game. Every time she pops up, I'll blast her out of me. It'll be like Whack-a-Mole.

No, that's too New Agey. I think I need some medical intervention. I need a doctor to find some Gaia antibodies. Some kind of serum that'll flush her out of my system.

Or maybe I should just go sit in a hot sauna and sweat her out of me. Maybe a high fever would burn her out. Maybe, with enough coffee, I could pee her out.

I don't know, though. If it were that easy, I guess hotels and spas would offer Love-Cleansing Weekends, where they'd give you a high colonic and you'd leave with no lingering love whatsoever. If it were that easy, people wouldn't write songs and poems and novels about their lost loves. If it were that easy. . . I'd be making out with Kai right now.

I think I'll have the Gaia virus for a long time. I'm just going to have to learn to live with it and all the accompanying symptoms: memories popping into my head at inopportune moments, lack of interest in other girls, the burning curiosity about what she's doing and who she's doing it with. I have to treat Gaia like a long-lasting but manageable disease. Like a heart murmur. Like arthritis. Like diabetes.

That's it. I've got Gaiabetes. Hah.

The thing is, there's only one person who would think that was funny. Only one person on the planet I could share that joke with. And you know who that is.

Gaia.

Oh, man. Someone get me some insulin.

It was
difficult for
Gaia to
reconcile this **not**
kind man with **in**
her image
of the **kansas**
serial **anymore**
killer
formerly known
as Loki.

# GAIA TURNED AROUND IN HER AIR-

# Reminiscence

plane seat and peered over the top at Jake. He had pushed his seat all the way back and was snoring with his mouth open. She sat back down and turned to Oliver.

"If sleeping were an Olympic sport, I think he'd be heading for the gold right about now," she said.

"It's very impressive. I wish I could sleep like that. Years of being an agent really trained it out of me," Oliver told her. "That coma was the first uninterrupted sleep I've had since I was in my twenties."

"So it was good for something."

"It was good for a lot of things." Oliver gave her a look. "It brought me back to you."

"I like how they show the movies on the backs of the seats now," Gaia said. She wasn't ignoring Oliver's overture purposely. She just didn't know how to respond to people when they said sweet things to her.

"Yes, but with all that new technology, they couldn't come up with better entertainment?"

Gaia laughed. "You didn't like the feature presentation?"

Oliver shook his head. "Those kids might be easy on the eyes, but they both looked embarrassed in that last scene. Like they didn't want to be there any more than I wanted to be watching them."

"The romantic comedy," Gaia said. "Boy meets girl,

boy loses girl, girl comes to her senses. . . boy and girl get paycheck."

They both laughed. It wasn't that funny, but the flight was long, and they still felt a little uneasy with each other.

"We need to come up with our cover story," Oliver said.

Gaia was relieved to have something businesslike to talk about. "Yeah, I guess we can't announce to customs that we're there to rescue my secret agent father from kidnappers."

"Especially since we don't know how deep this goes. Anyone we meet could be in on this. We don't know who has him, exactly, and the government of Siberia could be involved."

Gaia hadn't thought of that. "Do they know we're coming?"

"I don't think so, but we have to be prepared for anything. When we go through customs, we should say we're all one family. The passports have the same last name, so we should be all right."

"Sounds like a great plan. I'll try to be very sisterly toward Jake."

"It shouldn't be hard. You two seem like good friends."

"I guess we are. And it shouldn't be too difficult for you to play my dad. You're his twin—it's not exactly a stretch."

Oliver became quiet. His face blurred into an expression Gaia couldn't quite read. "What's wrong?"

"Oh, nothing."

"Something. What is it?"

"It's just—" Oliver shook his head. "When you said that, I had such a clear memory of you as a baby. At about four months old. You know, that's when babies start having real personalities."

"I wouldn't know." Gaia grimaced. "Babies."

"Oh, but you were a wonderful baby," Oliver told her. "You always had this wise expression. This wide-open smile. You woke up with that smile, like you were excited to see what the world had in store for you. My adoration for you was only obscured by my envy for my brother."

This reminiscence made Gaia's skin crawl. By the time Gaia was born, Oliver had been forbidden from visiting her parents' home. The only way he'd have had any idea what she was like as a baby would be if he had seen her behind her parents' back. This minor detail had obviously slipped Oliver's mind just then. But it reminded Gaia that the man she was dealing with was both twisted and tragic.

"That was my biggest mistake," Oliver continued. "Instead of tormenting myself with envy, I should have made my own life. Though I wouldn't have been able to have a child. And even if I could have. . ." He shot an embarrassed smile at Gaia. "Well, I just don't see how she could have been more wonderful than you."

It was difficult for Gaia to reconcile this kind man with her image of the serial killer formerly known as Loki. On the other hand, he clearly loved with the same frightening intensity that he'd hated with. And the last thing Gaia needed right now was more intensity.

"Oliver, come on. Don't you think we should catch up on our sleep?" Gaia asked gently, hoping that her suggestion wouldn't be taken as an insult. The irony of the scenario could have blown her mind if Gaia had let it. Here she was, protecting the feelings of the very man who'd taken her mother's life in cold blood. But now wasn't exactly the time to contemplate life's little curiosities.

The plane hummed though a bank of clouds, and Gaia put her headphones on and closed her eyes. She looked over at Jake, who was passed out and drooling. At the moment she could think of nothing more appealing than joining him. Something told her there wouldn't be a lot of time for sleep once they got there.

## THE RUSSIAN AIRPORT WAS AS

different from JFK as an airport could be. About the only thing they had in common were the **A Record** airplanes. The New York airport had a mall's worth of food shops and magazine stands. This place was clean, but it was distinctly more low-rent than the gleaming American version. It was clear to Gaia that she was not in Kansas anymore.

They hadn't checked any luggage, so she, Oliver, and Jake hitched their carry-ons onto their shoulders and began strolling toward the exit.

"*Tsst, tsst.* You vont cab, nice lady?" A slimy-looking guy approached them, wearing a shoopy-sounding vinyl tracksuit and sporting a moustache that would have made a porn star proud.

"No, thanks." Gaia shook her head, and Oliver and Jake moved in more closely to her. She looked around for security guards, but there didn't seem to be any. As they stepped out through the sliding glass doors, Gaia got the very distinct feeling that something wasn't right.

"You vont cab, yes?" The guy sidled up to them again, and this time he had a friend. A beefy friend.

"No," Oliver said firmly. Jake looked at him, waiting for a sign that they should fight. But Gaia knew the sign wouldn't come. Not now. They were trying to avoid detection. And getting in a fracas—that would be a dead giveaway. Three tourists with fighting skills like theirs? Not likely.

"This way," Oliver said, and led them back toward the airport door. Their way was blocked by two more locals. They eyeballed Oliver, Jake, and Gaia as though they were adding up how much everything they were carrying would net them in resale.

"Dangerous to leave airport without a cab," the first guy said. "Not safe. I know these men; I can help you get away from them."

"Yes, all right," Oliver said. "Let's get into the cab. Can you put this in the trunk?" He acted as if he were handing the guy his tote bag, then swung it into his face and turned to run.

"Come on!" he shouted, but Gaia and Jake were already heading along the sidewalk to the well-populated area on the other side of the airport.

Gaia heard their shouts as her feet thudded along the pavement. She'd been here five minutes and was already in trouble. This had to be a record.

"Who are those guys?" she shouted to Oliver.

"Nobody," he shouted back, as they rounded a corner and saw a clot of black cars and security guards. Lord only knew what godforsaken corner of the airport they'd wandered into. Bad rescue party. Bad!

Oliver slowed them down and looked behind him. Their four local assailants were standing in a forlorn-looking huddle; the big beefy guy lit a cigarette in defeat. Then they turned and headed back to the side exit of the airport.

"Those are some brazen muggers," Jake said. "Are you sure they're not after us specifically?"

Oliver shook his head. "There's no way. Men like

that seem to pop up wherever there are tourists, over here. They're leftovers from the old Soviet Union."

"It's good we didn't fight them, then," Gaia said. "Too bad, though. It would have been easy."

Oliver patted her on the shoulder. "That's my girl," he said, shaking his head.

Oliver got in the front seat of the cab and murmured to the driver in expert-sounding Russian. Despite the seriousness of their mission, Gaia felt something. . . nice. Comfortable. She knew she was on her way to her dad, and she was making the trip with people who seemed to know her. To understand her. Well enough to tease her, in fact. In spite of her annoyance, she looked out the window and smiled.

"Cheerleading team," she muttered out loud. "You guys can go to hell."

I know I'm on a serious mission. I know that at any moment we could be attacked and I could be in the fight of my life. Worse, I know that this journey to find my father could end in horrible disappointment.

So why do I feel so. . . almost normal?

Maybe it's the anticipation, the closeness of the possibility that I'm going to see my dad. Or maybe. . . just maybe. . . being with Oliver and Jake actually feels comfortable to me. Maybe I'm actually learning to trust people.

Two of them, anyway.

It's the strangest thing. Oliver I have no reason to trust, except that he's spent the past few days trying desperately to prove himself to me. I mean, every once in a while I get a bit of a freaky feeling from him, but let's face it: Evil or kind, he's kind of a freak. And Jake I've only known for a few weeks. Yet

GAIA

every time I need to rely on
either of them, they seem to come
through for me. Maybe that's par
for the course on planet Earth.
But on planet Gaia, it's unheard
of. In fact, it's downright
against the laws of nature.

I actually have to will myself
to pull back, feel less, trust
less, be more suspicious. That's
never happened before. It's like
my polar ice caps are melting.
Global warming, you might say.

So the question remains: Is
this a new springtime for me? Or
is it an ecological disaster of
world-ending proportions? I won't
know till this is over.

I wish I could just relax and
enjoy it in the meantime.

But if that were possible, it
wouldn't be planet Gaia.

GAIA, JAKE, AND OLIVER SETTLED into their four-seat compartment on the train. The station itself was gorgeous—pink marble, arched ceilings, and amazing Russian architecture. Gaia had to admit it: The place was almost as grand as Grand Central. But the trains themselves—at least the one that was destined to travel southeast, to Siberia—were decidedly less grand. On this one, she, Oliver, and Jake had passed down a narrow corridor, squeezed between aged wooden walls, and now found themselves sitting on red vinyl seats with their knees touching. A Formica table folded out from the wall, and a well-used pack of cards sat in a magazine holder, along with a copy of *Mademoiselle* from 1998.

# Soul-Vomit

"This is cozy," Gaia said.

"It smells like old socks," Jake pointed out.

"I think that's actually the food."

"If you think this is rough, you'd have made horrible agents," Oliver told them. "I've had to eat creatures you'd both call an exterminator to get rid of."

"Nice," Gaia said.

"What's the grossest thing you ever ate?"

Oliver thought for a moment. "Termites. I really didn't like the termites. I tried to swallow them whole and they moved around in my throat. But

84

crunching them was worse. It was a lose-lose situation."

"Termites." Gaia shrugged. "I'd rather eat something small than have to bite into a big water bug."

"I ate those in the Philippines. They're not so bad if you batter-fry them."

"Mmm, this conversation is making me hungry," Oliver said. "Let me see if there's a cafeteria car on this train. If I can't find anything, we'll have to dip into our rations, but I'd rather save those for an emergency."

"Don't go too far," Gaia said. "I wouldn't even know how to start looking for you." The face she turned up to him was struggling to remain impassive, but both Jake and Oliver could see she wasn't sure of herself, not at all. Fearlessness was one thing—emotionlessness was another. Maybe it was the huge scope of this mission, or maybe it was the stress of finally getting near her father—she was showing signs of wear and tear. It made them both feel very, very protective.

"Don't worry," Oliver promised. "I won't even touch the food if it looks dangerous."

Gaia pulled her feet up under her in her seat and turned back to Jake. "So I think we have some time to kill," she said.

"About twelve hours or so."

"What are we going to do?"

"I'd say we could play poker, but this deck only has fifty cards."

"Well, that's an interesting metaphor," Gaia muttered, taking the deck and shuffling through it to count the cards herself. "Sometimes I don't think anybody's playing with a full deck."

"Funny," Jake said.

"Then why aren't you laughing?"

"Because it's not, really."

He went silent and sat back, looking out the window. Gaia appreciated that: the quiet, without the awkward silence. The chugging of the train along the tracks, in a mesmerizing rhythm, was the only conversation. Gaia counted the cards again, and again. Then she started sorting them into suits, in order. Then a distant memory made a ghost of a smile flit across her face.

"What?" Jake asked.

"Oh, I don't know."

"Come on. I'm bored."

Gaia rolled her eyes. "When I was a kid, I had a deck of cards that was, like, ancient. And a couple were missing. But I wanted to learn to play cards, so. . . someone made the extra ones out of those index cards. You know, the ones people use to take notes on?"

"The ones David Letterman throws at the audience," Jake added.

"I guess. Anyway, so there were, like, forty-nine cards, and then these three bright white ones with the suits and numbers written on them, so whenever you tried to play anything, it was so obvious that the other person had a nine of clubs or whatever. It just didn't work." Gaia gave a quiet laugh. "I guess it's not really funny, it's just—it was funny that we thought it would work in the first place."

"It *is* kind of funny," Jake said. "Who did that, your dad?"

"Oh, no. It was. . . someone else." Gaia studied her cards.

"I mean, duh."

"What?"

"Obviously it was your mom."

Gaia's forehead wrinkled slightly, as if a headache were whooshing through it, then smoothed as if nothing had happened.

"Yeah. My dad was too organized and anal to come up with a goofy plan like that."

"You've never talked about her. Not to me, anyway."

Gaia shrugged.

"I'll tell you about mine."

"You don't have to."

"Okay."

Jake went silent again. Gaia reorganized the cards yet again, this time putting the two black suits together before moving on to the red. She marveled at how interesting a pack of cards could become when you needed a distraction. Something to keep you from blurting out your feelings in some kind of ill-advised self-revelatory soul-vomit. She forced herself to put the cards down and leaned back in her seat, putting her sneakers up on Jake's side of the compartment.

*Cha-chug. Cha-chug. Cha-chug.*

"I don't remember her as well as I'm supposed to," she mumbled. "I mean, I knew her until I was twelve. It's not like she—it's not like I lost her when I was a baby." It was a good lie. It kept Gaia from having to reopen the wounds, and it was believable enough. Jake couldn't possibly know about Gaia's sterling memory.

"The memories fade a little," Jake agreed, without pressing further. "It's disappointing."

*Cha-chug. Cha-chug. Cha-chug.*

"Did you, uh. . . I mean, do you ever think about stuff you said? To her? Your mom?" asked Gaia.

"You mean bad stuff? Like when I acted like a baby?" Jake asked.

"Well, you *were* a baby. But yeah."

"Um, I guess I do. But my dad sent me to a therapist for a while, right after it happened. And the therapist kept telling me that I was just acting like a normal kid, and that my mom knew I didn't really think she was a giant mean poo-head."

Gaia gave a snorting laugh. "Well, you got your money's worth out of that therapist."

"I know." Jake laughed, too. "But I gave myself a really hard time, anyway. I think I replayed every bratty moment I ever had with her, after she was gone. I was sure that I had made her life absolute hell."

"Huh."

The cards became fascinating again. This time, Gaia started poking them into the space between the glass window and the wall so that they stood plastered against the scenery outside. Then she studied the king, queen, and jack of diamonds as they stood there, gazing calmly back at her like a little nuclear family.

"Yeah," she said.

"What?"

"I can see how you'd do that."

*Cha-chug. Cha-chug. Cha-chug.*

"Did you do that?" Jake hazarded.

Gaia looked up at him, then snatched the cards out of the window and put them back into the deck.

"Forget I asked," he said.

"Sorry." Gaia gave an apologetic shrug. "It's not something I ever talk about. But the last conversation we had was a fight."

"You and your mom?"

"Yeah. I mean, I was twelve. Have you ever met a twelve-year-old? They're horrible."

"I'm sure you weren't—"

"Oh, please."

Jake laughed. "Well, I guess judging from the Gaia I know now, you might have been a tiny bit difficult."

"I was just annoyed all the time. Pissed off around

the clock. My body was doing all these wacky things, and my training was going horribly."

"I think that's normal."

"Yeah, maybe."

Gaia was silent as she remembered the rest of it. The whole idea of becoming a woman had freaked her out. She'd thought her boobs looked like fat blobs, and her center of gravity had been totally off. And her hips—she couldn't shop in the boy's department anymore. Her mom had seemed so comfortable in her skin, so beautiful and perfect; Gaia had seen herself as a ridiculous imitation. But she hadn't been able to find the words to explain how she felt, so she'd just acted like a bratty bitch.

The morning her mother died, Gaia had thrown a fit over something. God, she couldn't remember what. Breakfast, maybe? She'd wanted coffee and her mom had insisted on something more substantial. That's what moms do. And Gaia had acted like she was being asked to eat worms. She'd flown into a rage and left the house to go for a run. Loki had pulled the trigger just as Gaia had stepped back into the house. Her mom was dead before Gaia ever had a chance to apologize to her.

Gaia had never told anyone about that fight with her mother. In fact, even when she thought back to that day, she rarely touched on that episode. She felt too ashamed. What had she been so angry about? Why hadn't she—?

"You know, if you buy a pack of cards in Italy,

there's no queen," Jake said, taking the pile of cards from the seat next to Gaia and handing it to her. She took it gratefully and started shuffling them back into random order.

"No kidding," she said.

"Yeah, these are American cards. Or British."

"Why would you know that?"

Jake shrugged. "I have no idea. It's just a random fact stuck in my head."

Gaia envied Jake's state of mind. He seemed so relaxed and carefree. Why did she have to be so somber? Why was she forever wreathed in deep thought and regret? It wasn't as if Jake hadn't had tragedy in his life. And yet here he was, fully capable of levity. Why *was* she thinking of this now? Because she was missing her dad? Because she was bored and had too much time on her hands? Or was it because Jake made her feel comfortable enough for old feelings to bubble to the surface?

Ugh. If that were the case, Gaia was in big trouble. Now was *not* the time to start getting comfortable with Jake. She was glad when the feeling started to dissipate and she could think about something else.

"I hope you don't regret coming along," Gaia said to Jake.

"I don't," he said. "This is way more exciting than going to school. Besides, how could I miss all of this?" He waved his hand, taking in the dingy compartment, the musty smell, and the grimy window.

"I didn't mean for you to get sucked into my screwed-up world."

"I'm not sucked in. I'm fine."

"Well, I'm not." Gaia returned to studying the scene outside her windows, trees whipping by too quickly to discern one from the next, while mountains sat serenely in the distance. "After this, I want to chill out. For a long time."

"What's a long time?" Jake asked, arching an eyebrow. "You wouldn't last a weekend without a crisis to distract you."

"Try me. Try me and see how happy I'd be."

They rode in silence again. Friendship settled over them like a blanket, making the silence relaxing and not awkward. When Oliver slipped back into the compartment, they both just looked up at him, unsurprised.

"I got some sandwiches," he said apologetically. "I'm not sure what's in them, exactly."

Gaia bit into one and chewed thoughtfully. "I'm not going to think about it too hard," she said.

"Good move."

"Can't I just wait for the rations?" Jake said.

"No. Here, eat. Jake, we're going to be arriving at Obestoblak in about two hours," Oliver said. "Gaia and I will travel from there to the prison on snowmobiles."

"Oh, awesome," Gaia cheered.

"I want you to stay in town and wait for us," Oliver went on. "There's no reason for you to come along. You haven't been trained for this kind of mission, and if you want to stay behind and just keep things coordinated there, it would be a great help."

"That's a load of bull," Jake said, realizing a little too late that he needed to show Oliver the proper respect. "And I mean that with all due respect, sir. You don't need to make up phony excuses about needing things coordinated. Just level with me."

"Jake!" Gaia shot him an infuriated glare.

"I'm serious. Oliver, if you think I'm going to be a liability, that's one thing. I don't want to drag you down. But I think I can do this, and there's no way I'm going to sit around cooling my jets in a hotel while you guys go up to the prison. I want to come along."

"I don't know if you understand what this entails."

"I understand enough. I want to come along." He held Oliver's gaze steadily.

Finally the older man shrugged and sat down. "Fine. Then we'll spend the next few hours going over the plan. But you'd better not crack under pressure."

"You worry about yourself," Jake said, with that swaggering self-assurance that was beginning to grow on Gaia. Jake was cocky, but at least there was something there to back it up. Which made all the difference in the world.

"I've spoken to some people I used to know in the black market," Oliver told them. "They've put some snowmobiles aside for me, in a shack near the inn where I'm going to take some rooms. . . ."

Gaia listened to the plan as it unfolded. The relaxing motion of the train stopped having its soothing effect. The sound of the wheels slowly turned from a rhythmic lullaby to an energizing drumbeat. They were getting closer to where she needed to be. The battle was about to begin, and like an animal with its hackles up, a domesticated dog whose instincts kick in with `a primal urgency,` she felt her energy start to gather and focus for the task ahead.

She was ready.

I know I'm sitting still, because my legs aren't moving. My arms are at my sides and my butt is on a seat. But I'm also hurtling forward at a hundred and twenty miles an hour on this train.

My dad told me once that the worst part about his work was the waiting. The exciting stuff, he said, comes in bursts. The rest of the time you're sitting around praying for your investigation to get to the next level or for your informant to crack and give you something juicy. If you don't have patience, you'll never get anywhere, he told me.

Is that why I'm opening up like this? Are my feelings rising to the surface because time is stretching out before me? Do cops on stakeouts have major memories and revelations dogging them in the wee hours of the morning?

I don't know. But it's kind of nice to actually feel my feelings, even just a little. It's cool that Jake doesn't ask for more. If he did, I'd probably just clam up.

It's weird, the way my feelings are just kind of unfolding of their own accord. Like a complicated reverse origami.

The question is, can I fold them back up when the action hits? We're getting closer and closer to my father, and when the time comes, I want to be totally focused. I'm finally going to get him back, and I don't want to screw things up with stray emotions that I don't know what to do with.

How fast is this train going? I wish it would go faster. Less time on my hands and more action—that's the cure.

Only, these feelings... . they actually feel kind of good. Everything in moderation, I guess.

Together
they used
their
Oliver-
issued
night- **firearms**
vision
goggles to
find their
way through
the snow.

# THE INN WAS A RAMSHACKLE STONE

building that sat dejectedly on the outskirts of what Gaia supposed had once passed for a town. Behind it, a weird annex made of prefabricated corrugated sheet metal walls stuck out from one side, mak-

## Haphazard Angles

ing it look as though an alien ship had landed in the wrong place and then abandoned the wreckage in search of a prettier landing spot.

"Definitely not staying here," Jake muttered.

"Look at the mountains, though," Gaia pointed out. In the distance, a range of rocky peaks rose up into clouds so thick, they looked like smoke; they seemed to go on forever. "How close are we?"

"Farther than you think," Oliver said. "But close enough to get there if we can get our hands on the snowmobiles. Come on, let's go see if we can make contact."

They went inside. It seemed like the owners of the inn were trying to imitate an American bar they had seen on a postcard. A Budweiser sign was mounted behind the bar, but it didn't light up—it just sat there, dust covered, like an ancient artifact. The room was dim and smelled like stale smoke and old beer. Metal folding chairs sat at haphazard angles; the bar itself had wooden paneling and a plastic top. It was the most depressing place Gaia had ever seen.

Oliver began speaking in a low voice to the man behind the bar, who eyed him suspiciously. He kept shaking his head. Gaia tried to listen in, but they weren't speaking Russian; it was some kind of dialect. Finally she saw some money exchange hands, and Oliver led them back out into the light of the outside world.

"We have to meet a guy here later," he said.

"Are you sure?" Gaia asked.

"I'm sure that's what this guy told me. Am I sure that's what we're going to do? No," he said. He led them around to the prefabricated annex.

"This is their idea of expanding the property," he explained. "Nobody stays here but traveling tradesmen, so there's no need to impress the tourists. These are guest rooms. This whole area's been poor for a thousand years. There's nothing you can't get for a few dollars, but they're also used to getting as much as they can for the money. They'd rather kill us and take all our money than trade with us and just get some of it."

As if on cue, the man from the bar stepped out into the cold yard and stood eyeing them. Then he motioned for Oliver to join him inside again. Gaia made a move to follow, but Oliver put a hand on her arm.

"Stay here," he said. "Check around back and see if you can find the snowmobiles. I'm pretty sure they're going to be in that garage over there."

A cracked concrete structure stood under a huddle of trees. Gaia nodded and waited until her uncle had gone back inside the building to walk over and peer inside. Sure enough, two snowmobiles sat under tarps in the gloom.

"How old are those things?" Jake whispered.

"I don't know, did Edsel make a snowmobile?" Gaia answered. "At least they won't have a lot of fancy bells and whistles to figure out. Come on."

She stepped into the gloom and found a can of gasoline, which she used to fill up the two tanks. She was getting impatient. Oliver needed to come out here, now. If they couldn't buy or bargain for these vehicles, they should just take them.

Jake stood outside, keeping watch.

"Gaia," he said in a low voice.

"Yeah?"

"Can you get those started?"

"Yeah, I think so. Why?"

A shot rang out, and Gaia stopped asking questions. She revved up her engine, and Jake jumped on the other snowmobile; they shoved them forward, busting through the flimsy and ancient garage door, and shot out into the diamond-white snowy field.

Oliver was running toward them, his backpack flapping behind him like a cape; Gaia pulled up next to him, not even stopping as he hopped on behind her, and maneuvered away from the inn, where the bar guy and two friends were yelling and shaking firearms at them.

"Making friends?" she shouted, as she followed Oliver's pointing finger up a pathway in the woods.

"I paid them, but it wasn't quite enough," he shouted back. "They wanted more. That's what we were negotiating."

"This is their turf!" Gaia yelled back. "Aren't they going to come after us?"

"No! They're fine! That was a successful business transaction, if you can believe it. Otherwise, believe me, we'd be facedown in a snowdrift!"

Gaia laughed into the wind that whipped across her face, burning her cheeks with both sun and ice. "I don't think Jake knows that!"

Jake was ahead of them. He peered back once in a while to make sure they were still on his tail, but he was in no hurry to slow down. He looked slightly panicked. Gaia felt more alive than she'd felt in a long time.

"That was good," she shot back over her shoulder, after revving the engine a few times and finding a comfortable rate of speed. "I wouldn't have known how to handle all that."

"You pick things up as you go along," Oliver told her. "Some things don't really change. I haven't been in this area in—oh, twenty years, twenty-five? But business is business wherever you go."

"If you call that business," Gaia laughed. "Imagine pulling that at Tower Records."

"We'll try it when we get back."

Gaia grinned into the wind as she steered her snow-mobile up into the foothills of the mountains. Oliver really knew his stuff. She was really glad to be on this mission with him, strange as it was to be working with her old enemy—and her father's twin brother. She felt like after years of stagnating, she was learning a million things every second. And even though she was driving the snowmobile, she felt him steering their mission in the right direction. She had made the right decision for once. She was sure of it.

## TOM MOORE LAY ON THE ICY-COLD

concrete floor of his cell, meditating deeply. If he concentrated, he could force his body to stop shivering, even though every breath left a puff of vapor above his head. Going even deeper, he felt his consciousness recede until he was nothing but a point of light in a vast darkness. He was in a state of deep, deep trance. From the outside, it looked like he was passed out cold. The awkward position he had put himself in would signal to the guards that he wasn't just having a midday nap. They would have to come in and investigate. Soon, he hoped. Before he froze to death, unprotected and exposed.

## Seizure

Vaguely, from a million miles away, he sensed that yes, a guard was slowing outside his cell, peering in to see what was happening. He heard the guard's footsteps fade down the hall, then return with another set of feet. Now two pairs of eyes looked warily into the cell. For a long time. Studying him, seeing if he was faking.

He *was* faking. But they didn't know that.

He heard them whispering back and forth, trying to figure out who to tell and what to do. One of them, the fat one, said they should leave him alone until dinnertime. The other one was afraid he'd die and they would get in trouble for it. Back and forth, back and forth. Finally he willed himself to give a convulsive shudder. It set off a gagging noise in his throat; he hadn't planned it, but it worked wonders. Convinced he was having some sort of seizure, both pairs of boots thumped away down the hall, then returned with medical personnel, who loaded him onto a gurney and wheeled him down to the prison infirmary.

His eyes fluttered open of their own accord, and from his post deep inside his own trance, Tom saw the mountains looming up around him. The prison was in a sort of a basin, set deep inside the mountains. He wasn't even sure which range this was, and even if he had known, he didn't know how he'd survive out there long enough to get to civilization. But this wasn't the time to worry. He had to gather data.

There were probably caves in the mountains. He

could survive in a cave. If he could just overpower these two guards, get outside the compound somehow—but no. This was a fact-finding mission. He had to be patient—wasn't that what he had told Gaia? He had to stick to his plan. A hospital facility was always less guarded than the actual cells. He could catch someone off guard here as they puzzled over his strange comatose state.

"Mr. Moore," a voice called out in accented English. "Mr. Moore. Thomas. Can you hear me?"

*I hear you knocking, but you can't come in,* Tom thought, willing himself deeper into his trance. He was inside the hospital now; the mountains no longer cradled him. A doctor was the only person near him. If he had to, he could strike out now. He tried to perceive everything going on around him.

It was strange. The doctor didn't seem to be examining him. He had taken a few exploratory probing movements, checked his pupils, but now Tom seemed to be. . . alone? Or was someone standing next to his gurney, eyeing him?

He wanted to look around. This was frustrating. His concentration faltered as he strained to figure out what was going on. Was someone in the room with him? Had they called someone else in? Why was it so quiet? He thought he heard someone breathing. What was—?

He felt the gurney gripped tightly; it gave a sudden lurch, and he felt himself pitched toward the floor.

Instinctively, he sprang up and threw his arms out to break his fall, then rolled to protect himself, ending up in a crouched position, unharmed—but completely awake. Too late, he realized he'd been tricked. Tom Moore looked up to see a smirking doctor in a lab coat shaking his head at him.

"So clumsy," the doctor said, kicking the gurney toward Tom with a violence that seemed out of place with his house-of-healing surroundings.

"Yeah, that gurney seems to be a little wobbly," Tom growled.

"I mean you, Mr. Moore. Your attempt to fool me was quite clumsy. Amateurish, even. I might have expected that sort of foolishness from one of our normal prisoners—the murderers and petty criminals that make up most of our population. From you, it's quite disappointing."

"Why are you keeping me here?" Tom asked. "What kind of criminal am I, according to you?"

"I'd tell you," the doctor said, his smirk deepening until it was infuriatingly smug, "but then I'd have to kill you."

Tom took the invitation and leapt across the room toward the doctor. The two guards went for him immediately. One held him down and the other punched him over and over until the doctor raised a hand to stop them.

"This is hardly what I expected," the doctor said,

more to himself than to Tom. "Very unimpressive indeed. Hold him," he told the guards, and they did, while he injected Tom with something that deadened all thought almost immediately.

"Take him back to his cell," he said, yanking the spike out of Tom's arm with an agonizing twist of his wrist. "He is pathetic. Don't call me again on his behalf. He can die in there for all I care."

In his last moments of consciousness, Tom realized with perfect clarity that he was not going to be able to get out of this place. That even if he did, he would be lost in the white wilderness beyond the walls of the prison. There were no caves he could live in, no path to take; there was nothing but the false bravado he'd used to temporarily deceive himself. But he had lost the strength for self-deception. This wasn't the toughest situation he had ever been in, but it was going to defeat him.

Why? Because it came at a time when he was already emotionally vulnerable. He was worried about Gaia, pining for Natasha, furious at Loki. His only hope now was to steel his mind, rid himself of emotion, and focus on retaining his sanity.

Steel his mind. The mind that was slipping into unconsciousness with terrifying speed.

Steel his—

**The** apartment on East Seventy-second Street must be the most comfortable place on earth. Except for that terrible couch— the one that Natasha loves so much. That thing is the *least* comfortable place on earth, with its red velvet and mahogany details. But other than that, the apartment is perfect.

I love how Natasha has decorated it. The brick red of the living room is a bold choice, but a good one, and the curtains give it an elegant feel. Too many of those apartments get taken over by families that make them too casual, that don't take into account the grandeur of the good, old building. Natasha understands that. She created a space that acknowledges the beauty of the architecture but is still easy to live in. She can do that, bring together things that seem like they could never meet. It's one of the reasons I fell in love with her.

The girls' room could use some

work—you can see how different their personalities are. Tatiana's a good, kind girl, and her side of the room is as well ordered and tidy as her emotions. But Gaia—well, she's a bit more chaotic. If she'd just do her laundry once in a while. I don't know how she gets any sleep in that bed; it's like she can't get used to the fact that we have a stable environment now. Maybe Tatiana will rub off on her, just a little.

I thought that after Katia died, I'd never feel close to anyone again. The pain of losing her, of losing the warmth and safety of our little three-person society, nearly drove me insane. For months I couldn't even process the simple fact that she was gone. I'd wake up and reach for her. People kept telling me it would get easier, but it didn't. Not really. Once you see true evil you never feel right again. Sometimes you can't get what you want. Sometimes it's ripped from you. And then your heart doesn't just break—it shatters.

Then I met Natasha. She's

fascinating, warm, intelligent—
she's the only woman after Katia
who I've felt I could give my heart
to. The thing that did it for me,
though? The way she opened up to
Gaia. I know how difficult my
daughter can be. And yet Natasha
tried and tried with her, just
because she loved me. Or maybe
because she saw the real girl under
Gaia's shell. Either way, she
earned my eternal respect.

For a few brief hours, I had a
glimpse of how our lives could
entwine together. I saw Natasha
at my side, I saw Gaia relax and
laugh and come as close to happiness as I've seen her since she
was a child. I know—I *know* I
could give her the stability that
was taken away from her. If I
could just protect her and be
there for her, that would give
her the space to feel like a normal kid, a normal teenager. Maybe
she could be happier then. It
wouldn't make up for all the
years I was gone. But it would at
least be something. I'd be her

father again. I just have to get back to her.

Which means getting out of here. This prison. These walls enclosed by mountains wrapped in snow.

Who put me here? Loki. There's no doubt in my mind that the choking fit that led to the blackness from which I awoke here was caused by one person. Not person—entity. Thing with no humanity.

Who ripped me from Natasha? Loki.

Who robbed me of my Gaia yet again? Loki.

And who am I going to make pay for all this pain, when I finally get free?

Loki.

Loki's behind this. But I have a family to get back to, and for them I'll keep my mind steady. But before I return to that comfortable red room, there's one man who's going to pay for his sins in blood so red, it would make the perfect complement to that uncomfortable couch.

Loki.

# AS THEY BUZZED UP THROUGH THE

**hyper**

mountains, the darkness moved in around them like a cloak. Oliver finally signaled that they should pull over and meet just under the crest of one of the peaks.

"How are you holding up?" he asked. "Are you tired, or can you keep going?"

"I'm pretty sharp," Gaia said.

"Yeah, this air is keeping me awake," Jake agreed. "Besides, we had so much sleep on the train."

"Good. It'll take the rest of the night for us to travel down the inside of this mountain. Come with me."

They trudged to the top and looked down. "See that ring of lights?" Oliver asked. They nodded. "That's the prison. That's where your father is, Gaia."

Gaia felt a surge of excitement. If she'd been awake before, she was downright hyper now.

"What are we going to do?" she asked.

"We're going to hit it just at dawn. I want you to study the maps I gave you on the train. The two of you are going to sneak into the camp at this location, here, where there's a blind spot that the guards can't see, caused by the rock formations. It's a serious weak spot. I assume they never thought anyone would attempt a rescue."

"They didn't know who they were dealing with, did they?" Jake asked.

"Good," Gaia said. "So we sneak in. Any idea where he's being held?"

"I'm going to guess in here, the innermost tower," Oliver said. "You'll have to figure out a way to enter undetected. Gaia, cover your hair with this cap, and try to walk like a man."

"According to the girls at school, I already do that," she said.

"Well. . . good, then, I suppose. For now." Oliver moved on. "Now, if you're discovered—and chances are you will be—I want you to use this." He pulled out a nasty-looking pistol.

"You need to show me how to use this," Gaia said, eyeing it doubtfully. "I'm not that into guns."

"It's not really a gun. It shoots flares. Shoot it into the air when you want to signal that you're leaving the prison yard. Then Jake can find you at a designated meeting area."

"Is it going to hurt anyone?"

"Not really." Oliver shook his head. Gaia eyed him dubiously.

"Seriously," she said. "Those prisoners have nothing to do with my dad. I don't want them hurt."

"Gaia, I know what you're thinking. This isn't a Loki trick. Just aim the gun toward the sky and no one will get hurt. It's just to get you out of there safely. I promise."

A promise made by an old enemy, now a new friend. It was the best offer Gaia had at the moment. She would have to take it.

"Fine," she said. "Now show me which way to go."

The path shone pale in the deepening twilight. "I'll set up camp here," Oliver said. "We're far enough away that we can rest and let Tom recover if they've mistreated him in any way. Then we can start back."

"Jake should stay," Gaia pointed out. "He's injured. And he shouldn't be on the front lines."

"They'll recognize me," he pointed out. "I'm the exact twin of their most precious prisoner. I can't be seen in there."

"All right." Gaia gazed down the path, toward the lights and barracks that held her father. "I'm ready. Jake, you?"

"I'm good," he said, replacing his goggles. "Oliver, you're sure you'll be okay up here?"

"By the time you get back, I'll practically have a hotel built," he promised. "Get going."

Gaia and Jake slid down the mountain as the darkness gathered. The night would only last a few hours, and they had to hit the prison just before daylight. There was no time to lose.

**Dad!** Can you hear me? I'm out here.

Shouldn't he be able to tell I'm coming for him? In all those corny TV movies, fathers and daughters seem to know everything about each other with one wink. They sense all sorts of things, as if a telephone wire connects them at the heart.

Then again, in all those Shakespeare plays, the daughter dresses like a boy and her dad doesn't realize it's her. I don't know what kind of dumb dads were running around in the seventeenth century, but it's right there in the plays. So maybe he can't tell I'm coming. Maybe with my hair under this watch cap, he won't know it's me. I'll be like Viola or Rosalind, and in the end I'll get everything I want.

I think I can see the rock formation Oliver was talking about. Off to the side there—yeah. The maps were really good. I don't know how he did it. Must have

been satellite photos or something.

   I can't believe it, but everything he comes up with keeps
checking out. No matter how suspicious I am of him—and I'm not
sure I'll ever be one hundred
percent convinced of his
sincerity—he keeps coming
through. I couldn't have gotten
this far without him. And now I'm
within spitting distance of my
dad. It's so odd. But no odder
than the plot of a play where
twins end up finding each other
on the streets of Verona, thirty
years after they lost each other
at sea. I guess stranger things
have happened.

   Of course, that was fiction.

# AS INSTRUCTED, GAIA AND JAKE

parked their snowmobiles. Under the cover of darkness they built a makeshift fort to camouflage the vehicles and keep them protected. It took a while, and Gaia could feel the darkness starting to wane, hinting at gray around the edges.

**Riot**

"Are you ready for this?" she asked Jake.

"Yeah. I'm going to go in there and set off a series of explosions. The guards are going to assume they came from some of the inmates trying to cause a distraction so they can escape."

"You've got those fireworks?" Gaia asked.

"I've got everything, and it's all still dry. With any luck, the guards will be so disorganized, they'll split up in too many directions to notice us," Jake said as he dug a stake into the ground to anchor the fort.

"Right. And the inmates—they'll either start fighting amongst themselves or take advantage of the confusion to try to escape themselves." Gaia kicked her stake to make sure it was stable.

"And that's when we bust your dad out."

Gaia grinned. "Yeah. That's when we bust my dad out."

"You excited?"

"What do you think?" Gaia packed away her grin and gave a deep breath. "Okay. Let's do this thing."

Jake nodded. Gaia could just make out the outline

of his head in the inky blackness. Together they used their Oliver-issued night-vision goggles to find their way through the snow to the rocky outcropping that would give them access to the prison. They entered easily. Just as Oliver had told them, there was a fissure in the wall that gave them access to the main yard. Gaia ran across the yard to the tower.

Her heart raced as she entered the building. She knew she was close. She could sense her father's presence. She entered the building and ran up the dank stairs. He was sure to be at the top; that was the most difficult place to escape from, because it could be seen from everywhere in the prison.

Rounding the last flight, she saw a cell at the end of a hallway. Inside it was a figure in a gray uniform, head bowed. It couldn't be so easy. But apparently it was. There, right before her eyes—

"Dad!"

The head came up. In an instant, Gaia saw the face that was so much like Oliver's, but now instantly recognizable as her father's. She had found him. After what seemed like a lifetime of wondering, thousands of miles crossed, and an immeasurable amount of worry, she'd found him. Her father, Tom Moore. Her heart bloomed in her chest till it almost choked her with emotion.

Except something was wrong.

"Dad?"

Yes, technically, Gaia was standing in front of her father, Tom Moore. But he didn't know it yet. Gaia's heart broke when she saw what had been done to him. He'd been beaten, she could see that immediately. But there was something worse. He looked defeated, and he blinked at her as though he thought he might be hallucinating.

"I wish you were real," he said in a low voice.

The words pressed into her heart like a red-hot cattle brand. He didn't even recognize that she was real? What was going on?

"I *am* real, Dad! It's me!"

Forcing herself to act instead of worry, she ran forward and yanked on the door. She jimmied a crowbar between the bars and snapped them open, reaching through to grab him and break through whatever dream state he was in.

"Dad," she said.

His eyes peered out at her, red-rimmed and haggard. She shook his collar. He jerked back, as though he hadn't expected her to actually reach out and touch him. To Gaia, it felt like she'd been slapped. She threw her arms around him and squeezed.

"Come back," she begged. "Come back. It's me. It's Gaia. I'm really here." Her voice broke and she fought back tears. "Dad, don't do this." She pulled back, smoothing her hands across his face. He studied her with a puzzled expression.

"Come on," she moaned. "Hey!" She shook him a

little. Finally, his eyes widened. A spark entered them. Relief flooded Gaia's veins as their eyes connected for real.

"Gaia," he said, his voice husky and harsh. He hugged her back, crushing her in a desperate embrace. She waited to hear him say something, ask how she got there, tell her he loved her.

"*Behind you,*" he whispered. Without needing to think before she reacted, Gaia turned with her foot already in the air and caught a guard straight in the gut. The guy fell backward into his partner, who ran yelling down the stairs.

"*Jake!*" she shouted, knowing he was just outside in the yard. In response, she heard a whoosh and a pop, then smelled acrid smoke. Immediately, shouts filled the courtyard.

The prison riot was on.

Wiping out
at seventy-
five miles
per hour
would turn
them both **nerve**
into **endings**
red smudges
in the white
snow.

# Face-to-Face

TOM MOORE WATCHED IN AMAZEMENT as he realized his hallucination was real. His daughter was here; she had appeared out of nowhere, as if his mind had created her out of the raw material around him. She beat both guards, the ones who had beaten him, and then she turned around to where he was standing, still, in the opened prison cell.

"Dad. *Dad*. Come on. We've got to go."

"I'm groggy," he explained. "Some sort of drug. Knocked me out."

"Well, the air's cold enough to wake you up." She took off her own coat and put it on him. He followed her out.

"How?" he asked. "I can't figure out how."

"I'll explain later. Right now, we've just got to get out of here."

They hurried down the stairs. Tom felt like an old man. He was trained to handle harsh conditions, but this prison had been the most brutal place he'd ever experienced. Even in the short time he'd been here, the cold had sunk into his muscles, robbing them of strength. He'd barely been fed at all. And his lungs felt weak. He was embarrassed to be seen like this.

At the bottom of the stairs, he stopped Gaia. "Be careful," he said. "Those guards have a supervisor, a doctor. He's a brutal man—and he has some sort of interest in keeping me here."

"I'll watch for him. Right now, we need to head across the yard there. Do you see where we got in? There was a fault in the wall and we broke through."

The yard looked like a scene from a war movie. Men dressed in the thick, burlaplike uniform of the prison had broken en masse from their barracks, panicked by the acrid smoke, and were running in all different directions. Tom could see that a group of them had ganged up on some of the guards, repaying them in kind for the cruelty they'd been shown. There were fistfights going on all around them, and bricks were flying through the air like concrete-colored missiles. It was hard to see through the smoke and chaos. But the noise helped jar him out of his grogginess and his mind started to focus.

"I see it," answered Tom.

"I need to find Jake in all this mess. Wow."

"We can't look for your friend now," he said. "We need to get out of here ourselves. If you planned this properly, he'll know to meet us on the outside if we can't be found."

"Hang on," Gaia said, scanning the early dawn sky. Was she waiting for a helicopter? Tom didn't see how that would work. Where would it land? Suddenly there was a loud popping sound, and a flare shot up into the air. Gaia's eyes followed it to its source and she grinned.

"I can't believe that worked," Gaia said, shoving Tom

in the direction of the exit. For the next few moments, he knew nothing but the need to run, as he avoided flying fists, bricks, and even bodies. A few others had found the broken wall and were piling out. They only had a few moments before the guards discovered it, too, and began shooting at anyone trying to escape.

Once outside the walls, they ran straight toward the woods, where they were joined by a young man Tom didn't know. "You did this?" he asked the boy. "You're Gaia's age. How did this happen? What's going on?"

"Nice to meet you, Mr. Moore," the young man said. "I'm Jake Montone." He turned to Gaia. "We need to get the snowmobiles and get back to Oliver. I don't like how this thing is going down," Jake said, as he departed for the makeshift fort.

"Oliver?" Tom gasped. He wheeled around, yanking his arm out of Gaia's grasp. "Please don't tell me you're working with my brother. Is that who brought you here?"

Gaia looked at her father, horrified that Jake had let the secret slip so soon. He would have had to find out sooner or later, but she'd thought she'd have the trip up the mountain to soften the blow. "Dad, this isn't the time. Let's just get up the—"

"What kind of a deal did you make? Do you have any idea how much danger we are in right now?"

"Yeah, Dad. There's a riot going on and—you hear that? Those are gunshots. We need to get on the snowmobiles now."

"I'm safer inside that compound than out here with Loki. He's using you, can't you see that? He must have lost control of my abduction, and he used to you get me back—now he's going to kill all of us."

"It's not like that," Gaia shouted over the increasing noise of the riot. "He was in a coma. He had some kind of brain conversion while he was under. Sometimes when people suffer loss of oxygen to the brain they emerge from their comas a gentler version of their former selves. In this case, Loki just went back to his Oliver personality. He helped us put this trip together—he put it together for us. Dad, I know it's hard to believe, but he's really sorry."

"Sorry?" Tom asked, with an incredulous stare at his daughter. She almost withered under its heat. He didn't raise his voice, but his body language was unmistakable. He was furious.

Jake buzzed up on a snowmobile. "Is everything all right?" he asked. "Mr. Moore, can you ride on the back of this with me?"

Tom turned to Jake. "Thank you for your help—but my daughter and I aren't going with you."

"What? Dad!" Gaia said.

"There's no way you'll get back without the snowmobiles," Jake said. "And the rations. And the supplies."

"We'll manage," Tom said, taking Gaia's arm protectively.

"Dad, listen," Gaia said. She turned to face him.

"Jake's right. We're dead meat on our own. Even if you're still suspicious of Oliver, you've got to trust me enough to know we'll be all right. If we go with him, maybe something will happen. But if we don't, there's no chance of survival. And there's no turning back," she added, with a toss of her head toward the now-mounting flames inside the prison walls.

Tom gazed into Gaia's eyes as if he were trying to gauge whether she'd been brainwashed or not. It was a legitimate question. Loki had been a master of manipulation—Tom himself had been fooled by Gaia doppelgangers, though not from this close up. But there was no time to think it over carefully. He had to act quickly.

"Sir?" Jake asked. "If one of those bullets hits my gas tank, we're going to have some trouble."

"All right," he said. "I'll go with you." He climbed on the back of the kid's snowmobile while Gaia buzzed on ahead. She was right. He had no choice—for now. But he was going to watch carefully for a chance to grab his daughter and get away from Loki. Or use this opportunity to get revenge.

He didn't know what Loki was up to now, but he was about to come face-to-face with his old nemesis. What did Loki want? What was his plan? Tom wasn't sure. But he knew that, bottom line, it had to be evil. And being this close to Loki was going to give Tom the opportunity for revenge he'd always wanted. The temptation was beyond unbearable.

I don't think I could be more worried if Gaia were actually my own daughter. I've been watching since I finished setting up camp. Everything is in order. The food is ready, the coffee is brewing. Now all I can do is watch from my perch up here on the mountain. Gaia's down there somewhere, and she's with my brother.

My brother. How am I going to face him?

Tom has every right to detest me with all his heart. I ruined his life—and even tried to take it. I nearly destroyed Gaia time and time again. I have been behind every painful betrayal of the last five years, and there have been many of them. Too many to count. Too many to remember. The flashes that come to me nearly drive me insane with regret and remorse. A lifetime of penance couldn't make up for what I did.

Still, here I am. I brought Gaia to him, and I'm going to carry him out of here on my back

if I have to. It's the least I can
do. I owe him that much. After
that, if he still wants to hate
me, I can't stop him. But at least
I can prove to him that I can be
trusted with this one task.

I can hear shouts and gunshots.
The prison is boiling with rioting
prisoners. I saw the flare, so I
know Gaia found her father. Did
they get out? If I see two snowmobiles climbing toward me—and I
think I do—then they did.

The shouts. The gunshots. The
prisoners are rioting. Why am I
drawn to the sound? Is it familiar? Is there something I don't
remember from my Loki years that
is being set off now? The sound
is so familiar—

It's like there are two of me.
As I gaze down the mountain, I'm
horrified by the danger and chaos
in that prison. But I worry. Is
Loki still alive inside me? Is he
relishing the shouts? Does the
clamor sound as pleasant as the
laughter of children to him? If
he's here, I can't sense him. But

I'm worried that I will. If he appears out of my subconscious, I'll have to lock him up, keep him out of my way.

Concentrate on the pain, the horror of it, the worry about Gaia and Tom. If I can keep that fresh, I can remain myself and keep them safe from him. From that part of me.

Hurry up, Gaia. Get Tom up here so I can see him safe. So I can apologize like a man. This is the most terrifying thing I've ever had to do—not because I'm afraid he'll harm me, but because I have to admit what I became, what I was. What might still be, deep inside. Facing Tom will be the hardest thing I've ever had to do.

And I'd just as soon get it over with.

Hurry up, Gaia.

# GAIA PULLED UP FIRST. SHE JUMPED

## Hostility

off the snowmobile and ran to Oliver.

"He's not doing so great," she said.

"Was he injured?"

She grimaced. "I mean, he's a little wasted. He doesn't look so hot. But that's not the problem."

Oliver looked up at her, curious.

"It's going to be really hard for me to convince him you're trustworthy," she blurted out.

"Well, of course. We expected that." Oliver returned to his food-preparation activities, stirring a pot of beans carefully. Gaia watched him. He was nervous, anyone could tell.

"I guess I just thought he'd have more faith in me," she said quietly.

Oliver looked up at her. "Gaia, your father and I were bitter enemies for most of your life. You can't erase that in a few days. Don't expect too much of him right now. This is a huge shock. And it's not the only shock he's going to have to deal with. Don't forget, he has no idea that Natasha and Tatiana turned against him. This is going to be quite a blow."

Gaia breathed in sharply. She knew she was going to have to deliver that news, too. This was just getting harder and harder. She'd finally gotten what she wanted—she had found her father and delivered him

129

from prison—and she felt almost nothing but `nerve endings`.

Jake buzzed up behind Gaia in his snowmobile and pulled it up right next to hers. He was completely casual about it, like he was pulling into a parking spot at the mall. Gaia had to smile. The guy handled himself like a pro.

"Hey!" She plastered on a smile and ran toward Jake and Tom. "Come on over. There's food. . . ."

Tom climbed off the back of the snowmobile and stalked over to Oliver. She could see that his eyes were aflame with fury. "Dad, come on," she said. But he walked past her as if she wasn't even there. Oliver put the metal pot down on the fire and moved away from the flames, instinctively taking himself away from the vulnerable situation. Tom grabbed him by the collar and shook him furiously. The weakness brought on by his imprisonment was gone. Empowered by his anger, Tom was suddenly a tower of strength, lunging at his brother full force.

"What's your game?" he asked, grabbing Oliver by the collar.

"I know this is strange," Oliver told him, hands in the air. "I'm not here to hurt you."

"Do I look like an idiot?" Tom asked, shoving Oliver backward. "Do you think I'm a fool? You expect me to eat food you prepared? So you can poison me again? You've done enough. I don't know why you're pretending to help me or how you've fooled Gaia, but

I'm not falling for it. Go. Get out of here. Find your own way back to civilization."

Tom punctuated his tirade with little jabs at Oliver's chest. Oliver stepped backward slowly, absorbing the blows, hands in the air in surrender. Finally Tom gave him a shove and he tripped, falling backward into the snow.

"Out of here," Tom repeated. "Take a snowmobile and go."

"Dad, stop!" Gaia shouted.

"Tom. Listen," Oliver said, getting up and standing at a wary distance. "I'm not going to fight you. You need me to get out of here."

"I need you for nothing," Tom screamed. "You want to help me? Bring my wife back."

Oliver winced as if he'd just been pushed again. "I'm so sorry," he said.

"Sorry about what? About killing my wife?" Tom asked.

"That wasn't *me*."

"No, it was Loki. And Loki is who, exactly?"

Oliver bowed his head in shame.

"I'm not hearing an answer. Who is Loki?"

"He's me. He *was* me. Loki was me, but I'm not him anymore. You have to believe me."

Tom reached for the handle of the pot on the fire, ready to swing it at Oliver and let the boiling soup and the heavy iron finish him off. Gaia stepped in, using techniques she had learned from Tom himself to paralyze him momentarily.

"That's enough," she said. "Dad, you and I are going to sit over here. Oliver and Jake will build a new fire. Right?"

Oliver nodded. Jake looked dubious.

"Come on, Dad, sit down. Come on." Tom allowed himself to be led to the fire and sat down. Gaia crouched next to him for a moment, putting her arms around his shoulders. She suddenly felt very protective of him. She'd rescued him, but he wasn't out of the woods yet—literally or figuratively.

"This is a lot to take in," she said. "Maybe you're right, and maybe I'm just being an idiot about Oliver. But we're okay for now. Just hang in there with me."

Tom nodded. Gaia got up and went to Oliver and Jake, who were already busy setting up their alternate camp.

"Oliver," she said. "This is weird. I mean, it's awkward. You've been so great, but—"

"Your father is showing me the same suspicion you did," Oliver acknowledged. "It's understandable. Be patient with him."

"Oh, I am," she said. "I just hope you will be, too."

Oliver nodded, giving Gaia a reassuring smile.

"I think it's also the imprisonment—the torture. His mind isn't quite working at full capacity. He told me they pumped him full of all kinds of drugs. He doesn't even know what they are."

"And without a laboratory, we don't know, either," Oliver said. "So I'm up against Tom's legitimate suspicions plus his lowered capacity to be reasonable. The trip back to New York should be quite interesting."

"Well. . . I guess it'll be like any other dysfunctional family reunion," Gaia said.

She looked toward Jake. He seemed freaked out. She didn't even know what to say to him. As far as he knew, Oliver was a great guy who'd been helping them. He didn't really know Gaia's long history with Loki, just the broad strokes. She couldn't risk telling Jake any more than that. In this case, too much information could be a dangerous thing. Now, though, she wished she'd prepared him for how scary Loki was. Just to give him some perspective. She suddenly felt a wave of guilt for having let him come along. For not having let him make an informed decision.

But she couldn't worry about that now. Her priority was Tom. Her dad. He wasn't doing so great. She had to nurse him back to health—and get the last of those drugs out of his system so he could return to his normal self.

She tromped back over to the Gaia-and-Tom fire and sat down on a folding camp chair next to his, in the shelter Oliver had constructed. "So we'll rest here, then go to Moscow and get the plane back to the U.S.," she said.

Tom gazed at his daughter. The grizzle of his unshaven face made him look older than he was, older than his brother. The red rims of his eyes could have been the result of sadness or illness—it was hard to tell. Finally he nodded.

"How's the food?"

He looked down at the bowl of beans in his hands. "I haven't been able to bring myself to eat it."

"You need your strength," Gaia said gently. "Here, look." She dipped a spoon into it and brought it to her mouth. "Ow! It's hot. But it's fine."

Tom nodded again and took the spoon back from Gaia. She wrapped him in a blanket that looked like tinfoil and rubbed his shoulders. She hated seeing him like this.

She was suddenly ravenous, and tucked into her own bowl of food with an enthusiasm she hadn't known she had. She wanted to get the meal over with and get moving. At least with the buzz of the snowmobiles in her ear, she wouldn't have to listen to the uncomfortable silence between her father and her uncle.

"This is kind of good," she said.

"Probably because we're so hungry," he answered. "Gaia, thank you. Whatever else is going on, I can't believe you made it all this way. I thought I was lost in there."

"I couldn't sleep till I found you," she told him. "There was no way."

"Do I really look that bad?"

Gaia laughed. "You've looked better, I guess. Do you think you can drive?"

"I'd be happy to."

"Good. I'll ride with you, Jake will ride with—on the other one. Okay?"

"Fine."

They sipped in silence again.

"The game plan," she finally told him, "is that we're going to travel back on the train, but instead of being passengers, we'll hop on the freight cars this time."

"Sounds wise," he said. "That's a good plan."

Gaia's heart skipped a beat. *Funny how your dad's approval always gives you that warm feeling,* she thought. *Even when you just had to bust him out of jail.*

She wanted to get going. Get out of this odd isolated location, with this odd group. Funny how all the easiness of the last few days had vanished. She hoped her dad would come around soon, before she developed an ulcer from all this hostility.

*Maybe it's a dysfunctional family,* Gaia thought, *but it's my dysfunctional family.*

**Okay,** I found my dad. I
haven't had a second to process
all of this. Here I am, riding
down the side of a mountain
behind him, hanging on to him for
dear life. I've been hugging him
for hours, but I still don't feel
like I really have him back.

Maybe there's only so many
times you can lose someone and
get them back. Maybe after a certain number of times, your heart
says, "Enough. I'm not going up
and down anymore."

Or maybe he doesn't seem like
my dad. My dad is physically
strong and incredibly sharp-wit-
ted. Even when he's angry, he
doesn't let his emotions get away
with him. He should be able to
deal with Oliver, even if he
thinks he's secretly still Loki,
until we get back to New York.
And he should be able to see that
I've assessed Oliver and trust my
judgment about him.

I mean, I'm not an idiot. I
understand my dad's point. When

Oliver was Loki, he was absolute undiluted evil. Caused us pain beyond measure. Hurt people thoughtlessly. Almost for the sport of it.

But I've checked him out. And I believe he's changed. And if I can investigate him and come to that conclusion, Dad should trust my instincts.

Then again. . . then again, maybe I *am* wrong, and Dad's right. I mean, we both trusted George Niven. He was Dad's oldest friend, the person he'd left me with to take care of me, and nei-ther one of us could tell he'd hooked up with a wife who was trying to kill me. And then there was George himself. He got Dad captured in the Caribbean.

And me? Everything I believed in has fallen apart. I thought I could trust Natasha and Tatiana, until I found the gun used to shoot at me hidden in the very same bedroom I shared with the little creep. So maybe I'm not as smart as I thought.

This is complicated, but I
have to go with the plan. Unless
Oliver shows some reason for me
to stop trusting him as much as I
have, I have to let him guide us
home. That's how missions like
this work. I have to take care of
my dad, get him healthy, and hope
his emotional outbursts go away
as the drugs leach out of his
system. And I have to follow
Oliver's lead.

Thank goodness I have my dad
back. He's reminding me to think
critically about everything and
everyone. Maybe when we're on the
train, I'll have a chance to talk
to him—really talk this through
and fill him in on how Oliver's
been acting. Maybe together we can
figure out how much to trust him.

Because right now, I want to.
And this is one thing I really
don't want to be wrong about.

I'm guiding this snowmobile across the frozen tundra, with my daughter on the back. The air is cold and refreshing. The snow is bright and sharp. But I don't feel right. I do not feel right at all.

Part of it is physical. The buzzing in my ears? It could just as easily be the snowmobile's engine—or it could be an internal ringing, the siren song that hits just before unconsciousness. I shouldn't be driving this thing. But I can't admit to Gaia how sick I still feel.

Yes, the food was nourishing and good. But I took many beatings in the short time I was in that prison. And those drugs. . . whatever they were, they've diminished my capacity to react reasonably. They are clouding my judgment. I'm useless as a father right now. Useless as an agent.

But if Loki finds out how diminished my abilities are, he's sure to strike—sooner than he'd

planned. At least this way, if I
fake feeling relatively healthy,
I can buy enough time to get back
to normal.

Focus, Tom. Focus hard.
Everything rides on your ability
to steer this snowmobile—and this
mission—as much as you can.

Then again, I have to confront
the possibility that Gaia trusted
Oliver for a reason. I raised her
to have a critical mind. And Loki
has given her enough reason to
hate him for life. She's certainly not naïve, nor is she naturally trusting in any way. Maybe
she sensed something in him that
has really changed.

Difficult as it might be to
believe, I have to accept that
possibility. I'm an agent, after
all; I'm supposed to be able to
consider any possibility, no matter how unlikely.

What a concept. My brother,
Oliver. . . could be my brother,
Oliver, once again. I buried him
years ago, deep in my heart,
accepting and mourning him as

dead. Because he was dead to me. Now, the idea that he might be resurrected. . . I don't know what to do about that. Right now, I can't even process it. I can't admit to myself how much I have missed my brother over these years, and how fantastic it would be to have him back.

My God, what if what Gaia says is true? What if Oliver is back from the dead, and Loki is really gone?

I can't focus on that now. I have to keep my defenses up as much as possible. I have to work to control my emotions. I have to fight to keep my mind focused and functional. And I have to appear much healthier than I feel.

It's a tall order. But I've fought tougher battles. And won.

I'll win this one, too.

I just hope that hum is the snowmobile after all.

# GAIA PICKED HER HEAD UP AND

peered down the mountain. In the distance she could see the railway yard. The trains were lined up, ready to rejoin the regular rails and return to Moscow. They could hop on one easily, if they could figure out which was the next to go. Otherwise they'd have to wait till one moved, then board while it was still rolling slowly. That was less safe, but surer. She tucked her head back into the wind-free zone behind her father's back. They were still a long way away; it would be a while before they got there. She tried to calculate in her head how fast they'd have to move and how much time they'd have to get on the train, mentally rehearsing the moves she'd have to use, flexing her muscles to keep them warm.

Gaia relaxed as much as she could on the back of the snowmobile. It wasn't as cozy as the train car. For one thing, the wind was freezing wherever her skin was exposed, and she had to keep shifting so she wouldn't get frostbite. Not to mention that this was a snowmobile, not an upholstered couch on steel wheels: She couldn't exactly lean back and have a snooze. But the steady buzzing of the engine and the smooth sailing of the journey were enough to lull her into a state of calm.

Until she sensed something strange. Like when she

was riding the subway and it took on too much speed. Or when she was in an old elevator and it dipped unexpectedly before stopping at a floor. She picked her head up again. She could see Oliver and Jake up ahead, on the right, and she squeezed her father's arm to make sure he saw them, too.

She felt a distressing lack of response. Something was wrong.

She shook Tom's shoulders and felt the snowmobile waver in response. She couldn't even tell if he was conscious or not. But it was clear something was going drastically wrong. Gaia clung to him for dear life as the snowmobile skipped over the snow at a ludicrous speed. Wiping out at seventy-five miles per hour would turn them both into red smudges in the white snow.

She had to get it under control—and fast!

Tom and Oliver, identical in every way, sat on opposite sides of the *which one?* fire, both glaring into the flames.

GAIA POUNDED ON HER FATHER'S
**peculiar** back, trying to wake him from whatever stupor he was in as they sped across the snowy plane. Her fists bounced off him like pebbles, he was so steely and tense. She shouted at him, then reached as far forward as she could and grabbed the handlebars of the snowmobile. It was tough—she could barely reach—but if she shoved herself forward, she could just get a handhold. She tried to squeeze down on the hand brakes. The bike slowed, but wobbled again because her balance was off. Gaia let go and they sped up again.

To make matters worse, they had almost caught up to Oliver and Jake. The two of them were looking back curiously. She tried to shout to them to keep away— that she was out of control—but the words were whipped out of her mouth by the wind. She just prayed they'd steer clear—literally.

The next step was going to be tricky. She could lose a leg if they landed wrong. But if it was her leg versus all four of them in a midsnow collision, she'd have to make the sacrifice. It was a gamble she had to take.

This was where having no fear came in handy. She knew pain might be coming, but that didn't stop her from doing what she had to do.

Gaia wrenched the steering mechanism to the left,

yanking herself and Tom off course and causing a sickening lurch. The snowmobile, like a puzzled horse, tried to stay on course, but the sudden change of direction threw it completely out of control. Gaia pushed forward so she'd be flung back when the snowmobile crashed, which it did almost immediately. She landed on the icy crust of snow with a brutal crack. Tom landed facedown and spread-eagle, like a snow angel, and the snowmobile spun wildly a few times, then lay on its side, still buzzing, then shorting out and stalling with a hopeless cough.

It was a good thing they were close enough to the railway, because the snowmobile was dead.

Oliver and Jake pulled up immediately. Oliver hopped off and ran over, first pulling Gaia to a sitting position.

"Gaia! Are you all right?" he asked. "My God, what happened? Did you lose control?"

"Uh. . . I don't know," she said, thinking fast. Had her dad tried to kill Oliver in a fit of drug-induced rage? Had he briefly lost consciousness? Was he sicker than she realized? Whatever the case, it wouldn't be smart to let Oliver know there was any weakness at all. Just in case there was more Loki in him than she thought.

"Get Dad," she said. "Here, let me." She stood, wincing in pain at the wrenched feeling in her leg, and ran over to him. She flipped him over on his back and was relieved to see him blink up at the darkening sky. He turned his head toward her.

"Your nose," he said. "You're bleeding."

*Oh, crap.* She swiped the blood away and tilted her head back.

"I'm fine," she said. "The snowmobile lost control. Right, Dad?"

She peered down at him sidewise, hoping he'd play along.

It took him a moment longer than it should have, but his mind clicked into sync with hers.

"It lost control," he agreed. "Damn thing must be fifteen, twenty years old."

"Well, at least it got us here," Oliver said. "I'm glad you're all right."

Jake looked at Tom curiously, but he was busying himself taking care of Gaia's nose.

"What happened?" she hissed up at Tom.

"I'm not sure," he said. "I think I lost consciousness."

"Is that really what happened?"

They stared at each other, wary. Gaia wasn't sure if her dad was all the way back from his drug- and prison-induced weakness yet. Tom wasn't sure he could—or should—admit to her how weak he really was. So the silence blossomed between them, replete with the aroma of distrust.

But they were father and daughter, after all. The

moment passed, and they stood up, trudging behind Jake and Oliver toward the rail yard.

Since they couldn't actually enter until well after nightfall, they set up camp in the woods at the edge of the plain, in view of the railway yard but far enough away that they wouldn't seem suspicious. They set the temporary shelter up, all vinyl and space-age metal rods. It was surprisingly comfortable, creating a little igloo of warmth. They built a fire, creating a ring of wood to house the unlikely element of heat in the frozen tundra. Oliver unpacked more of the aluminum foil–style blankets.

"I'll never understand how these work," Gaia said. "They're warmer than fur."

"They used to sleep under shiny metal blankets on *Star Trek*," Jake pointed out. "I knew that show was ahead of its time. It always looked kind of uncomfortable, but now I get it."

Gaia smiled at him gratefully. Okay, so things wouldn't be as easygoing as they'd been on the train ride up to the prison. But if she could just get everyone talking, maybe she could reevaluate Oliver's trustworthiness—and assess how incapacitated Tom was.

It seemed impossible, though. Tom and Oliver, identical in every way, sat on opposite sides of the fire, both glaring into the flames like they were waiting for a phoenix to hoist itself up and into the sky. Their low-slung camping chairs sagged, not just under their weight, but under the weight of their respective bad feelings. Tom had pounds of suspicion, and Oliver, it seemed, had pounds of guilt.

Gaia spread a blanket on the ground and sat between them, facing the fire. If her dad was high noon, her uncle was 6 P.M., and she was three o'clock. Time for a truce — of sorts.

Jake sat down next to her. With a rush she realized she'd barely spoken to him in the last twenty-four hours or longer. It was strange—she'd missed him. And she wanted to talk to him now. To explain the strange tension between her father and Oliver. From his point of view, her dad was probably just a peculiar, scattered, ungrateful jerk. If you didn't know he was shot full of sedatives, and that Loki was a seriously evil overlord who had taken over Oliver's consciousness for the better part of the last twenty years, you might have thought that.

But this was no time for an intimate tête-à-tête. She had to play ambassador.

She cleared her throat. "So, did I mention that my dad and my uncle are twins?" Gaia asked. Ostensibly she was talking to Jake, but she said it loud enough for everyone to hear. "My—my mom used to tell me that when they were kids, they dressed alike. Not by choice. She said their mom made them. Their mom had a picture with both of them in sailor outfits. She couldn't even tell which was which, they looked so similar. It always cracked her up."

"Sailor outfits," Jake said, playing along. "I didn't know they really made those."

"I saw the picture when I was a kid. It was pretty funny. Dorky. Extremely dorky."

A silence so loud it seemed to scream settled over the campfire. It crackled hopefully, but neither man said a word.

"My dad was kind of a nerd," Gaia said. "They both went to Columbia University."

"Oh, my dad's dying for me to go there," Jake said.

"I couldn't stand those sailor suits," Tom muttered, staring into the flames. He didn't sound angry. But he didn't sound exactly friendly, either. "I put mine on to make Mother happy, but I did feel extremely. . . dorky."

"I didn't mind," Oliver said. "It was clean and white. That appealed to me."

The two of them were addressing their comments to the fire, not to each other.

"Yes," Tom added after a pause. "Oliver did like things neat. His side of the room was always well ordered and tidy."

"And Tom made a point of not being neat," Oliver said. "Right after that photo was taken, he ran off into the woods. Came back so covered in dirt, bark, and sap, the suit would never get clean again. Mother had no choice but to throw it out. That was the end of our naval careers."

Gaia gave a snorting laugh, which set her nose bleeding again. She had to tilt her head back, pack snow on it, and lean against Jake. Which almost made it pleasant.

"So you stopped dressing alike?" she asked.

"Yes," Oliver said.

"No, not really," Tom disagreed. "We had a lot of the same clothes. You just couldn't tell because mine were always several shades darker than his."

"Hah." Gaia gave a less snorty laugh.

Silence blew in again, but a less uncomfortable version this time. Gaia watched the two men. They weren't looking at each other, but their conversation—stilted, not quite easy, but a few sentences of conversation nonetheless—had limped along with nobody punching anybody else. They'd even shared a little family memory. Okay, so they weren't exactly skipping down memory lane together. But this was a step in the right direction.

She stared into the flames, skootching a bit closer so that the heat enveloped her. The blanket reflected the heat back onto her, and the one around her shoulders kept it next to her skin; it was very, very cozy.

She knew she should take this moment to tell her father about Natasha. The longer she waited, the harder it would be. She stared at the flames licking at the wood and dancing up and down. This was so nice. Like being next to a fireplace.

This was the first time Tom had relaxed since the rescue, she told herself. She didn't want to shatter his calm. Obviously this particular imprisonment had been harder for him than most of his adventures. Maybe it was the drugs, maybe he was getting older. Maybe it was because he'd only escaped another prison two weeks before and hadn't quite gotten over that one. But if she told him about Natasha, she'd make it worse. Better to let him gather some strength before giving him more bad news.

She'd tell him later.

## JAKE WATCHED GAIA DROWSING BY

the fire. For the first time, he was hit by the full oddity of this situation. He was a high school student from Manhattan who'd had his eye on an interesting-looking girl. And now he was in the middle of nowhere on another continent, looking at that same girl, who had

## Weapon of Mass Destruction

turned out to be more interesting than anyone had a right to be. It was nuts.

Gaia's head gave that falling-asleep nod, then jerked back up. Her eyes darted left and right, to make sure her dad and her uncle hadn't seen. Then she pulled her knees up to her chin and rested her head there, looking into the flames again. Something dangerous was happening here. Jake sensed that. Dangerous in a different way from the bricks being flung at him or bullets grazing his shoulder. Something about the way Gaia pulled her cap down over her forehead, or stared into the flames, or scratched her nose (angrily, like it pissed her off by itching) gave Jake the feeling that she could destroy him more completely than any weapon of mass destruction. He was falling in love. At least, he thought he was. With Gaia. And that seemed more perilous than any of the other stuff.

Her head slid off her knees and she pulled them up more tightly, still not able to get comfortable. Jake knew that the safe thing would be to stay right where he was, maybe organize some of their camping gear a little better or scrape out some extra food from a pot. But the safe thing had never appealed to him. He walked over to Gaia and sat down on her blanket, leg-to-leg and hip-to-hip. Gaia didn't give him a look. She didn't give him a wisecrack. She just, miraculously, laid her head on his shoulder, without a word.

Jake sat rigidly, not sure what to do. He couldn't think of anything to say. He didn't want to ruin the moment—if it *was* a moment. Was it a moment? Was he having a moment with Gaia Moore? Now it was his turn to look back and forth from her dad to her uncle. All he wanted to do was put an arm around her shoulder. No, if he was going to be honest about it, what he wanted to do was lay her on her side and curl his body around her, keeping her warm and—for a few minutes, anyway— safe. Not that she wanted saving, but somehow that only made it even more imperative that he take care of her.

But talk about dangerous: She basically had `two dads who could kick Jake's ass in a heartbeat.` Not to mention that she could, too. His arm stayed where it was.

"How are you doing?" he finally murmured in a low voice. He was answered with a long, slow snore.

"Oh. That's good," he answered.

He tried to listen in on Oliver and Tom's conversation, still droning on over his head. But the campfire was awfully warm. Plus there was Gaia's body heat. And the comfort of being so close to her. It was pretty irresistible.

Funny how anyplace could feel cozy if you were with the right company, he thought.

And then he was asleep, too.

# THE PIERCING BLAST OF A TRAIN

## A Dad-Sized Arm

whistle jolted Gaia and Jake awake. They both sat up, blinking, realizing they'd been pretty much curled up together. Gaia also realized she'd been drooling.

"Ugh. Sorry," she said. "My head feels like a science experiment. What's going on?"

The sky was a deep violet color, almost black; the only lights were the ones from the rail yard. It had to be three in the morning. The fire was gone, stamped out and covered in snow by Oliver, while Tom was packing away the last of their camping equipment, except for the blankets Gaia and Jake were using.

"Give me those," he said. "Are you awake? Sorry, I know it's late."

"No, I'm fine." Gaia stood and folded one of the blankets. Jake folded the other one. Then he took some snow and rubbed it across his face.

"Man, I was really out," he said.

"Shake a leg," Oliver said, handing one of them a pack. "Come on, that's our train right there. It should be coming past us in a few minutes."

The train chugged out of the railway yard, moving toward them slowly. But as it got closer, Gaia saw that it was going faster than it had seemed. The four of them started running at top speed. Tom hopped on first, then Jake, and then Gaia was supposed to go. She just didn't make it the first time, so she kept running. Oliver hopped up easily.

Gaia could feel the train moving faster. She didn't want to be left behind here. She also didn't want to be the reason everyone else had to jump off. This was stupid. She had to get on. The big black open door of the freight car loomed over her, but she was just a little shorter than the two men and Jake, and she couldn't quite reach the metal handle.

"Gaia!"

She looked up to see an arm reaching for her. A dad-sized arm. She reached up for it and grabbed, and felt her feet leave the ground. As she twisted around, yanking her legs up so she could step on the small metal ladder-steps without getting herself chopped to bits, she suddenly realized she couldn't tell which man had grabbed her, Oliver or Tom. She looked up, still clinging tightly to the steps, ready to swing herself inside the door.

"Come on!" he yelled.

The only light was from the moon; they looked so alike. Was it Oliver? Was it Tom? Did it matter? There was a time when she hadn't even known which one was her father in the first place. So maybe it didn't matter. Maybe family was family, for better or for worse.

She reached out her free arm and grabbed him around the shoulders; his arm snaked around her and pulled her firmly into the train. She was safe. Whoever had done it, she was safe.

**Amazing.** Crazy and amazing. Over the years, I've had an interesting and varied relationship with the concept of "dad." First my dad was the head of my perfect little nuclear family— though it was a little intense, I'll admit. I was cut off from the rest of the world and homeschooled, and reading *The Canterbury Tales* in Middle English at the age of ten, not to mention being trained harder than a circus performer in the fighting arts. So first my dad was my taskmaster and coach.

Then he was gone, and I was furious. I had no dad at all for what, five years? The whole time I was dealing with my mom's death.

Then I thought Oliver was my dad. And Oliver was evil, so I had an evil dad.

Then I found my real dad, and found out he was my real dad, and saw the letters that told me he had loved me all along. So I had a dad again. A great dad. The dad I'd always wanted.

GAIA

Then my evil not-dad became my. . . well, my dependable uncle. And now my dependable uncle is acting like. . . a dad.

I don't know—I've spent my life feeling really unfortunate. I mean, I *have* been unfortunate. I've had a lot of horrible, horrible things happen to me and to the people I love. But maybe this is one way the universe is making it up to me.

Maybe that dad-face is finally going to be a face I can trust without asking myself who's behind it. Without wondering, "Is it my real dad? Is it the dad who's on my side?" Maybe anyone who looks at me with those eyes and that expression is someone I can count on. For once in my life, maybe I don't have to process that one bit of visual information.

All I know is, whoever grabbed me got me on this train. The arm that pulled me in was strong and safe. And I don't care which of those twins it belonged to. I trust them both. They both—sort of—feel like my dad.

Maybe there was a Hallmark card she could send. A soft-focus picture **lost** with fancy script: *Just Wondering If You're Still Evil?*

# Quadrupled

THE FREIGHT CAR WAS AS LONG AS three taxicabs at least, and huge inside. Gaia was amazed. The only time she'd seen one of these had been in an electric train set, and it had been, well, about the size of her foot. It smelled musty, like too much stuff had been moved in and out of its ancient interior without a trip to the trainwash. It was an unidentifiable smell—sort of like grain, plus electronics, plus feet.

"Well, this is cheerful," she said.

She stood near the door, carefully holding on to the wall, feeling the slightly violent swaying of the train beneath her feet, and tried to figure out how to get comfortable. Finally, they all gingerly dropped to the wooden floor, which was somehow harder than concrete, and stared out the doorway at the rushing fields and woods they were passing.

"Well, the trip here was a lot more comfortable," Jake said. "What I wouldn't give for that pack of cards right now."

"Or the mystery sandwiches," Gaia laughed. "I'm freezing. I mean, literally. Should we yank that door closed?"

"At least partway," Tom said. He and Jake gave it a couple of tugs, and the ancient metal creaked its way close to shutting. Now the biting wind couldn't get to them, but the gloom was quadrupled. They huddled as near the dim moonlight of the doorway as they could.

Gaia and Tom were on one side of the door, Oliver and Jake on the other. There was nothing to do now but wait to get to Moscow. They rode, swaying with the train's movement, waiting.

"The trip up was much easier," Gaia said. "I feel bad."

"No need to apologize. This is the best way," Tom said. "They are going to be on the lookout for me. We can't be seen hopping into first class just a few miles from the prison I got out of. That'd just be asking for trouble."

"I guess. It was a nice ride, though. It's a shame they stuck you in a prison here—the mountains are gorgeous, and I saw some people who looked like they were on a horseback-riding trip or something. It looked like fun. But I'm sure you weren't noticing the lovely mountain peaks from your cell, huh?"

"Well, I've learned to find the good in whatever crazy situation I find myself in," Tom said. "Over the years, you know. You've had to do the same thing, haven't you? You found Washington Square Park even when you were living with George Niven and hating it."

"Well, it's a skill I could improve upon," Gaia admitted. "I mean, it's not something I work at. It's a lot easier to just be pissed off all the time."

"That, you've got a talent for," Tom teased.

Gaia laughed.

"Thank you," he added.

"For what?"

"For coming to get me. I'm quite sure that whatever Oliver did—and it's clear he did a lot—you were behind it. I know how you are. I wish you hadn't run such a risk, but I do appreciate it. And I'm glad to be out."

"Well, it was no problem." Gaia patted her father's leg. "Just another family adventure. I just wish I could have gotten here sooner. I felt so horrible, sitting around in the city while you were God-knew-where."

"I'll never know how you tracked me down. . . ." Tom shook his head. "This is no life for you to be leading," he said. "Too much danger, too much upheaval. You haven't had a moment to just be a normal girl, not in your entire life. When we get back, things are going to be different. We're going to settle down and be a family."

Gaia's chest began to tighten. She'd known that the subject of family and future would come up eventually. She just wished it didn't have to be now. But it *was* now. There was no more avoiding it. She'd have to tell her father the truth about Natasha and Tatiana. She'd just have to plunge right in and not let herself think about it.

"Dad," she started. Her voice cracked as she spoke. But her father didn't stop to let her speak. He seemed transported.

"You, me, and. . . I guess you know Natasha and I are going to get married. We'll really be a family. Just pick up where we left off when I got poisoned and kidnapped. We'll finish that dinner, but this time I won't choke. That's a promise."

Gaia was silent.

"Gaia?"

*Now,* she commanded herself. *No more waiting. Just jump right in before he has another opportunity to interrupt.* She steeled herself, then took in a deep breath.

"Sssh!" Tom held a hand up.

Gaia stared into the darkness. She'd been so focused on the terrible truth at hand, she hadn't heard whatever was making him nervous. She was about to say something when—

"*Ugh!*" she shouted.

A pair of rough hands had reached out from the darkness and grabbed her around the throat. Clearly they weren't alone on the freight car.

# GAIA ROLLED FARTHER INTO THE

pitch blackness with whoever had grabbed her. The stench was choking. Her attacker hadn't bathed in a long, long time, which meant he **Crunch**

probably wasn't well fed, either. If her eyes would just get used to the darkness, she could beat him, no problem. But she had no way to gauge where he was, or whether he had friends.

"Gaia!"

"What happened?"

"There are squatters on the train—agh!"

From the sound of it, the others were being attacked, too. This was some way for their story to end—they'd made it out of a prison riot only to get jumped by some rail-riders for their pocket money? That wasn't going to happen. She stood, but the rocking of the train threw her down again. She felt hands scrabbling down her body, trying to find a wallet or money hidden in her pockets.

"Don't get fresh," she spat, using the distraction to jam an elbow into her attacker's face. She felt bone crunch against bone as his nose took the blow; maybe she'd broken it. That'd level the playing field a bit.

She crouched in the darkness, wishing she could get her back against a wall. "Where are you?" she yelled. "Dad! Open the door, someone open the door!"

She heard some "oofs" and "ughs" as Jake and Oliver and Tom fought their own individual battles, and then finally she heard the door roll wide open. The moon had risen while they were inside, and it spilled brilliant white light so bright it actually hurt Gaia's eyes. It was a good thing the night was clear. If she hadn't been able to see, she didn't know if she could have taken these attackers.

In the light, though, she could see what she was up against: not much. The vagrants were half-starved. The man who had attacked her looked young, but old before his time. He was missing every other tooth, and his hair was falling out—not from male-pattern baldness, but from malnutrition. It was obvious that he and his companions had spent too many cold nights eating too little food. And they were used to getting no resistance at all from the people they robbed.

Gaia's assailant jumped at her again. This time, she pulled her punches. A real blow from her could kill him. She wasn't ready to have blood on her hands. Not for this. She shoved him back and he grabbed her around the waist, trying to knock her to the ground once more. He was surprisingly quick. Plus, he was used to the swaying train and knew how to use it to his advantage. She tumbled back and hit the wall with her head. Momentarily dazed, she took a second to regroup.

"In the middle," Tom shouted. Their best bet, the four of them, was to somehow get back together and form a unified front at the center of the car. But the rail-riders were determined. Someone grabbed Gaia's hair, slammed her head against the wall one, two, three times. It made her angry more than it hurt.

"Cut it out," she growled. "*Ow*. What the—?" She grabbed her own hair and yanked it out of her assailant's grasp. She came face-to-face with a girl about her age, but filthy and visibly defeated by a difficult life.

Gaia was too angry to care. She decked the girl with a swift punch and kicked the other guy out of her way.

She got to the center of the car, where the other three were already together, and they stood back-to-back (-to-back-to-back, since there were four of them) to face the vagrant attackers. She thought there were about eight of them, but there might have been more. That explained why it smelled so bad in here. And now it was freezing, as the wind blew right in the wide-open doors. They all stood glaring at each other, the vagrants looking for any sign of weakness, Gaia and her crew just hoping they wouldn't have to do any more damage. Their packs had already been taken, dragged off to a corner to be plundered. The rail-riders had really hit the jackpot.

"Now, we're not going to need our camping supplies any longer," Tom said. "But I hope our travel documents are somewhere handy?"

"In a belt under my clothes," Oliver said. "Only. . . oh."

"What?"

"Well, the one that attacked me, he ripped it off. I can see it over there. That one has it. See?"

Gaia wanted to roar with frustration. A pint-sized man with enormous ears and spindly fingers had the belt in question. "That guy?" she asked. "I mean, we can take him. If someone gets my back, I'll go get it."

"Hang on," Tom said. He spoke in Russian, asking for the belt, and promising the rail-riders to give up everything else if they could just have their passports.

The guy answered with a laugh. He had a point. Why give up anything?

"We're going to have to go for it," Gaia said. "Come on, just cover me and I'll get it."

Without warning, Oliver leapt from his post and wrestled the belt-stealer to the floor, easily and handily, taking the belt without much of a struggle. The other vagrants started to attack, but he shoved them back with a vicious windmill kick that sent two of them flying—one nearly out the door.

"Oliver!" Gaia yelled. "That wasn't in the plan."

"Sorry. Too much discussion," Oliver said.

"But you didn't have to—"

"I had to get this back."

He had a point. Then again, his attack had been more vicious than Gaia thought necessary. But it broke their attackers. Any aggression the little hangdog band of enemies had had left was now spent. They settled down, almost literally licking their wounds and going through their newly acquired backpacks, pleased with all the camping equipment and, of course, the food.

"Should we try to get the rest of the stuff back?" Jake asked.

"We really don't need it," Tom said. "We probably would have dumped it all before getting on the plane. Easier if we travel light."

"He's right. May as well let them keep it," Oliver added.

Without another word, Gaia, Jake, Tom, and Oliver sank to the floor, making a little star, with their legs as the points sticking out. They were going to have to spend the rest of their trip vigilantly watching and making sure they kept the rail-riders at bay so they could keep the belt Oliver had fought so viciously for. There was no time for a heart-to-heart. Giving Tom the bad news about Natasha—that would have to wait.

Gaia sat, feeling an uneasy wave of confusion rising inside her. Oliver was good. She trusted him. He'd helped her all this way. But at the same time, that last confrontation—it had made her nervous. Fed into the suspicion her father had reawakened in her. If it had been Jake who'd taken the belt back with such fury, she would have chalked it up to being overenthusiastic and young. If it had been Tom, she'd have excused him because he was freaked out and tired and obviously having some kind of difficulty readjusting.

But it had been Oliver. And even with all the new-found trust he'd earned, Gaia found her mind returning immediately to Loki.

Who'd gotten that belt back? Oliver—or Loki?

Gaia needed to know. But it wasn't exactly the kind of thing you could just blurt out as a question. Maybe there was a Hallmark card she could send. A `soft-focus picture with fancy script`: *Just Wondering If You're Still Evil?*

Guess not.

Anyway, all she could do now was sit tight and hope to get to Moscow in one piece, with the other three in tow. She could figure the rest out later. For now, everybody in her little circle seemed trustworthy enough.

For now.

## HOURS LATER, GAIA NOTICED THE

little sliver of scenery she could see through the slats of the door changing rapidly.

**Faux Goatee**

"We're getting close to Moscow," she said.

"What's the plan now?" Jake asked. "The train's slowing."

"We'll ride it into the station," Oliver said. "From there I can get us to the Metro, which we can take to the airport."

"What, like the subway?"

"Yes."

"Is that wise?" Tom asked. "I'd think the police would empty these freight trains before the homeless got to the city."

"Not in Moscow," Oliver told him. "The homeless problem is so big here, the homeless live in the train stations. There aren't any shelters. And if any police hassle us, we can bribe them easily."

"How do you know all this?" Gaia asked.

"Better that you don't know," he told her, and she heard that uncomfortable chord sound in her heart again. As Oliver, her uncle was mighty helpful; as Loki, he couldn't begin to make up for his horrible acts. After her initial rush of joy over having such a great ally, she was beginning to mistrust him again. . . or maybe her dad's attitude was rubbing off on her. Either way, she felt sort of lost.

The pale light of dawn vanished as they entered a long tunnel. It was too late now, anyway. They were on their way to the Moscow train station. If Oliver was right, they'd have no problem.

In short order, Oliver turned out to be a hundred percent right. The inside of the train station was like an underground version of the ritzier, normal station above. The minute the train stopped, their companions—now loaded down with their new, stolen camping equipment—filed off politely, saying good-bye to one another like tourists leaving a hostel on a backpacking trip, and barely glancing back at Gaia and her miserable little huddle. She finally shifted her position, feeling a horrible stiffness in her joints after so many hours of tense watching and waiting.

"Well, no sense sitting around," she said, and

hopped off after them. Tom, Oliver, and Jake followed after her. "Where to now?" she asked Oliver.

"This way," he said. "There's an entrance to the Metro system that's supposed to be for employees only. Follow me."

Tom looked around warily as they walked through the station. Gaia wasn't sure if he wanted them to stick with Oliver or set out on their own. She took him by the arm. "How are you feeling?" she asked him. "Are you still groggy?"

"I wasn't groggy," he snapped. "Just a little. . . disoriented."

"Okay, sorry." Gaia said. "Are you feeling better now?"

"Yes, I am. I'm just not sure about this," he told her.

"I know. What do you want to do?"

He turned toward her and studied her face. "What do you think we should do?"

Gaia blinked, a bit surprised. "Well. . . ," she said. "Actually, I think we should stick with the plan. Things have gone fine so far. And I don't want to leave Jake with someone potentially dangerous. If something goes wrong, it's three on one—I think we'll be okay."

He kept looking at her. "You really do, don't you? You trust Oliver."

She shrugged. "I think it's safer than taking off on our own." She paused a moment. "And yes. I actually feel okay about him."

Tom vanished into his thoughts for a moment. "I

have to tell you something," he said. "I'm really not well."

"I know," she said.

"Yes. Of course you would." Tom squeezed her arm back. "I'm going to have to follow your lead on this."

"Oh."

Gaia didn't want to take the lead on this. The consequences were so enormous. Besides, since she'd reconnected with her dad, she'd grown used to having him around for the big questions. Or at least wishing he was around to make the big decisions. Now he was here, and he was telling *her* to make the call?

That was a twist. Like being on a train where the conductor asks the passenger what stop is next.

But if that was the way it was going to be, she'd have to go with it.

"Okay," she said. "Then we stick to the plan." She tried to feel as confident as she sounded.

"I'm going to be watching carefully," he added. "I'm going to be watching Oliver for any signs of Loki. If he pulls anything suspicious—"

"It's okay." Gaia rubbed his bicep reassuringly. "I think it's going to be okay. It's one stupid plane ride—how much could go wrong?"

The minutes she said it, she wished she'd kept her mouth shut. He shot her a smile. "Let's just get back home and sort it out then," he said.

"Jake's got good news," Oliver said, slowing down

to join them. "He saved the pack that had the disguises in it."

"Jake!" Gaia cheered. "Look at you! How did you hide that?"

"I think they just didn't see it in all the confusion," Jake told her. "It was much smaller than the other packs and it was stuck behind me when we were sitting with our backs to each other."

"That's pretty impressive, Jake," Gaia said. Jake waved her off—he already knew how impressive he was.

They stepped into a utility room to pull their new act together. Oliver stuck an elaborate blond beard on his face—not too shaggy, but thick enough to cover the line of his jaw and make him look totally different. With his hair under a wig, he was unrecognizable.

Tom, on the other hand, went midlife-crisis groovy: he slicked his hair back with gel and lengthened it with a fake ponytail. Jake swapped a couple of items of clothing with him—a trendier sweater, too-young jeans.

"Wow, you look kind of slimy," Gaia commented.

"Well, thank you," Tom grumbled. "I'm so glad I had a daughter."

Gaia laughed. "Well, it's better than looking like an escaped prisoner. Maybe I should travel with you, and you can pretend I'm your girlfriend."

"That's much too disturbing," Oliver said, shaking

his head. "Gaia and Jake are going to be boyfriend-girlfriend, college kids traveling abroad. Tom and I will be on our own. We're going to travel in separate Metro cars from this point forward."

Gaia stopped laughing and turned to Oliver. She wanted to make sure she got the plan straight. And his expression was grave.

"Tom knows what I'm about to say. From now on, we do not know each other. This is the most dangerous leg of our trip. We're the most vulnerable here. We still do not know exactly who took Tom, but if the government is involved, they're going to have agents looking for us at the airport."

"They can't hold us. We can cause an international incident," Jake said.

"They can't arrest us legally, but they can 'disappear' us—we can be kidnapped easily. Try to stay in sight of official police whenever possible. Everybody have bribe money ready. And if you see someone else captured, keep going. An airport isn't the place for any kind of vigilante justice. Security is too tight. And if we all get taken, nobody knows where we are. The only chance we'll have is if one of us gets out and contacts someone to help us."

"And who the hell would that be?" Gaia demanded to know. "I needed you to get here in the first place."

"Don't worry. Your father has even better contacts than I do," Oliver pointed out. "But if worst comes to worst, I left information in my apartment. Whoever makes it back to the States can start the process over again. Or not," he said, with a glance at Tom. "That would be your choice."

He handed out their documents, rubles, and tickets. "Well, it's been nice knowing you," he said. "The Metro is down this corridor and to the right. You're taking the yellow line to the airport. Can't miss it." The door flopped shut behind him, and Oliver was gone.

Tom turned to Gaia. "Okay, I'm sticking to the plan," he said dubiously. "I hope you're right about this."

Gaia hugged him, careful not to dislodge his `faux goatee`. "I'll see you on the airplane," she said. "Just be careful."

She and Jake held hands—almost like a real couple, Gaia thought. As they left the closet and boarded the train, she saw their reflections in a window. It was amazing: After the night on the gross train, the days camping, they looked just like a shaggy hippie couple. It surprised her a little to see herself looking so normal. What surprised her more was how much she liked it. Not just looking normal, but looking normal holding hands with Jake.

She pulled her hand back. Not rudely. Just kind of slipped it out of his and pretended to be looking for something in her pocket.

"What are you looking for?" Jake asked. "Everything okay?"

"Yep, fine," she said, patting her leg like she'd just found whatever it was. The conditioned response she'd been having against normalcy had passed. When Jake reached for her hand again, she couldn't think of an excuse in the world not to let him.

And it felt really good. To let him hold her hand.

He looked down at her, smiling, like they were both in on a secret plan. Which, of course, they were. Except Gaia had the sudden realization that there was more between them than a shared mission and a Siberian adventure. She tugged his hand and looked up at him.

"I don't want you getting any ideas," she said.

"Ideas?" he asked.

"About us. When we get back to New York, we're still just friends. Really good friends. But that's all."

Jake looked at her, then shrugged nonchalantly. "Yeah, okay."

He kept her hand in his and gazed out the window of the train. Gaia tried not to feel disappointed that he wasn't arguing his case.

"You're okay with that?" she asked.

"Sure," Jake said. "Just friends. That's okay."

Once they arrived at the airport, Gaia and Jake stepped off. She looked up and down the long platform; sure enough, Oliver had been in the first car, her father in the third. She tried to pace herself so she'd always remain about thirty feet behind them—not so close that they looked like they were traveling together, but not so far that she couldn't keep a close eye on everyone in her group.

The act of entering the airport and looking for their gate was easy. All they had to do now was get through the metal detectors and walk onto the plane. The airport was mobbed with people, teeming with tourists and business travelers. There was no way someone was going to mess with them here. Besides, the guards were about a hundred times more serious here than in JFK Airport in New York. For one thing, they carried Uzi machine guns. For another thing, they looked like they knew how to use them.

Gaia almost started to relax when Oliver made it through the metal detector and headed up the ramp toward their gate. She could see Tom's black ponytail as he waited his turn to go through the metal detector. Near him were two local police officers who looked no more official—or trustworthy—than the one who'd tailed her on the L train. They walked over to Tom, asking a few questions.

"I'm sure it's all right," Jake murmured, returning the squeeze she didn't know she was giving his hand.

It wasn't. It didn't seem to be. Now they pulled him out of the line, off to the side. He was answering their questions calmly, giving a perfect imitation of an annoyed but cooperative dude on the move. But they were eyeing him in a way that made Gaia uneasy. She started to move toward him. Jake jerked her hand back.

"We're on orders not to stop," he said.

"But Oliver's through," she said.

"Gaia. Orders. Stop it," Jake pleaded.

Gaia took her eyes off her father to make sure Oliver was through. If she saw him board the plane, she would go after her dad. Jake could go back with Oliver, and at least she'd be here to keep him company—with the kidnappers. Or in jail, or whatever. She wasn't going to leave him—

That was strange.

"What the—?"

Oliver had stopped to look back. He seemed to glance through the metal detectors, as though he were checking on them. She saw his eyes pass over her, then stop on her dad. Oliver's demeanor seemed to change a bit. He stiffened. What was he thinking? He was supposed to keep moving. His own orders.

She watched as he moved backward slowly, smoothly, almost like he was on roller skates. Without even turning around, he stepped inside a doorway and disappeared.

It was not the gate to the plane. Oliver was off course. She had no idea where he was, what he was doing, or what was happening.

*He's deserting us*, she thought. The thought

struck her with the full force of agony and betrayal. *My God. My dad was right. He turned us in, and now he's going to get his payoff. And I'm going to be captured next.*

She looked up at Jake. He'd seen Oliver disappear and looked puzzled. He turned his eyes to her.

*How do I tell him?* she thought. *We're dead. Oliver's gone. We're about to get snagged, and there's not a goddamned thing we can do.*

It was amazing
to watch how the
mirror-image
men, Tom in his
goatee and
Oliver **shatter**
in his regular
face, dusted
themselves off
in exactly the
same way.

GAIA WATCHED IN HORROR AS TOM desperately but quietly tried to talk his way out of being detained. She couldn't stare at him openly—she was still hoping not to be recognized herself—so she was stuck in a frustrating and spastic dance of stealing quick glances and then looking away as if she didn't care.

**Uzi Attention**

But even the other passengers were beginning to notice what was going on. None of them liked the attitude of the pseudocops/kidnappers—Gaia knew that was what they were—hassling Tom. Before any real officers had a chance to notice them, the kidnappers took Tom by the arm and started to lead him away from the metal detectors.

Gaia stepped forward to interfere. All bets were off. If Oliver wasn't going to stick to the plan, then she wasn't going to either.

"Look," Jake said.

Oliver was stepping back out of the door. But he had taken off his disguise. Gaia breathed in sharply.

"Is he an idiot?" she asked.

Oliver patted his pockets as if he were just a regular Joe Tourist who thought he'd forgotten something. He stepped over to the metal detector and spoke to a security guard. The guard nodded, and waved Oliver. . . back through to the main terminal.

"Oh my God, where's he going?" Gaia breathed.

"He's going to get caught for sure," Jake said.

"I think. . . oh my God, I think that might be the point."

Oliver—Oliver, with his twin-of-Tom face—stood at the other end of the bank of metal detectors, looking around like a lost tourist. Showing his face to anyone who might be curious about him. Or looking for him. Or looking for someone who resembled him. Sure enough, almost immediately, he was approached by two more fake cops.

Gaia looked back over at Tom. His kidnappers had stopped short as their walkie-talkie squawked. The ones on the other side—the ones with Oliver—spoke intensely into their walkie-talkies. Each group was convinced he had Tom Moore, the escaped prisoner from Siberia. And each was telling someone—some central operative, giving them orders—that they had him.

If it hadn't been so nerve-racking, it would have been funny, Gaia had to admit. First Tom's captors tried to walk him out the door. Then they were ordered to stop, and the other captors headed for the opposite door. Neither group could see the other—by conicidence, Gaia and Jake were situated perfectly between them. But both groups were starting to attract attention. And neither wanted to give up their prize or lose credit for bringing in the quarry.

Gaia could guess exactly what was happening. Each group was trying to take credit for capturing Tom Moore. And each side was saying, "Those other guys don't have him. They have the wrong guy. *We* have the real Tom Moore." And as far as they knew, they were right. But the guy in the middle had to be getting frustrated.

Gaia just hoped he'd get really frustrated.

It was absolutely brilliant, what Oliver had done. By seeming to be Tom Moore, he'd created a perfect decoy. He had successfully confused the operatives so much, they were tripping over their own feet and messing up their own plan.

Of course, if it backfired, he'd be in that Siberian prison instead of Tom. Gaia watched anxiously, dividing her gaze spasmatically between her father and her uncle. The bad guys were waiting too long. They were arguing too much. They were attracting attention to themselves. Airport security attention. Uzi attention. . .

With a rush of relief, she saw similar packs of legitimate lawmen approach the two packs of would-be Tom-takers. Asking why they were bothering these tourists. Sending them on their way.

"Oh my God," Jake said. "They did it."

"*He* did it," Gaia added. "Oliver did. He distracted them long enough to get the real cops involved. He saved my dad."

"Again," Jake said.

Gaia nodded. She was painfully aware of that, and felt horrible for having thought there was even a dollop of Loki still in Oliver.

It was amazing to watch how the `mirror-image men`, Tom in his goatee and Oliver in his regular face, dusted themselves off in exactly the same way. Each one thanked the guard graciously, turned, and strolled unhurriedly through his metal detector. On the other side, they were both funneled into the same corridor, where they stood almost face-to-face, paused, and then walked, pretending not to know each other, to the gate.

By that time, Gaia was at her metal detector, too. She stepped through, then waited for Jake to follow her. She was surprised to find herself trembling from the tension of the moment. She had never seen such an elegantly choreographed yet accidental operation in all her life. It was high drama of the quietest kind. She swallowed hard and stepped through the gate onto her airplane. It was all she could do not to stop and jump for joy.

They were nearly there.

GAIA WAS WORRIED ABOUT THE plane ride back. She was going to have to tell her

**Suspicions**

father about Natasha, and that was going to shatter him. She wasn't sure if he was back in control of his faculties quite yet. She didn't want to risk a confrontation between him and Oliver. Regardless of the way he'd helped them, Tom would no doubt hold Oliver responsible for Natasha's betrayal.

As a precaution, Gaia made sure her father sat at the extreme left side of the plane, and that Oliver sat on the extreme right. She even put both men in window seats. She was going to straighten this out, once and for all, and she didn't want her father distracted by Oliver's presence. The last thing she needed was an argument on her hands. On a twelve-hour flight, no less.

Once she had Tom settled, she walked across to Oliver. He and Jake had found a travel version of chess and were setting up the pieces, arguing quietly over who would get to be black.

"Oliver," she said. "I saw what you did."

He didn't look up. "Are you going to yell at me for going against my own orders?" he asked.

She laughed softly. "No. It was amazing."

He lined up the black pawns on his side of the board. "It was the least I could do," he said.

"If you'd been caught—"

"I would have dealt with the consequences." Oliver looked up. "I appreciate what you're saying, but it's not necessary. I just did what needed to be done. And it worked."

Gaia shook her head in admiration. Oliver was proving himself again and again and again. She could see that Jake totally admired him, too. Of course, he didn't understand the extent of what Oliver had done as Loki. But it was obvious how hard he was trying now.

"You'll be okay over here?" she asked Jake.

"Yeah, of course," he said. "Go sit with your dad. We'll be back in New York in no time."

Her father. Who she was going to be sitting next to for the next twelve hours or so, with no excuse not to give him the worst news he could ever hear.

"Hey," she said, flopping into her own seat next to him. "Now we can relax, right?"

"I suppose." Tom's gaze slipped across the plane, toward Oliver. He was nervous. He knew what Oliver had risked to get him on this plane—but he was a good agent, and he wasn't letting go of his suspicions. Gaia decided to let it go. No reason to force the issue. If Oliver really were reformed, her dad would figure it out in his own time.

"I'm glad you gave him this much of a chance," she said. "And so far, so good, right?"

"Yes," Tom said. "Yes, you were right about sticking to the plan. I'm just—"

"I know. He did a lot of terrible things. It's really, really hard to trust a man who tried to murder his own brother. But the brain's chemistry operates in mysterious ways. You're probably wise to be cautious at this point. I just have to say that so far, he seems nothing but sincere to me."

"Keep in mind that he's a true chameleon when he needs to be," Tom said. "It wasn't so long ago that he was still wreaking havoc. Let's not forget, he wouldn't have had to rescue me if he hadn't sent me to Siberia in the first place."

"Well, we don't know that he did that for sure," Gaia said. "Let's not forget, he was in a coma the night you choked. That's what we were celebrating, if you recall."

"Yes, well, I'm not entirely convinced that that's what happened." Tom said.

"Well, you gotta feel for the guy," Gaia said, pushing her seat into recline mode. "I've been working really closely with him. It's not that he doesn't remember his old life. He remembers everything, and he has to deal with all the terrible things he's done. A normal person might kill himself if he woke up to find he'd destroyed the lives of everyone close to him. But instead of running away, Oliver's trying to make amends. It doesn't fix things, but it counts for something, don't you think?"

Tom's answer was a long, light snore. Gaia had to laugh. Well, of course. He hadn't slept in days. He had just survived a brutal prison experience. They were all exhausted.

She adjusted his fake goatee, sticking the moustache part more firmly onto his face. She was just so glad to have him back. If only she didn't have one last, horrible task to perform.

She had to break his heart.

# Nothing is ever what you expect it to be.

On the flight over here, I thought I'd be a wreck. I wasn't sure if my dad was even alive. I was anxious and nervous, yet I was enjoying myself. What was it? Anticipation? Hope? Looking forward to a big adventure? I remember talking to Oliver and being amazed at everything he said. Amazed that we were connecting on such a deep level. I was happy, I guess. Even with all the tension and worry, I was happy.

Now everything is okay. Dad is alive, and I've gotten him out of Siberia. We're heading home. When I dreamed of this trip, I imagined it would feel like a twelve-hour-long sigh of relief. Instead, it feels like slow suffocation. As devastated and betrayed as I felt when I found out about Natasha and Tatiana, Dad's going to feel worse. Much worse. Because he loved Natasha. And he left me with her. When he finds out she was a double agent, he's not just going to be heart-broken: He's going to feel guilty. And there's nothing I can do to stop him from feeling that way. I have my dad back, and I feel terrible.

How is that possible? *This* is supposed to be the happy trip. *That* one was supposed to be the tense trip. It's like the whole world has flip-flopped. For all I know, we're flying upside-down through Opposite World.

But there it is: The arms he thinks he's coming home to have been taken away in handcuffs. I've got to tell him, and I really don't want to.

God, I am such a coward. Maybe I can't feel fear, but engaging in emotional confrontation is my idea of terror.

I hope he sleeps the whole way back.

I know Gaia's father has been in a prison and that he's been drugged. And Gaia told me a little bit about how her uncle Oliver used to be a total asshole. I mean, I didn't get all the details, but she definitely hinted at some very dark stuff. Still, it seems like her dad could be a little more grateful.

I've never seen anything like this trip. Everything was orchestrated perfectly, and even when things went wrong, Oliver figured out a solution with lightning speed. I don't see how anyone could doubt the guy's sincerity.

Don't get me wrong: I'm sure there's a good reason for all the bad blood. But from where I'm sitting, it seems like someone as smart and sharp as Gaia's dad could read this guy and see something good in him. I mean, Gaia herself isn't exactly the trusting type. How long did I have to wait around before I could even get her to talk to me? Yet she managed to find some common ground with Oliver. Enough to get herself here.

Not that it's any of my business. But when I peek across at the other side of the plane, I see Gaia watching her dad sleep, and there's so much love in the way she looks at him. More than that. Much as I think she'd hate to admit it, I think Gaia idolizes her dad. And I just hope the guy deserves it. I hope he knows something I don't, and that the hostile feelings he has toward Oliver are based in reality.

Oliver's an amazing man. I could see myself learning a lot from him. If he's done something beyond forgiveness, I don't want to know. There's too much to learn.

# TOM BLINKED AND OPENED HIS

eyes. Looking down, he could see New York off in the distance. He had slept for ten straight hours. He looked to his right. Gaia was awake, and she was smiling at him.

"I was out," he said.

"How do you feel?"

He thought about it for a moment. "Much more like myself," he said. "Much better." She handed him a small bottle of water and he drained it. Its refreshing coolness gave him an extra charge. He sat up and stretched.

"I was having the most fantastic dream," he said. "We were already home, and redoing that last dinner before I got kidnapped. Only this time it wasn't interrupted. I can't wait to get home."

"Uh, Dad. . ." Gaia's face fell.

"What's wrong?"

"I have to tell you something."

Tom was silent. He could tell it was bad news. Something Gaia was afraid to tell him, that was plain enough.

"Something happened to Natasha," he said. "Someone did something to her."

"Not exactly," Gaia said. "God, this is hard. I don't know how to start. . . . I started feeling suspicious when someone shot at me one night in a Ukrainian church. I was supposed to be meeting someone there."

"Shot at you!" Tom gripped Gaia's arm.

"I'm fine," she soothed him. "I got out of there. But after that, I tried to figure out who had set me up. Eventually, all the clues seemed to point closer to home than I would have liked."

"You're not saying—"

"I searched the apartment. Natasha and Tatiana's apartment. And I found a gun. The same gun that someone shot at me."

"It was planted. It was a plant."

"No. I hoped so, too. But then Dmitri helped me set up a sting. I let them think I'd be alone at a vacant lot in Brooklyn, and they showed up. . . and tried to. . ." Gaia's voice trailed off.

"You can't be serious."

"They tried to kill me, dad. Tatiana almost got away. And Natasha. . ." She couldn't look at him. "Natasha said horrible things. About us. About you."

"Natasha?"

Gaia stole a peek at her dad's face, then immediately wished she hadn't.

"I'm sorry. It's true. The CIA came and took them to jail. I had to make a deal with Tatiana to find out where you were—now that I found you, I have to call to let them know they can be jailed together. But they both admitted it. Proudly. They weren't who we thought they were."

Tom's face folded into a tight, closed-up package.

"But we're still a family," she said.

He didn't move.

"You and me. We have each other. Not that that's the same. But it's something."

His eyes closed. He nodded slowly. "Of course," he said. "Yes. We have each other."

But Gaia had blown out a candle, and Tom's soul was dark as a result. Any idiot could see that.

*Poof.*

And it was
Gaia's
words, the
ribbon of
air **piercing**
coming out
of her
mouth, that
had done
this to him.

# THERE ARE CERTAIN THINGS A KID

should never have to do—even a kid who's been on her own since she was twelve. And breaking her father's heart is one of them. Gaia stood outside herself and watched, her gut melting with the pain of it, as her father stared straight ahead. Behind his impassive face, she knew he was flicking through his Rolodex of memories, reliving every moment with Natasha, then smacking himself with the reality that each kiss, each kind word, each loving gesture had been a cold, empty lie. Trying to wrap his mind around the staggering loss. And it was Gaia's words, the ribbon of air coming out of her mouth, that had done this to him, choked off the only good thing in his life. Dug up the seedling of the future that he'd nurtured.

Their little hopes for a normal family had been blown apart in one tiny conversation, whispered from the aisle seat to the window seat.

The worst part was that no matter how hard she tried, Gaia couldn't soften the blow. She was so goddamned clumsy with her words, she felt like she had made it worse. When she fought, everything made sense, she could measure her strength to that of her opponent. But this? Words? Feelings? She couldn't control how hard they hit or how they made someone feel. She'd had chance after chance on this long trip, and she had put it off so long that the information had just come out in a `diarrhealike rush`. Gaia hated herself.

"Dad?" she asked, lamely. "Are you okay?"

"I'm fine," he said. He looked down, avoiding her face, as he unbuckled his seat belt. Gaia realized that the plane had landed and taxied all the way to the gate in the time she'd been in agony over this. She hadn't even noticed. She unbuckled herself and stood up. They started the long, slow shuffle to the front of the plane. In the other aisle, Oliver and Jake were making the same journey, the two men yards apart in space and miles apart in emotions. Gaia realized her father would never forgive Oliver now. He would be sure it was Oliver who'd turned Natasha against him. It was one more nail in the already-sealed coffin of their relationship.

She locked eyes with Jake and tilted her head toward the exit. He made a confused face. She eyeballed the exit again, trying to indicate to him that he should take Oliver and get him into a separate cab. She didn't know how upset her dad would be. She didn't want a confrontation in the airport. But it was no use. She just looked like `a head-bobbing, eye-rolling idiot`. Jake just shrugged, and Gaia stopped to tie her shoe so they would at least be forced to leave the plane first.

Out in the airport, Oliver and Jake waited for them. Tom walked slowly, his head bent toward the floor. Gaia approached them.

"I was thinking, we'd probably better split up. There isn't enough room at the Seventy-second Street apartment for all of us; you can stay with Oliver in Brooklyn till he decides it's safe for you to go home. Does that make sense?"

Her words hung in the air. Jake and Oliver looked curiously at Tom, who gave them the super–poker face. He stood there like a pillar of concrete.

"We'll see you soon?" Oliver asked. He directed his question toward Gaia, ostensibly, though he was looking at his brother.

"Sure. Sure, we will. After everyone gets settled in and rested," Gaia said, taking her father's arm.

Oliver, sensing that this would be the wrong time to force a brotherly moment, turned away, heading for the doors to the taxi stand. Jake hesitated and looked at Gaia.

She looked back.

"I'll call you?" he asked.

"Definitely," she said quickly.

"Not because I'm getting ideas," he said.

"Of course not. Just to hang out."

"Right." He nodded.

The block of concrete to her left was no help. Gaia felt as awkward and exposed as a fresh septum-piercing. The truth was, she was the one with ideas. About Jake. Serious ideas. And that was the last thing she needed: more romantic entanglements. Ed, she missed terribly. He just knew how to make her laugh like no one else. And she loved him for that. And Sam. . . She wasn't sure how she felt about Sam, but it pretty much wavered between guilt and lingering love. But after this intense little adventure, she thought Jake was maybe the only guy who had ever understood her—who would ever understand her.

Yikes. She wondered whether that was good or bad. If you know there's nobody out there who can understand you, you've always got a buffer zone, something they can't penetrate. But if you think someone actually *does* get your inner workings. . . you set yourself up for danger.

Being alone seemed like the obvious solution.

Except that when she was alone, she was miserable.

I've never wanted to hug someone so much in my whole life. The last few days have been so intense. I swear, Gaia and I lived a lifetime together. She told me so much about herself—more than she's ever told anyone, I'm sure of that. That's a huge deal. And a huge responsibility. I just wish there was some way I could tell her I understand that, and that I'm not going to let her down.

Who am I kidding? The most surefire way to make Gaia run screaming for the hills is to say that to her directly. It's probably a blessing in disguise that her dad and uncle had to split up before I could try to get my arms around Gaia—or kiss her. I need to take some time to chill out so I don't scare her off. Ease back into my regular life.

My regular life. Wow. That sounds so far away. I guess a lot of people would feel as if they couldn't wait to get back to some

old familiar ground, but I just
want to tell this cab to turn
around and go back to the airport
so I can get on another plane.
I've heard that war reporters get
addicted to adrenaline and can't
function if they're not trying to
type on their laptops while
they're dodging bullets. I think
I understand them. I'm never
going to be regular again. I'll
do what I have to do—bide my
time, keep my grades up, train
until my body's a perfect weapon—
but I'm going to do this again.
And again and again. Maybe I'll
join the CIA, or some other spy
organization I don't even know
about. I'll have to do my
research. But I'm never going to
be Regular Guy.

   Never have been, and now I
know I never will be.

GAIA OPENED THE DOOR TO THE

East Seventy-second Street apartment slowly. Empty apartments
have a smell to them, of dry heat
mixed with dust. She wished they
didn't have to come back here. To
the house of hope. To the bed
where Tom and Natasha used to
sleep. But there was nowhere else to go.

**Another Univers**

At least her dad seemed calmer. The taxi ride had
been good for him, apparently. At least he wasn't talking to himself anymore.

"You can have the first shower," she said, giving him
a smile. "I'll order up some food, how about that?
Pizza? Or something more nutritious? Um. . . burritos?"

"Whatever you like," he said, with a tired smile that
was supposed to be reassuring but just looked. . . tired.
"Something that will go down easy. My stomach—"

"Yeah. Like soup or something. I'll figure it out."

"Okay."

"There's ointment and stuff in there. Oh! Wait a second." She darted into the master bathroom and swept
all of Natasha's feminine belongings—her cosmetics,
her shampoos—into a bucket and shoved it all under
the sink. She'd change the sheets on the bed while he
was showering. She was going to make this as easy as
possible for him. She'd do anything to have him back.

She stepped out of the bathroom, letting him go

in, and closed the door behind him. *Phew.* First things first: Gaia had to call Dmitri and tell him to give the go-ahead to send Tatiana to her mother's jail cell. She didn't want to give them that. But she had made a promise. She picked up her cell phone, sitting in its charger on the floor next to her bed, and hit the speed-dial. The old Russian man answered on the first ring.

"I'm back," she said. "He's here. Everything's fine."

"That's good," Dmitri said. "Are you all right?"

She sighed. "Sure. But telling him about Natasha was horrible. I felt so bad."

"It can't be helped."

"I suppose. But you can tell them Tatiana can have her little reward."

"I'll do that." Gaia heard the line click off and looked at the screen, ready to dial the diner downstairs, when she noticed the little envelope at the top of her screen.

A message.

She listened and was shocked to hear Sam Moon's voice. It sounded like he was a million miles away, like a voice from another universe. Another lifetime. But when Gaia thought about it, she realized that she had just seen him the other day. On Broadway, when she'd come out of Urban Outfitters. He had moved to an apartment. He was restarting his life without her. Now he was calling her.

"I wanted to tell you where I'm working," he said

in the first message. "I mean, not where I'm living, or anything. I still need more time. But, ah, free food and all. I know how you like that, so if you want to come by. . ." He left the address, and hung up.

And there was another one. "Hi. Uh, yeah, so you didn't come by and that's cool, but I wanted you to know you can. I know yesterday I said I still needed time, but I didn't mean that completely. I've been thinking a lot about it, and I think with a little distance I can understand a bit better why you were so guarded. Why you acted the way you did. I came on too strong, and that was, you know. That was my deal. So I won't do that again." He paused. "I think I'm ready," he added. "I'd really like to try again. I'd love to give it a try. So. Call me. When you feel like it."

What? What did this mean? Gaia felt a tightening in her chest. Two messages in a couple of days. From Sam. From Sam Moon. Sam Moon had called her. Sam Moon had called Gaia Moore to say he wanted to give their relationship another shot while she'd been in Siberia battling the unknown operatives who had kidnapped her father, with the help of her formerly evil—possibly not evil—uncle and a random guy who was now her best friend.

But not just her best friend. He was someone whose heart seemed to match hers, and it was all she could do to stop herself from thinking about him.

Life. Life was just bizarre sometimes.

**Dear** Dad: Sorry I had to
break your heart. Sorry I can't
fix anything. Most of all, I'm
sorry I'm thinking about Sam and
Jake when you need me the most.

I'm also *really* sorry we're
not on that freight train, fighting with thieving vagrants, or
building a shelter in the middle
of the frozen steppe, or even
running around in the middle of a
prison riot. Because all those
things were easier for me than
figuring out this knotty little
conundrum.

Sam was the love of my life.
Is. Was. Is. Was.

Jake is the best thing that's
ever happened to me. But I don't
know what I should do about it.

Neither one of them should
matter, because you're here,
and you're hurting, and I have
to be there for you—not flying
off the handle every time a guy
calls me.

So please excuse me if I'd
rather fly off to somewhere even

GAIA

farther than Siberia to kick some
ass—any ass. Any ass at all.
Because you know what? It's easier. Matters of the ass-kick are
easier than matters of the heart,
any day.

And you heard it here first.

# here is a sneak peek of Fearless™ #30: FREAK

The last
thing she
wanted right
now was to
**trepidation**
open a
can of
emotionally
overwrought
worms.

# GAIA MOORE WAS HAVING A MOMENT

## Damn Guardian Angel

she'd probably remember forever. She was one of those rare people who had burned-in-her-memory moments all the time, but this one was different from the norm.

This one was good.

A good memorable moment was atypical in Gaia's screwed-up life. The awful ones. . . well, those came up all the time.

Like the moment she learned her mother was dead. The moment she realized that the man she thought was her father might actually be her evil uncle, Loki. The moment Mary passed away. The moment Sam was kidnapped. The moment some Loki operative fired shots at Ed. The list of gut-wrenching, miserable, devastating moments went on and on.

But a light, content, all-is-right-with-the-world moment—that came almost never. And when she realized she was having one, instead of automatically thinking of the few things that were still wrong—things that could crap all over the moment like a giant pigeon—Gaia just smiled.

For once, she was going to let herself be happy.

"I like this," Jake Montone said, lying back next to Gaia on the big mound of rock near the Columbus

3

Circle entrance to Central Park. "Who would've thought there was actually a place in this city where you could see stars? Actual ones, I mean. Famous people I've been seeing everywhere lately. It's like you get one warm day and they suddenly come out of hiding. I was almost nailed by Brad Pitt on rollerblades this afternoon in Union Square."

"Jake?" Gaia said, the back of her skull searching for a smooth bit of rock to rest on.

"Yeah?" he asked. He turned his head so he was looking at her profile.

"Shut up," she said.

"Right."

Ever since Gaia, Jake, and Oliver had returned from their little smash-and-grab job in the former Soviet Union (they'd smashed a fortress and grabbed Gaia's dad, Tom), Jake had been prone to these little fits of verbosity. Just every once in a while. Like he was a little kid who was still psyched up from a trip to an amusement park and couldn't contain his bursts of excitement. Gaia would never have admitted it, but somewhere deep down she kind of thought it was cute—in an irritating sort of way.

A jagged point bit into the back of her head and she moved again, sighing in frustration. Jake sat up, slipped out of his denim jacket, bunched it into a ball and moved to prop it under the back of her head. For a split second Gaia thought about refusing, making a crack about his chivalry and turning it into a joke, but she stopped herself. Instead she just lifted her head, then leaned back into the Jake-scented softness.

Ah. Pillow. Just one more thing to make the perfect moment last.

*All is well,* Gaia thought, taking a deep breath. She almost didn't dare to believe it, but it was true. Her father was home, safe and sound. Her uncle had been living for days now as good old normal Uncle Oliver, with no signs of Lokiness whatsoever. There was no one out there hunting her down, tracking her every move, plotting ways to take her out.

And to top it all off, she had a new friend. A real friend. Surprisingly enough, Jake Montone had turned out to be, contrary to all snap judgments, a non-moron. He was, in fact, freakishly true. Supportive. Noble almost.

"I can't believe that guy actually gets to have sex with Jennifer Aniston," he said suddenly, his brow furrowing beneath his dark hair.

Okay, so he was also still a guy. But he had already saved Gaia's life, accepted her increasingly psychotic family situation with none but the pertinent questions asked, *and* dropped everything to come to Russia with her to save her father. In a short time he'd gone beyond the call of duty, friendshipwise. He'd gone beyond the call of duty for a damn guardian angel.

"So, anybody at school ask where you were for the past few days?" Jake asked.

"Not really. The teachers are used to me disappearing, and no one else notices."

*Except Sam,* Gaia thought, her heart giving an extra-hard thump. *Sam noticed.* Sam had noticed to the tune of eight messages on her answering machine. Gaia had been more than a little surprised when she'd heard his voice over and over and over again on the tape. The last time she'd seen the guy he'd basically told her to get out of his life and stay out. By the time she was done listening to his messages it was fairly clear that he wanted the exact opposite.

*I need to call him back,* Gaia thought. But even as her brain formed the suggestion, the rest of her felt exhausted by the mere thought. The last thing she wanted right now was to open a can of emotion-ally overwrought worms. She'd much rather just stay where she was—lying on her back in the park, staring at the sky, with Jake's warmth next to her, keeping the goosebumps at bay.

"So, listen," Jake said, propping himself up on his elbow and turning on his side.

Gaia swallowed and her stomach turned. It was a loaded "so listen." The kind that was usually followed by either an unpleasant announcement like, "So listen, I'm moving to Canada." Or by an awkward silence–inducing question like, "So listen, do you want

6

to go to the prom?" Not that Gaia had ever been asked to a prom before, but she could still identify the appropriate "so listen."

She stared at the sky and held her breath, waiting for the ax to fall, not sure which ax would be the quicker, less painful one. Gaia had been getting the more-than-a-friend vibe from Jake for a few days now, but she'd chosen to ignore it. Mostly because acknowledging it would require acknowledging the fact that she was also attracted to him, and Gaia was definitely not ready to go there.

Not just yet.

Whenever she allowed herself to admit she liked a guy, only anguish ensued.

"I was wondering if you might want to—"

Jake's question was interrupted by a sudden, blinding light that was directed right into his eyes. He held up his hand to shield himself, and the beam moved to Gaia's face. She squinted against the stinging pain and sat up, her boots scraping against the grainy surface of the rock.

"What do you kids think you're doing out here at this hour?" an authoritative voice asked.

The light finally moved away and Gaia was able to distinguish the outlines of two New York City policemen through the pink dots that were floating across her vision.

"Just hanging out," Jake said, pushing himself to

his feet. He was slightly taller and more than slightly broader than either of the men in blue.

"Yeah, well, not the safest place to just hang out these days," the chubbier of the two cops said, eyeing Gaia as she stood. He shone his light along the ground, looking for beer cans, crushed joints—anything that would allow him to give Jake and Gaia more than the usual amount of hassle.

"We've had a number of attacks in this area of the park in the past few days," Cop Number One said. "I suggest you two move it along for your own safety."

"Sure," Jake said, leaning down to grab up his jacket. "No problem."

He used his jacket to nudge Gaia's arm, and they turned and scrambled down the side of the boulder. Gaia sighed as she fought for her footing on the steep side of the rock. She appreciated what the cops were trying to do, but they'd obliterated her perfect moment. Of course, they might have also saved her from an awkward, embarrassing, tongue-tied conversation with Jake about his "so listen." Little did they know they'd just added "rescue from ill-fated romantic interludes" to their duties as New York's finest.

Gaia jumped the last few feet to the ground and landed next to Jake. He shoved his arms into his jacket and straightened the collar as they started to walk. For a few blissful seconds there was total silence—aside from the faint honking of car horns somewhere out on the streets that surrounded the park.

Then Jake tried again. "So, anyway, as I was saying—"

"Hey! No! Help! *Help!*"

It took Gaia a split second to realize that she wasn't hearing her own desperate get-me-out-of-here pleas, but actual shouts of panic.

"It's coming from over there," Jake said, taking off.

Gaia was right at his heels, slicing through the trees in the direction of what was sounding more and more like a struggle. They suddenly emerged into a small clearing and saw not one but two middle-aged women in jogging suits, flattened on their backs by four men in full-on black. Two of the men held each victim down, while the other two yanked at their clothes.

Gaia took one look at the tear-stained and desperate face of the woman closest to her and felt her fingers curl into fists.

"Hey!" Jake shouted at the top of his lungs.

All four men stopped and whipped their heads around. At the instant of surprise, Jake and Gaia both launched themselves at the clothing-gropers and knocked them off their victims. As Gaia tumbled head over heels with her man, she saw the two women struggle to their feet.

"Go!" Gaia told the joggers, as she flipped the assailant over and dug one knee into his back. A second guy wrapped his arm around her and yanked her off his friend.

The stunned, shaken women pulled themselves together, then wisely turned and ran. Gaia was thrown away from her second man and she had to fight for balance. The second she found her footing she got her game face on. Jake was working his best `Matrix-worthy moves` on his two guys as Gaia's men circled, leering at her.

"We got the girl, Slick," one of them said, punctuating his statement by spitting at her feet. "Aren't we lucky?"

Slick looked Gaia up and down slowly. "You said it, buddy."

*If you're feeling so lucky, come and get me,* Gaia thought. *Quit wasting my time.*

Slick came at her then with a clumsy one-two punch, which she easily blocked. She thrust the heel of her hand up into his nose, waited for the satisfying crack and the spurt of blood, then turned around, hoisted him onto her back and over her shoulder. He landed on the ground in front of her, clutching his nose, rolling back and forth, and groaning in pain.

Gaia looked up at his friend and lifted her eyebrows. "Ready?"

He let out a growl and ran at her. Gaia was about to throw a roundhouse at him when Jake shouted her name. She looked up at the last second and saw a third guy coming right at her from her left. Glancing at his trajectory, Gaia quickly ducked, crouching as low to the ground as possible. She smiled when she heard the *thwack,* then stood up and slapped her hands together.

Both of the thugs were laid out on the ground, unconscious. They'd smacked heads coming at her and knocked themselves out. It was almost too easy.

"Amateurs," Gaia said under her breath, stepping over one of the bodies.

"Nice work," Jake told her, reaching out his hand. They slapped palms and Gaia noticed that the fourth guy was also unconscious, crumpled into a seated position against a tree.

"You too," she said.

They both looked up when they heard rustling in the dark and the huffing and puffing of approaching men. The two cops who had roused them from the boulder came skidding into the clearing, hands on their holsters. They took one look around at the men on the ground, then gazed at Gaia and Jake, stunned.

"What happened here?" Chubby Cop asked, looking impressed against his will. "I thought we told you two to move along."

"And we did," Jake said, opening his arms. "You're welcome."

Cop Number Two shot Jake a wry smile as he knelt

11

down to cuff Slick. "And now you can hang out while we get your statements, wiseguy," he said.

Gaia and Jake exchanged a quick smile and leaned back against a thick tree trunk to wait, catty-corner from one another. The side of Gaia's shoulder pressed into the back of Jake's, and she didn't move away.

"They're gonna take credit for this, aren't they?" Jake whispered.

"Probably," Gaia replied.

"Figures. I feel like Batman. I keep kicking ass and there's no one I can tell about it," Jake said. Then he smiled and nudged his shoulder back into hers. "'Cept you."

Gaia felt the corners of her mouth tugging up slightly. What was wrong with her? Was she actually *enjoying* flirtation?

"So, Gray's Papaya after this?" Jake asked as the cops roused the two knuckleheads who had run into each other.

Gaia's stomach grumbled. "Definitely."

She tucked her chin and turned her face away from him, smiling for real. She'd been doing this forever— beating up toughs in the park, ducking or dealing with cops, then going for a postfight midnight snack. But she'd been doing it forever alone. And she'd always thought that was the way she liked it. Yes, actually—that was the way she *had* liked it.

But now . . . now she liked having someone there.

She liked having Jake to share all this with. She liked having an . . . ally.

*Huh. Maybe it's true,* Gaia thought, an evening breeze tickling a few strands of her long blonde hair against her face. *Maybe things* can *change.*

# TOM MOORE SAT AT THE SMOOTH

**Venom**

metal table glaring across at the prisoners. His spine was straight, his fingers clasped into a knot, his elbows just slightly off the edge of the table top. He breathed in and out deliberately, maintaining his composure—maintaining his calm.

*Just another set of criminals. Just another day.*

"Are you going to say anything?" Natasha asked.

"I'll ask the questions," Tom spat back instantly. He could taste the **venom** in his own mouth.

*Just another set of criminals. Just another day.*

Tatiana blinked but remained otherwise impassive. She looked small and wan, her light skin translucent and green in her bright orange jumpsuit. The monstrous cuffs circling her tiny wrists were almost comical. Even though it was impossibly cold in the interrogation room, there was a line of sweat visible above her upper lip. It was taking a lot more effort for Tatiana to remain composed after days of stony, obstinate silence in her cell. Far more effort than her more experienced, more world-weary, more spy game–weary mother.

Tom shifted his gaze to Natasha again. Her dark hair was pulled back in a low braid that hung heavy and smooth down her back. She wore an amused smirk on her face. The face he had once held, once kissed, once touched with the tenderness that he'd formerly reserved only for his wife—his one true love.

His stomach was shot through with hot acid bitterness. He could only hope the nausea wasn't apparent on his face.

"That's fine," Natasha said finally, shifting slightly in her iron chair. "It's just that you're not. Asking questions, that is."

"Who were you working for?" Tom asked flatly.

The smirk deepened. "You don't want to know that, Tom."

"Don't say my name," he snapped. "You don't have that right."

Maddeningly, the smirk turned into a smile.

"Who were you working for?" he repeated.

"I want to talk about a deal," she said.

Tom got up and threw his chair across the room, the noise slicing his eardrums as it clattered and crashed. Tatiana flinched as he leaned his knuckles into the table and got right in Natasha's face.

"You tried to kill my daughter! You tried to *kill*

Gaia! And you have the audacity . . . the unmitigated *gall* to sit here and talk to me about a *deal*!?" he shouted, his eyes so wide they felt about to burst.

She didn't move. She didn't blink. And suddenly Tom Moore knew. He knew that he was going to grab her. He saw his hands around her throat. Saw himself choking the life out of her. Who would blame him if he did it? The woman deserved to die.

"Agent Moore!"

The door to the cinder block–walled room flew open and Director Vance stood on the threshold, his intimidating former-Navy-Seal, former-NCAA-basketball-player frame blocking out the light from the hallway. He pressed his full lips together into a thin line.

"That's enough, Agent Moore," Vance said in his rumbling baritone.

Tom didn't move. His knuckles turned white against the table as he continued to glare into Natasha's unwavering eyes.

*I told this person I loved her. I thought I was going to be with her forever,* he thought. The visions he'd had of him and Natasha together, of making a family with their daughters, flitted through his mind, whirling together in a sickening tornado of colors.

"Agent Moore, I'm not going to ask you again," Vance said, stepping into the room.

The whirling suddenly stopped. Tom swallowed

hard and struggled to focus on Vance. Ever so slowly, some semblance of balance returned to his mind and he realized what he was doing. He was letting Natasha get the upper hand. He was letting her have the whole game. He pushed himself up and smoothed down the front of his blue suit jacket, hoping to regain some shred of dignity.

But when he glanced at her again it was clear from the expression of triumph on her face that all was lost. He couldn't handle being around her. He'd just proven it.

Tom turned and followed his director out of the room and into the monitoring space just beyond. A couple of agents stood in front of the one-way mirror that looked over the interrogation room and they averted their eyes when Tom entered. The second the door was shut behind him, Vance turned on Tom, his dark eyes livid, his deep brown skin flushed with anger.

"Moore, don't you ever let me see you lose your cool like that with a prisoner again, you understand me?" Vance spat, leaning in over Tom. "You know what you were in that room? You were that prisoner's bitch!"

Tom pulled his head back slightly, unaccustomed to such severe scolding after his glorious tenure in the CIA. Still, he knew on some level that Vance was right, so there wasn't much he could say.

"I'm sorry, sir," he said, swallowing his pride. "It won't happen again."

"Damn right it won't. Because you're going home,"

Vance said through his teeth.

It took Tom more time than absolutely necessary to process this. The man couldn't be suggesting that he was taking Tom off this case. Didn't he know how invested in this he was? He had to find out who had kidnapped him, who had ordered his daughter to be killed. He had to find out for sure whether or not his brother, Oliver, was involved, as he so highly suspected.

"What?" Tom spat out finally. "No! Sir, I—"

"You heard me, Moore," Vance said, straightening his tie and shooting a death glare at the few CIA personnel who had conspicuously stepped into the room to watch the proceedings. "These particular prisoners obviously have you more than a little on edge." He paused for a breath and looked at Tom sorrowfully, almost pityingly. "You're taking a little time off," he added, causing Tom's heart to sink with the finality of it all. "Starting now."

GAIA OPENED THE DOOR TO THE **Manic** East Seventy-second Street apartment on Friday after school and immediately went on alert. She lifted her hand, telling Jake to stop and wait behind her, then pushed the door open the rest of the way as slowly and quietly as possible. Something was wrong—she could feel it.

There was a crash in Natasha's—no, her *father's*—bedroom. She and Jake glanced at each other. There was someone here.

*Dammit,* Gaia thought. *I knew it wouldn't last.*

She tiptoed toward the living room, her rubber-soled boots soundless on the hardwood floor. For once, Gaia was clueless as to who she might find. Could there be a *new* enemy? Was it even possible?

Footsteps approached, confident and loud and not remotely trying to be stealthy. Gaia flattened herself against the nearest wall, around the corner from the hallway, and braced for a fight. That was when her father emerged into the room, all smiles.

"Hey, honey!" he said, shuffling a few envelopes in his hands. His dress shirt was unbuttoned at the top and the sleeves were rolled up above his wrists. "I didn't hear you come in!"

Clearly, Gaia hadn't fully acclimated to civilian life. The idea of coming home to her *father* of all people was still so very strange.

Tom's eyes flicked to Jake, who was now standing outside the door to the kitchen, his muscles visibly slackening.

"Hey, Jake," Tom said as Gaia forced her fingers and her jaw to unclench.

Her father breezed by her and sat down at the head

of the dining-room table, where there were dozens of neatly arranged piles of bills and papers. He started pulling pages out of the envelopes, sorting them, and tossing the envelopes into the kitchen garbage can, which had been temporarily relocated.

Gaia finally moved away from the wall, eyeing her father. This was all very weird. Not only was he home in the middle of the day, but he was doing paperwork—something she hadn't seen him do . . . ever. When her mom had been alive, that had been her territory, and since then, her father hadn't been around for enough days in a row to even know that there *were* bills.

On top of it all, there was an odd air about him. He was humming. His foot was bouncing under the table. Her father was normally cool, aloof, sometimes intense, but always in a quiet way. Just then he was acting. . . well, hyper.

"Dad?" Gaia asked, tucking her hair behind her ears. "Everything okay?"

"Fine. Great, actually," he said, glancing up at her for a split second before returning his attention to the papers.

Jake moved into the room, stuffing his hands into the front pockets of his jeans and giving Tom wide berth. The two of them hadn't gotten along very well on the whole Russia excursion, and it was clear that Jake also sensed something off in Tom's behavior.

"I heard a crash in the bedroom," Gaia said, sitting down in a chair across from her father. She pulled her

19

messenger bag off over her head and laid it carefully on the floor. Normally she would have just dropped it, but something told her not to make any sudden noises or movements. Her father, though acting happy, was clearly on edge.

"Right, I broke a lamp," her father said. "I'll clean it up later."

Gaia looked at Jake and he tilted his head, giving her a look that said, "He's *your* father."

"Okay, so what are you doing home?" Gaia asked, glancing at her black plastic watch. "It's four o'clock."

"I decided to take some time off," Tom said, slapping a piece of paper down on top of a pile. Gaia felt as if he'd just slapped *her*. Her father taking time off? Was this some kind of new, previously unexplored reality? Before she could even formulate a question, her father paused and folded his hands in front of him, flattening a stack of what looked like contracts. "In fact, there's something I wanted to talk to you about," he said with a smile. "How would you feel about making a new start?"

"What kind of new start?" Gaia asked slowly.

"Should I . . . ?" Jake asked, motioning toward the bedrooms.

"No, stay," Tom said with a laugh. "I just wanted to ask Gaia how she'd feel about doing a little shopping this weekend."

Gaia's jaw dropped, but she recovered quickly and

snapped it shut again. That was definitely a phrase she'd never thought she'd hear. Not from her father, anyway. The things she heard most often from him were phrases like, "Stay off the radar," "I'll try to be in touch some time next month," and "Aim for the solar plexus."

"Shopping?" Gaia asked, slumping back in her seat. "For what?"

*Please don't let him say bras or something like that,* Gaia thought. *Like he suddenly wants to make up for not being there and for my not having a mother.*

Gaia didn't blame her father for his many disappearing acts over the years—at least not anymore—not now that she knew what he'd been doing on all those excursions and why. He'd been fighting the good fight. Protecting her—protecting the free world. It had taken Gaia a long time to accept that and move on. She couldn't handle it if he decided to take on the role of guilt-ridden father now.

"New furniture," Tom said. "Everything in this place belongs to Natasha and Tatiana. I think it's time we get some of our own things, don't you?"

A little stirring of excitement came to life in Gaia's chest. She hadn't thought of it that way, but her father was right. This place was going to be their home. *Their home.* She and her father hadn't had one of those in years. Why would they want it to be decorated by their evil archenemy?

"Really?" Gaia said, too unaccustomed to the idea of doing something as normal as furniture shopping with her father.

"Yes, really," Tom said, standing. He moved over to the end of the hallway and looked off toward the opposite end—toward the room Gaia once shared with Tatiana. "We can get rid of those two beds and get you a double . . . move out that old fashioned desk—I'm guessing it's not your style," he added with a grin.

Gaia liked what he was saying, but the way he was saying it was still odd. Almost manic. He was too excited about the prospect of shopping.

*But maybe he should be,* Gaia thought. *Maybe he wants some normalcy in his life as much as I do.*

She sat up straight and squared her shoulders. "Okay, I'm in," she said.

"Good," her father said, squeezing both her shoulders from behind. "We'll go over to Seventh tomorrow and hit the stores." He turned, hands in the pockets of his khakis, and looked around the living room. "It'll be a whole new start. Out with the old, in with the new."

Gaia smiled slightly and looked up at Jake, who was already staring right at her. She felt a flutter in her heart as their eyes locked.

*A whole new start,* she thought. *Out with the old, in with the new.*

# OLIVER SAT IN ONE OF THE FEW CHAIRS

**Rejection**

in his brownstone in Brooklyn, staring at the telephone on the table next to him. A half-empty bottle of scotch reflected the glow from the desk lamp that afforded the only light in the room. He took a swig of his drink and braced himself as the warm liquid burned down his throat.

*It's just a phone call,* he told himself. *You've taken phone calls from the president of the United States in your day. Just get it over with.*

He set the tumbler down, picked up the receiver, and quickly dialed Gaia and Tom's number. He had no idea why he was filled with such trepidation. Yes, there was a lot of bad history between him and his brother and niece, but that had all changed. They had fought side by side in Russia. They had escaped together. And even if he and Tom had been at each other's throats half the time, going through that experience together had brought them closer. He could feel it. Tom must have been feeling it too.

The phone rang a few times and he finally heard someone pick up at the other end. Oliver started to smile.

"Tom Moore," his brother said stiffly.

"Hello, Tom. How are you settling in?"

Silence. Oliver's heart thumped almost painfully.

"Tom?"

"I don't want you calling here again," his brother said, his tone impossibly cold.

"Tom. . . please, I just thought you and Gaia and I could get together," Oliver said, sitting forward in his seat. "Talk things over . . . maybe have a meal—"

"Until I know with absolute certainty that you had nothing to do with my kidnapping and with the threats to Gaia's life, I have nothing to say to you. And I don't want you contacting her," Tom said. "Do you understand me?"

Oliver struggled for words—a unique experience for him. Usually he could be smooth under any circumstances, could sweet-talk anyone and everyone he came into contact with. It was all part of his CIA training. But this . . . this flat out rejection from his only brother—his twin—was too much, even for him.

"Tom, I—"

"Stay away from my daughter, Oliver. Don't test me on this."

And with that, the line went dead. Oliver held the receiver against his face for a few moments, unable to move. He hadn't expected Tom to jump up and down and do cartwheels over the phone call, but this completely inhumane treatment was uncalled for. After everything he'd done to bring Tom home safely, everything he'd done to help his brother and his daughter, he certainly didn't deserve *this*.

Hand shaking, Oliver slowly lowered the receiver

onto the cradle. He took a steadying breath and lifted his drink again, downing the rest of it in one quick gulp.

*It's going to be okay,* he told himself, bracing his forearm with his other hand to stop the shaking. To stop the hot blood that coursed through his veins from pushing him toward the edge—toward anger. *He'll come around eventually.*

But his words were cold comfort to him, alone in his dark, unfurnished home. What did he have to do to get back in Tom's good graces? How many times would he have to prove himself?

**To:** Y
**From:** X22
**Subject:** Prisoner 352: Code name: Abel

There has been a security breech in subsector K. Prisoner 352 is AWOL. Unconfirmed reports state that a young woman, believed to be Genesis, along with two men were instrumental in the liberation of 352/Abel. They are believed to be en route to the States, if not already there. We await your orders.